The Prophecy

by

Lisa Zimmermann

Cover design by Jason Anscomb
rawshockdesign@gmail.com

Interior design by BAD PRESS iNK

ISBN: 978-1-0687203-2-1

published by www.badpress.ink

Dedicated to Fiona and Mina

May you continue to grow into strong and happy women

Prologue

It happened so fast that she couldn't even say what she noticed first. The blinding light that enveloped her, the earth-shattering noise that left her ears ringing for days, or the invisible force that hit her like an angry tsunami and blew her into the shelves behind like a rag doll, completely knocking the air from her lungs.

To her surprise, the impact when she landed on the floor wasn't really painful. The debris that rained down on her directly afterwards didn't hurt much either. Her mind, however, had a difficult time catching up with the events. Only seconds ago she had been standing behind the counter of the coffee shop she was working in, taking a sip from a silly Star Wars mug. And now she was face-down on the ground in a heap.

She still had the taste of coffee on her tongue when she slowly got back to her feet, a feat which was accompanied by a dull pain in her leg and her head. She didn't pay much attention to it right now, too shocked to feel properly.

The small old-fashioned bell that usually announced the arrival of new customers was still hanging from the ceiling, ready to release its silvery sound as soon as the door was opened. The only problem was that there was no more door.

She stared right into the face of a stranger who was

standing on the footpath on the other side of the street. His eyes were wide open, his mouth agape, and he was staring back at her as if she was a ghost. She could see that his lips were moving, but all she could hear was that loud ringing in her ears. She brought her hand to her face and when she looked at it, it was covered in dust and blood.

Her mind was finally able to catch up with what was going on and everything fell into place.

Sarah knew that life as she had come to know it was over. It had shattered into a thousand tiny pieces, just like the coffee shop around her. She heard something other than the ringing noise. A pathetic-sounding wail.

It took her a moment to realise that it was coming from her own mouth.

Chapter 1

'Damn,' Sarah O'Donoghue muttered quietly under her breath when the sound of the incoming train reached her. She immediately broke into a sprint, not wanting to miss it. She was late for work again. It would be the third time in two weeks and her boss, Steven Bailey, had already made a habit of looking pointedly at his watch when she entered the small coffee shop.

Sarah knew that he had a soft spot for her, and so far, he hadn't made a big deal of it, but even middle-aged coffee shop owners with a penchant for collecting Lego had their limits. She was testing his patience and no matter how much he liked her, he wouldn't allow this to continue for much longer. She didn't like her job much, but she needed the money. As she rounded the corner, she saw the taillights of the underground train vanishing into the dark tunnel. 'Damn,' she muttered under her breath again.

She ran her hand through her curly auburn locks that, together with the freckles on her otherwise pale face, gave away her Irish heritage. Her hair was one of the features she liked about herself, even though this morning she had barely had time to brush it. She had slept in, the reason she was late for work.

It had begun a few weeks back. She had never had trouble falling asleep, but for a few weeks now she suffered from severe insomnia and strange nightmares. Even if she fell asleep early, she woke at least two or three times every night with her heart racing and her palms sweaty. She could never remember exactly what she had been dreaming about but there was a strong feeling of threat and imminent danger following her. But more often she only was able to fall asleep in the wee hours of the morning, causing her to sleep right through her alarm clock.

While she waited for the next train to arrive her mobile phone buzzed in her pocket and she pulled it out. She had a text from Charlotte Martin, her best friend and co-worker at the coffee shop.

'Steven is furious,' it read, 'bring a good excuse.'

'Damn,' Sarah muttered unhappily, for the third time. She wasn't a morning person, there was no mistaking that, but today was worse than usual.

Steven's Place, as the coffee shop was not so imaginatively called, was located in Haleston's bustling city centre. The city had a little over three hundred and fifty thousand inhabitants which made living here very exciting for Sarah, who had escaped the boredom of the countryside early on in her life. She had always thought of England as a weird place. One minute you were in a busy city centre, but drive ten miles east, and you found yourself in an open field that appeared as though it had never seen a single trace of human existence. The world was a strange but often wonderful place, and for Sarah, England was at the heart of that vision.

The coffee shop was a small building that offered different kinds of coffees and teas, but also handmade sandwiches, scones, and other snacks. Only Steven,

Charlotte, and Sarah worked there. Then there was Rosy the cleaning lady, but she only came when the shop was closed and prepared it for the next day. The place had a few dining tables and was packed with customers exactly three times a day – in the morning, during lunchtime, and in the late afternoon, when commuters picked up a hot beverage and a snack on their way home.

As expected, Steven was waiting for her when she finally rushed into the shop. This time he didn't even make a show out of staring at his watch. Instead, he approached her directly. 'Sarah, can I have a word, please?' he asked. It was clear that it was more an order than a polite request.

Sarah followed him into the office at the back of the shop, quietly closing the door behind them. She knew what was about to come.

'Sarah, you are late for the third time within the last two weeks. I was fine with turning a blind eye the first two times, but I can't accept this kind of behaviour any longer. I need to keep things in order here.'

Steven carried on talking but Sarah drowned his words out. He had made his point clear.

When he stopped speaking, Sarah focused her attention back on him. 'I'm sorry,' she said. 'I promise it won't happen again.' There wasn't much else she could say. He hadn't even wanted her lame excuse.

'Is everything all right with you?' Steven wanted to know and to her surprise, there was genuine concern in his voice.

Sarah sighed. That was the question, wasn't it? Things were not right, but this certainly wasn't anything she was going to discuss with her boss.

'Everything is fine.' She looked up at Steven through her eyelashes. 'I appreciate your concern, but I promise I'm OK, and I will do better!'

Steven furrowed his brows. He wasn't buying it. 'If you insist. I'd much rather talk about it, but I can't make you discuss anything you do not wish to discuss. So go and get started with your shift. And you better bring your A-game today.'

'What did he say?' Charlotte interrogated her sometime later when the first rush of customers had left and they had a moment to take a breather.

'He gave me a warning,' Sarah replied, 'and then asked me if I was OK.'

Usually, her best friend would have made a funny remark about it, but this time Charlotte stayed serious. 'Are you?' She knew her friend better than anyone else.

Sarah considered not answering this, at least not honestly, but Charlotte would know anyway. 'No,' she finally admitted.

It had started about four weeks ago, right with her insomnia. Or maybe even before that. Sarah wasn't sure because, in the beginning, the changes had been subtle. She was missing a few seconds here and there, something she had barely noticed. But then about four weeks ago, something happened that convinced her she was losing her mind. She had been on her way home from work when she spotted a pretty dress in a shop window and stopped to study it in detail, thinking about how long she would have to work to be able to afford it. Working in a coffee shop didn't exactly come with a salary worth boasting about.

The dress had changed before her eyes.

While it had been silk and lace before, it was suddenly made of cotton, the fabric less shiny and rougher. The shape and the colours were about the same, but the buttons were different too. Instead of small pearls they now were made of horn.

Sarah had frowned, wondering if the daylight reflecting in the shop window was playing tricks on her eyes. But she also smelled something that hadn't been there before. It was an earthy scent, like forest ground after rain. How was that possible in the middle of a bustling city? It hadn't rained in days, which was already a miracle in this country. And there was the smell of horses. She had taken riding lessons as a young girl, so she knew that scent well. Blinking rapidly in confusion, everything had turned back to normal. She had checked her surroundings but no one seemed to have noticed anything unusual. The scent in the air was gone, and she only could smell the usual car fumes. The woman behind her was still talking into her mobile phone, and a father was dragging his two children behind him in annoyance on the other side of the street. Everyone was minding their own business. And the dress in front of her was made of silk and lace, with pearl buttons.

She had tried to convince herself that it had been her tired mind playing tricks on her, but the moment left Sarah with a deep feeling of unease. A feeling she hadn't been able to shrug off entirely since.

The days after the incident had passed normally and when she was convinced that it had just been the hard working day taking a toll on her, it had happened again. She usually used the public transport system since she didn't own a car. After doing her weekly grocery shopping, she had waited for the bus to take her home. The large red vehicle had turned around the corner when it suddenly changed into a horse and carriage. One second it was a bus, the next, it was four horses, pulling a large coach made of dark wood. Sarah's mouth had dropped open and she had stared at the animals, had seen the dark stains of sweat on their coats, had heard the hooves rattling against the concrete. It could only have been a few seconds and when she blinked, the horses were gone and there was a regular bus approaching. The other people waiting in line had behaved normal so they obviously hadn't noticed anything unusual. Numbly she had climbed the steps into the bus while wondering what was going on.

Was she losing her mind?

Ever since then, she had lived in a constant state of unease. She was always expecting it to happen and even now, when everything looked as it was supposed to, Sarah had the feeling that other images were just a blink away. Her reality had become fragile, the ground underneath her feet not reliable any longer. And combined with that inexplicable feeling of a looming threat above her head, this was the other reason she lay awake at night. She was scared to close her eyes because what if reality shifted when she opened them?

'You saw something strange again?' Charlotte guessed, pulling her out of her memories.

Sarah dropped her gaze, fearing that her eyes would betray the depths of her anxiety. 'Yes,' she admitted quietly. 'Yesterday. At home. My living room suddenly turned into an episode of *Twilight Zone*,' she jested, trying to take the edge off her words by making a bad joke out of it even though she didn't feel like laughing. She forced herself to voice her deepest fears. 'What if something is seriously wrong with me? What if I have a brain tumour?'

Charlotte studied Sarah sceptically. She hung the tea towel back over its rack and reassembled the coffee machine she had been cleaning before casually putting an arm around her best friend's shoulders. 'I think you're just tired and stressed. Maybe you need a break. Why don't we go out tonight? There's a new fancy club in town, and I haven't gone dancing in ages.'

Truth was, Charlotte was a sucker for nightlife and went out at least twice a week, so her last club night certainly wasn't ages ago. Right now, Sarah preferred to curl up in her comfortable armchair in her living room with a good book or binge-watch a show on Netflix.

Charlotte sensed her indecisiveness. 'No refusal! You are young and need to distract yourself. And you need alcohol, some loud music, dancing, and maybe a proper snog to take your mind off things. Maybe you'll even get laid. It's been a while, right?' She didn't even wait for an answer to her rhetorical question. She knew exactly what was going on in Sarah's love life. Or rather, what wasn't going on. 'I tell you what you are going to do. Tomorrow you are going to make an appointment with a doctor to get yourself checked out – even though I'm sure you're fine. But tonight, we're going dancing. I'll send the location to your phone and meet you there at nine.'

And with that, it was decided. It seemed as if rewatching *Supernatural*, one of her favourite TV shows, would have to wait.

The nightclub was packed, and the music was hammering loudly through the air. It smelled of alcohol, perfume, and sweat, a combination of scents that, according to her friend, were the hallmark of fanciness. If nothing else, at least they lay the foundations for the promise of a good night.

It took Sarah ages to make her way through the crowded dancefloor to reach the bar located at the other end of the room. She had tried to be optimistic about this evening, but the truth was, she wanted to be at home where it was peaceful and quiet. Netflix never made this much noise.

On the other hand, she knew that Charlotte was right. At home, she would only sit in her armchair in the small living room, pretending to read a book while her thoughts would circle about driving her crazy. She would google the symptoms of dementia and schizophrenia, and of course, at the end of the evening, she would be convinced she was either crazy or terminally ill.

After having to choose between a lonely spell of eating ice cream and overthinking, and going out with her friend, Sarah decided to give this night a chance.

She had even made an effort to dress up nicely in a low-neck top that showed some cleavage and tight jeans that hugged her curves in the right places. She had also put on some make-up and pinned up her hair, only leaving a few loose strands hanging around her face. For this place, she was still underdressed – she had noticed that as soon as she took her first steps into the building – but she didn't care. She felt pretty in her skin, and that was all that mattered.

Charlotte was nowhere to be seen but Sarah was early and knew that her best friend would be here at any moment. She ordered a beer and turned around to watch the crowd, taking small sips from the bottle. After a friend of hers had been drugged in a nightclub about a year ago, she didn't drink from glasses any longer and never let her bottle out of sight either. She didn't intend to drink much tonight anyway. She had work in the morning, and with her current punctuality record, drinking to Charlotte's standards didn't sound like a smart idea. That girl drank alcohol like a blue whale drank krill.

The crowd in the club was young, diverse, and colourful – exactly what you would expect from a new and fancy nightclub. With a little time to sink into the stool, and as the alcohol began to merge with her blood, Sarah began to enjoy the vibe.

There was a closed-off VIP area across the dance floor. It was heavily guarded by broad-shouldered security guys in black uniforms. It made Sarah wonder if there was a celebrity around tonight. It was not unusual for Haleston and according to Charlotte, this was the most popular nightclub right now. The music washed pleasantly over her, drowning out her thoughts and Sarah slowly relaxed and let her eyes wander around the room.

At first, he was only a face in the crowd. One among many faces. But something about him caught her attention. Maybe it was the broody expression, one that didn't quite fit into the group of cheerful faces. He certainly wasn't enjoying himself, and Sarah wondered if he had been dragged here by friends or if maybe he was on a date gone wrong. But just like her, he seemed to be alone, and he also clung to a bottle of beer, only occasionally sipping from it.

Since Charlotte was running late and Sarah had nothing better to do, she watched the man.

He seemed her age, around thirty, maybe a little older. He was taller than her, which wasn't difficult since she was a small woman. He was wearing blue jeans, boots, and a plain black but tight T-shirt that showed his muscles. He was not attractive in a regular sense. His nose was slightly crooked, his hair a bit too long. And then there was the scar. It started at the left side of his forehead, passed his eye closely, and vanished underneath his ear lobe. It must have been a clean cut because it was a straight line, and even though it was old and faded, it peculiarly marked his face. Parts of it were covered by some black hair that dangled from his forehead, but the rest was visible.

By the time she realised he was staring right back at her, it was too late. He had bright eyes, green or blue, an interesting combination with dark hair, and his gaze was intense. Embarrassed that she had been caught staring, she dropped her gaze and busied herself with her beer before she studied the room to see if she could detect Charlotte amongst the crowd. She hadn't meant to intrude on the man's privacy, and she certainly hoped that he hadn't interpreted her gaze as an invitation to flirt. She had gone through a nasty breakup a few months ago and flirting was the last thing on her agenda – even with Charlotte's repeated attempts to get her laid by introducing her to some of her friends.

After what seemed an appropriate time, she looked

up again and carefully peeked through her eyelashes in the direction of the stranger. He was making his way towards her.

Shit!

Sarah straightened her posture, feeling uncomfortable with the situation. But the closer he got, the more peculiar he seemed to her. The expression on his face was grim and not at all flirtatious. There was something in his eyes she couldn't read. Now that he was closer, she could see that he was older than she had first thought. He had to be in his mid-thirties at least. The situation felt so weird that Sarah quickly studied her surroundings to see if she was misinterpreting this. He was probably approaching someone else. But there was no one next to her and when she glanced back at him, he had stopped a few steps away, openly staring at her. Was that despair in his eyes? Sarah's worries about him chatting her up turned into confusion.

'What...'

Her speech was cut short as Charlotte jumped into her line of vision. 'Booya,' her friend yelled. 'Sorry, I'm late but see what I found!' She pulled someone closer. Or to be precise, two people. A man and a woman. Twins. Blond. Fairly good-looking and smiling expectantly.

'Ergh...' Sarah managed to say while she raised her eyebrows in a silent question.

'These two are Camille and Stuart. I met them outside,' Charlotte introduced them and pointed vaguely in the direction of the doors. It was typical for her to immediately make new friends. If there was a textbook definition for extrovert, Charlotte hit all the marks. Her best friend leaned forward and whispered happily into

Sarah's ear. 'She gave me that look. I might get lucky tonight!'

She had never made a secret out of being attracted to women and Sarah couldn't help but grin at her friend's excitement.

Charlotte stepped back, reached for Sarah's wrist, and started pulling her towards the dance floor. Sarah had just enough time to take the last sip of her beer and put the now-empty bottle back on the bar before she was pulled along.

When she finally remembered the peculiar encounter with the strange man, she glanced back over her shoulder toward the spot where he had been standing. But he had gone.

Chapter 2

The noise was almost physically hurting her, and she wrestled her arm out from underneath her blanket, flailing it wildly at her alarm clock in an attempt to stop it from beeping. She couldn't find it in its usual place, a fact that forced her to open an eye. 'Ugh,' she groaned when the headache hit her.

The alarm clock was still beeping loudly, and Sarah remembered that she had deliberately placed it on the other side of the room last night before going to bed to make sure she got up. Of course, it had gotten too late at the nightclub and of course, she had drunk way too much alcohol. But despite her worries, she had enjoyed herself. Stuart and Camille had been funny company.

Now though, feeling the typical hangover, she regretted staying out late, drinking too much, and being alive in general.

Groaning once more she sat up in bed, which was greeted by the intensification of her headache and a wave of nausea. On any other day, she would have called in sick, but that wasn't an option today. Not after yesterday's episode. It was time for some painkillers, a shower, and a strong coffee.

Charlotte looked exactly as Sarah felt, but at least both of them had made it to work and on time too. Her best friend was grinning widely, despite her hangover.

'Now that was an awesome night, wasn't it?' she inquired and handed her a large cup of coffee.

Sarah gratefully accepted, immediately taking a large sip of it. 'True.' She set the cup aside to put on her working apron, realising that she hadn't thought about brain tumours or losing her mind for the entire evening. If the hangover was the price to pay, so be it.

She reached for the coffee beans and refilled the machine to prepare for the first rush of customers, the scent of freshly ground coffee quickly filling her senses. 'How was the night with Camille?' she wanted to know with a grin while reminding herself at the same time to make that doctor's appointment during her lunch break today. It was time to face her fears and get a proper check-up.

A little more than three weeks later, Sarah was sitting in her physician's office, anxiously awaiting her results.

'You have a perfectly healthy brain.' The man quickly came to the point, while studying something only he could see on his computer screen. 'All the neurological tests we have carried out have shown no abnormalities. Everything in is perfect order. The MRI scan shows nothing either.'

He took his reading glasses off and peeked at her over the brim of the screen. 'Wherever your symptoms stem from, there is no physical cause for them. Did you ever have your eyesight examined?'

Sarah nodded automatically even though she hadn't. This had nothing to do with her eyes, and she knew it.

'Does this mean I could be going crazy?' she asked

but there was still relief in her voice. It was one thing to go nuts, but an entirely different thing to suffer from a possibly fatal brain tumour.

'Your symptoms might be stress-induced,' the physician replied and studied her from above the computer screen. 'I would recommend taking more breaks. Read books, maybe do some yoga? It helped my wife greatly with stress management.'

Sarah frowned at him. That was his recommendation? Yoga and books? How was that supposed to stop her from seeing things that weren't there? But then, she hadn't had any more episodes in the last few weeks. There had been no strange sightings, no hallucinations, and no nightmares either. Whatever this had been, maybe it was over. Maybe it had been some sort of temporary thing. And if it had gone and did not return, was it really important what had caused it?

Later that day after finishing her shift at the coffee shop, she walked into the local shelter for homeless people, a place where she regularly helped out on Wednesday evenings. She had started doing this voluntary work about a year ago when she had been particularly unhappy with her job situation. Serving coffee wasn't exactly a world-changing task and she had searched for something meaningful, even if it was just for one evening of the week. One of their regular customers had mentioned the homeless shelter just around the corner and after gathering her courage she had turned up there one day, offering to volunteer. Since then, she helped out here and loved it. By now, she knew all the regulars by name and had even started collecting spare clothing from her friends and relatives that she donated to the shelter regularly.

As usual she was greeted cheerily by Joe Holmes when she entered the building. Joe worked in the kitchen of the shelter. He had been homeless for a few years but had managed to settle down and nowadays was living in a small apartment. He was receiving social welfare from the government but worked here voluntarily every day. During the year she'd been here, he hadn't taken a single day off and she never had seen him sick either. The homeless respected him more than the people who were running this place since he had been one of them. This always came in handy when conflicts arose. He was a tall gaunt black man with a deep voice and a kind heart and Sarah liked him dearly.

'Sarah, my love,' he barked through the room as soon as he saw her, giving her his biggest grin, 'where have you been?'

'Hi Joe,' she waved before shouting back. 'Doctor appointments.'

She knew he would accept this as an explanation without asking further questions. This was a homeless shelter after all, and people usually didn't like to be asked questions. The truth was that Sarah had been too exhausted to come here last week because of her lack of sleep. Sure, there had been additional appointments and tests she had undergone but she had mainly been too anxious about her upcoming test results to sleep properly, and her mind had been foggy most of the time. After work, she only wanted to go home and curl up on her sofa. Today, she didn't feel too rested either but hadn't wanted to miss two weeks in a row.

She went into the small storage room at the back

that also served as an office and general junk room, where she stored her jacket and handbag. The shelter was in an old restaurant with a large open space in the front and a kitchen in the back. It was the perfect place for the soup kitchen that opened every evening. This was where she mostly helped out. Above the restaurant were three stories where the apartments had been turned into an assembly of single sleeping rooms.

Sarah put on her kitchen shoes, an apron, and a white cap she was forced to wear when working with food. She made sure that her curls were safely secured underneath before she left the storage room to meet Joe in the kitchen. 'What are we having today?' she inquired and tried to peek into one of the large pots behind Joe.

'Caviar,' Joe joked as usual but quickly fell serious. 'Chicken soup and a bread roll for everyone. The donations have been meagre for a while.'

Sarah bit at her lower lip. She had meant to talk to Steven about this. Maybe she would be allowed to put up a donation box on the counter of the coffee shop. She made a mental note to ask him about it first thing tomorrow morning. Her thought process was cut short though when the doors opened, and the first people came in for food.

For the next three hours, Sarah was busy handing out meals and cleaning the tables and dishes afterwards. Her feet already hurt from standing and walking the whole day at the coffee shop but the work here always left her content on a very deep level, so she didn't mind her sore feet. She was carrying one of the last rounds of dirty plates back to the kitchen when her eyes fell on a latecomer who was sitting at one of the tables, eating. He was one of four people left in the room and he had his back turned towards her. Something about him made her pause in her step, a small frown appearing on her forehead.

'New guy,' Joe said, noticing her interest in the man. He had been waiting for her at the kitchen door. 'Been coming here for almost two weeks now. He's a strange one. Doesn't talk much but doesn't cause any trouble either and that's fine with me.'

He took the dirty plates out of her hand and disappeared into the kitchen when the man turned around and almost immediately met Sarah's gaze as if he had known that she was going to be there. Her eyes widened in surprise. She had completely forgotten about him, but she recognised him nonetheless. That nose, the hair that was falling into his forehead, and the noticeable scar. It was the man from the nightclub.

Confused, she studied him while he stared at her with the same urgent intensity as he had at the club. He didn't look homeless but then, who did? Working here had taught her a lot about people and the first thing was that many of them didn't *look* the part. Some came here to simply get something to eat, a warm meal for themselves and their families. Those were the people falling through the cracks, the ones working for less than minimum wage, the single parents, or those heavily in debt. Seeing him here most likely was a strange, but simple coincidence. Her confusion, however, grew stronger when he got up from his chair, completely ignoring the remains of his meal, and made his way over to her. This time no Charlotte was jumping in his way and he came to a halt in front of her.

Sarah had to revise her estimation of his age once again. He was as young as she had originally thought but the hard expression on his face and the scar made him appear older from a distance. And there was a strange expression in his eyes she couldn't quite decipher. For a moment the two focused on each other before Sarah cleared her throat. 'Uhm, can I help you?' she asked in the lack of anything else to say. The man seemed to search for the right words, running a hand through his longish hair.

'Yes,' he finally answered. 'I need your help.'

Without elaborating any further he fell quiet, and Sarah raised her eyebrows at him in a silent question. This whole situation was weird but strangely enough, she didn't feel threatened. As far as she knew, he could be a puppy-killing mass murderer or an utterly mad person with a freakish obsession, but there was no bad vibe coming from him and she didn't think there was any danger. Not that she was going to test this out by taking him into a dark alley. Now, with the stray thought about the freakish obsession nestled in her mind, she couldn't quite shake it off.

His words pulled her out of her train of thought. 'This is a bit difficult to explain,' he said, appearing slightly embarrassed but the expression in his eyes had intensified and Sarah was pretty sure that it was despair. She noticed that he was speaking with a strange accent, one that she couldn't place.

'What is it?' she wanted to know, taking a small step away from him, suddenly scared by the intensity of the emotions he was radiating.

'If you would allow me to sit down with you some-where, I could explain it to you,' he responded. 'Please,' he added after reading the expression on her face correctly.

Her first reaction was to decline his request. She definitely wouldn't sit down with a weird, random stranger, listening to him. But the pleading in his voice was genuine and whatever it was he needed help with, he truly seemed to be desperate about it. But why her? She had never seen him before, except that night in the club, and she wasn't trained for this. The shelter offered psychological counselling once a week, and she told him about it.

The despair in his eyes grew and he grabbed her arm. His touch almost felt like an electric shock and even though she immediately tried to pull away from him, he held onto her tightly. 'No,' his voice was merely a whisper. 'It has to be you.'

There was no hesitation.

'Joe,' she shouted out loudly, calm but with an iron determination in her voice. The man immediately let go of her and took a step back, lifting his hands in a defensive gesture.

'Sorry,' he apologised, taking another step back to undermine his words. 'I didn't mean to scare you, but I really need to talk to you, it is very urgent.'

Joe's steps could be heard, approaching the kitchen door and the man added hastily. 'Meet me tomorrow night at the Pogues on Main Road.'

The Pogues was a highly frequented and quite nice Irish Pub in the City Centre. The man's eyes met hers and once again she could see that strange urgency and the despair lying in them. 'Please, Sarah!' And with those words he turned around, put the collar of his jacket up, and left the moment Joe stepped out of the kitchen.

The chef followed the disappearing figure with his eyes before his gaze fell on Sarah. 'Everything alright?' There was concern in his voice.

'Yes,' Sarah replied absent-mindedly and rubbed the side of her arm where she still could feel the strong grip of the man's hand on her skin. 'He was just being peculiar.' She turned around to Joe. 'But thanks for having my back.'

'Always,' the chef responded and smiled at her. 'You go home now,' he insisted. 'It has been a long day for you. I will take care of the rest and finish up here.'

'Thank you,' Sarah mumbled but her thoughts were miles away. She replayed the strange conversation in her head and realised what was bothering her about it.

How had he known her name?

Sarah didn't plan on meeting the stranger the next day at the Pogues but the entire incident wouldn't leave her mind either. She tried to shrug it off as simply a weird meeting. They had their fair share of people with all kinds of psychological problems at the homeless shelter, and Sarah had witnessed a lot during her time there. He wouldn't be the first delusional or psychotic person she had come across but something about him had seemed genuine, something that had been lying within his eyes, and she didn't think that he was just a random nutcase. Since she had been working with people for the majority of her life, she was usually a good judge of character.

But how had he known her name?

There was the possibility he had picked it up throughout the evening but he had been in quite late, and the soup kitchen had been fairly empty at that point, so that wasn't too likely.

Maybe he would turn out to be a crazy stalker after all? She took a deep breath and shook off the feeling of unease the best she could. There was nothing she could do about it anyway. She would have to wait and see.

The next few days and the weekend came and went without anything special happening and the longer she didn't see the stranger again, the more he faded into the background of her mind.

When she returned to work the next Monday, she knew that it was going to be a busy day. Charlotte had the day off because her aunt was visiting from overseas, so it would be only Steven and Sarah. Steven's shop was located on a busy corner that led into the financial district of the city and there were going to be many extra commuters around in the morning who needed a strong coffee just because it was Monday.

After the first rush was over, Sarah poured herself a cup and started cleaning the tables in the shop. Steven disappeared into his office to do some paperwork, leaving Sarah on her own. The small bell above the door rang, announcing a customer, and Sarah's insides turned to ice when she looked up and saw the stranger standing there. She quickly got herself under control and put her hands on her hips, glaring at the man defiantly.

'What are you, a stalker?' she demanded, taking a step closer to him. She had read somewhere that this would depict confidence, and she wanted to show him that she wasn't scared of him, even though this was a blatant lie. It wasn't a coincidence that he turned up here, and his appearance at the homeless shelter last week surely hadn't been one, either. She wasn't sure about the nightclub, though. Maybe that was where his obsession with her had started? She had never considered herself interesting or pretty enough to have a stalker but here he was. 'I want you to go now. Leave me alone. I'm not interested in you.'

The man lifted his hands in a placating gesture as if he had expected a reaction like this. 'I am not a stalker,' he assured her quietly, 'and I don't want to harm you,' he promised. Sarah realised that he had quite a pleasant voice. Warm and soothing. 'But I really need your help. I need to talk to you.'

Sarah's fear slowly turned into anger. 'I don't care what it is you want! I don't know you, why should I talk to you?' she snapped. She realised that allowing him to engage her in a conversation probably wasn't the best way to get rid of him, but her train of thought was interrupted by his next words.

'You don't understand,' he declared. 'You are in danger.'

Sarah froze, staring at the man in front of her, the cold fingers of fear reaching for her spine.

The stranger studied their surroundings nervously, glancing repeatedly at the street through the shop windows. 'I can't stay here any longer,' he said, 'but please meet me at the Pogues later after work. You need to listen to me. Please!'

And there it was again, the urgency and the despair in his eyes but Sarah couldn't care less right now. Before she could ask what he meant by danger, he turned and left.

Sarah considered following and confronting him, but

she remembered that Charlotte wasn't in today and she couldn't leave the shop. Also, the chill that had gotten hold of her spine kept her rooted to the spot. After a few moments, she slowly sank into an empty chair, the cleaning sponge forgotten in her hand while she stared at the now-closed door. Had he just threatened her? It had sounded more like a warning. But of what?

After what felt like an eternity, Sarah got up and went to the counter where she reached for her mobile phone.

'Why didn't you tell me about him before?' Charlotte accused her on their way to the Pogues later that evening.

Sarah was about to reply when she realised that she wasn't quite sure what to say. She hadn't deliberately kept this from Charlotte. Maybe she had thought that telling her best friend would give it too much importance. She shrugged apologetically. 'I didn't think it was that significant. I forgot about the club, and the shelter could have been a coincidence.'

'Today not so much,' Charlotte concluded. 'And he said you were in danger?'

'Yes, and I need to know what he meant by that,' Sarah explained. 'What if he knows something I don't? I know it's crazy to meet up with him but I can't ignore this. At the pub, there will be a lot of people so it's probably safe.' She gave Charlotte a quick smile. 'And you will be there.'

Charlotte reached out and squeezed Sarah's arm in a reassuring gesture while Sarah continued to speak.

'I don't understand all this secrecy and the paranoia

though. Why not sit down with me for a coffee at the shop and tell me there? It was completely empty. But he was...' Sarah fell silent while searching for the right words. 'He was desperate, Charlie,' she tried to explain. 'I mean really desperate as if there was much more to it. It was weird,' she shrugged again.

Charlotte linked arms with her. 'I won't let you out of my sight. And if he tries anything dodgy, I will totally kick his balls. And then I'll phone the cops, but first a kick to his nuts!'

Sarah laughed but her heart wasn't in it. She was nervous about the upcoming meeting.

Chapter 3

The Pogues was a mid-sized typical Irish Pub with old musical instruments and pictures of famous Irish poets and musicians hanging on the walls. It smelled of stale beer, and the wooden tables and chairs were marked by age and the many pints and customers they had carried. The two young women were greeted by some low fiddle tunes upon entering, and Sarah immediately spotted him. He sat at a table in the very far corner of the room, an untouched pint of Guinness in front of him. From his position, he could keep an eye on the door and saw her the moment she stepped in. He lifted his hand to wave her over, but Sarah went to the bar first to order a glass of water for herself and Charlotte. This was not the right time for alcohol.

Together the two women approached the corner table and Sarah slipped onto the chair opposite the man. When Charlotte was about to sit down, he stopped her in her tracks.

'I need to talk to Sarah alone,' he announced, and Charlotte froze, her gaze wandering towards Sarah.

'It's OK,' Sarah answered the silent question. 'Just stay over there and keep an eye on us.' She didn't even lower her voice, wanting the man to know that Charlotte was on watch.

'Listen,' Charlotte snarled, addressing the man. 'If you

touch even so much as a hair on her head, I will find you and make you pay, do you understand? Also...' she pulled her mobile phone out and took a snapshot. 'I have your picture now. Don't try anything funny, are we clear?'

'Understood,' the man replied, and Sarah was pretty sure that she could hear an amused undertone in his voice.

'You have a good friend,' he stated, once Charlotte was back at the bar, glaring at him openly.

'Yes,' Sarah responded. For a moment the two studied each other in silence.

'Thank you for coming,' he offered but Sarah saw no reason for polite conversation, she wanted to get this over with.

'Who are you?' she asked. 'And what do you mean when you say that I am in danger? Are you threatening me?'

The man took a deep breath and dropped his gaze to the scratched wooden table underneath his hands as if trying to sort his thoughts. 'My name is William Lawrence,' he began, 'and I promise that I am no threat or danger to you but to answer your question, I need to expand a little and tell you a story first.'

Sarah frowned while leaning back against the hard wooden backrest of the chair, crossing her arms in front of her chest in annoyance. He wanted to tell her a *story*? She wondered if coming here had been a mistake and if there was no hidden knowledge behind his peculiar behaviour after all. Maybe he was just a random nutcase after all.

He seemed to sense her thoughts and spoke up. 'The story is crucial for understanding the answers you seek.'

'OK then, go ahead.' Sarah gave in since she had nothing to lose anyway. She exchanged a glance with Charlotte who was watching them very closely, before settling in her chair, her hand wrapped around her glass of water to hold on to something.

'Let's pretend for a moment that there is another world,' William started to speak and Sarah noticed his soft accent she still couldn't place. 'It is a world very similar to this but different in some aspects. The biggest difference is that it is a world filled with magic, and even though most have forgotten that the magic exists, it is still there, inherent in the world and ensuring the balance of everything.'

Sarah scowled at him. This wasn't going in the direction she had anticipated. What on earth was he going on about? This time, William didn't even have to sense her thoughts since they were written all over her face.

'Just have patience and hear me out,' he pleaded quietly, and Sarah huffed but didn't object yet.

Oddly, she was curious to see where he was going with this. He appeared to be more relaxed than she had seen him before, but she noticed how his eyes regularly darted towards the door nervously as if expecting some sort of interruption.

'As I said, the existence of the magic is mostly forgotten in this world but there are a few who remember. They know that the world they live in will die if its magic dies. They dedicate their lives to protecting and guarding the magic, and therefore their world, against the void and extinction. They are called the Guardians and when they die, they pass on their knowledge to the next generation of Guardians.'

William fell silent and made sure that Sarah was still listening. When he was convinced, he continued. 'The world we are talking about worked like this for centuries, but the more time passed, the more the magic was falling into oblivion and there were fewer and fewer Guardians until finally there were only two left.'

Sarah studied him quietly, her fingers fidgeting with a beer mat. She had no idea where he was going with this but there was that urgency in his voice, the same one she had been reading in his eyes before and despite herself, she was captured by his story. She had no idea what this all had to do with her, but she decided to hear him out. She had read enough books to know that there most likely a sinister ending coming to his story.

'Something happened in that world and the two last remaining Guardians were killed long before their time and before there were new Guardians to follow on. With their downfall, their world was doomed, and dark times started. With no one to guard it, the magic didn't work as it was supposed to any longer. The balance was gone, and a horrible famine broke out that led to wars over resources. There were other things, like epidemic plagues and lack of clean water. The whole world turned into a place of chaos, pain, and death.'

William's gaze was absent-minded now as if he was able to see something she couldn't while he was staring out of the dirty pub window. Sarah quickly used that opportunity to glimpse over at Charlotte. Her best friend gave her a quizzical look and Sarah answered with a reassuring nod before she focused her attention back on William.

'People were dying, good people, and those who

didn't die suffered. Until then the people of this world had ruled themselves in peace and harmony but the calls for a strong leader grew louder and someone finally took the throne. His name was Drake Graham. He turned the world into an even darker place. He was hungry for power, not caring about the people and things got even worse.'

There was a painful expression on William's face and Sarah wondered why he was so moved by this story. Sure, it was sad but it was just a story, after all. She hadn't forgotten why she was here and even though he had been able to capture her attention with his tale, she wanted answers and not to swap ideas for a fantasy novel.

'Everything seemed lost since the last Guardians were dead, but they left something behind,' William's words interrupted her thoughts. 'A prophecy. It describes how the downfall of the world can be prevented and reversed, even if the last remaining Guardians have fallen.'

William studied her and once again Sarah was captured by the intensity of his gaze, but now there was also curiosity in his eyes.

'That's a fantastic story,' she admitted, 'but what does it have to do with me? Or with me being in danger, to be precise?'

William hesitated, but before he continued to speak his eyes caught something behind her. Sarah turned her head and saw two men entering the pub. They were laughing and talking to each other and there was nothing unusual to see. What was it that had William distracted? When she turned back, he was gone, and she stupidly stared at his now empty chair before she saw a movement out of the corner of her eye. It was William, hiding behind a group of people in the bar, his hood drawn deeply over his face, covering it in shadows.

Sarah's eyes followed him in confusion until he slipped through the door and was gone.

'What the hell?' Charlotte asked after appearing at her table. 'He disappeared like a Ninja.' She studied Sarah's face curiously. 'What did he want? And did he tell you why he thinks you are in danger?'

That night Sarah couldn't sleep. That in itself wasn't new but this time it was for a different reason. In her head, she kept replaying the weird meeting, the story William had told her and his sudden and strange disappearance over and over. William, if that was even his real name, had been so eager to talk to her and then he had disappeared like a ghost. As if he had feared those two men. But why would he? They hadn't even looked in their direction. And what had he tried to tell her with that story? He hadn't explained why she was supposed to be in danger. Would he approach her again?

It was no surprise that she was really tired the next morning, and her head felt foggy despite the strong coffee she had drunk earlier. She could have sworn that she had checked the street properly before crossing it, but the sound of screeching tires pulled her out of her fatigue and when she turned her head in shock, she knew it was too late. The vehicle was red, and it was approaching fast. Sarah noticed the little scratch at the left side of the bumper, and the small mark on the windshield that probably originated from a stone chipping. She also noted that the colour of the car perfectly matched the colour of her handbag today but she couldn't see the driver because the sun was reflecting on the windshield. Time seemed to slow down, yet Sarah wasn't able to move a single muscle, being completely frozen in terror while all those thoughts shot through her mind in overdrive. The car would hit her any second now, crash into her, and send her flying like a puppet. She would land on her head and be dead on impact. Or maybe, if she was lucky, she'd only be paralysed.

The grip on her shoulder was hard and forceful, something that certainly would leave a bruise, and instead of flying over the hood of the car she was pulled back forcefully, falling and crashing on the asphalt behind her, bumping her elbow painfully during the process. She was disoriented until Steven's face appeared in her field of vision. 'Holy shit,' he shouted, his face ashen, the eyes behind his glasses large. 'That was close, are you OK?'

Sarah blinked a couple of times while her mind tried to process what just had happened. If Steven hadn't pulled her back in time, she'd be dead now, or at least gravely injured. As soon as the realisation sank in, she started shaking uncontrollably while trying to get back to her feet. In the meantime, the car disappeared around the next corner. It hadn't even slowed down. With Steven's help, she managed to get up and shakily stood on her own feet. Her elbow hurt but other than that she was fine.

'That car came out of nowhere,' he said, supporting her. 'You are lucky I just walked past; I was on my way to the shop. I think you should sit down somewhere,' he added after taking a critical look at her face and Sarah agreed this was a great idea.

A while later she was lying on her sofa, covered with a blanket and Charlotte was fussing over her, asking her for the thousandth time if she wanted a cup of tea or coffee or maybe a proper shot of whiskey. Or all of it at once.

After the police had taken their statements and a description of the car, Charlotte had insisted on bringing her home, and Sarah had been too shaken to refuse. Steven had given them the day off. He had appeared as shaken as Sarah felt, and she had thanked him and hugged him tightly before saying goodbye. She owed him her life, and she didn't want to think about what would have happened without him today. Charlotte heated some soup and went out to the small shop around the corner where she bought chocolate, ice cream, and plenty of wine. She insisted on staying around, even cancelling her date with Camille for the evening; one of the twins from the nightclub. Sarah hadn't even been aware of the fact that Charlotte was still seeing her. Had her life revolved so much around herself that she hadn't even noticed what was going on with her best friend? That thought made her feel even more miserable than she already did, but somehow, the two women made it through the day until Sarah finally passed out, allowing sleep to pull her into blissful oblivion.

'How are you?' Steven asked as soon as she walked into the shop the next morning. Sarah smiled at him. It felt a little rusty, but it was genuine. She was grateful for him saving her life, and always would be.

'Still a bit shaken,' she replied, 'and my elbow is bruised. But other than that, I'm all right, I think. Is everything OK with you?' she wanted to know in return because Steven seemed miles away.

Her boss scratched his neck. 'I couldn't sleep because I have been thinking about the accident. Something about it was peculiar,' he said. 'You know, I walked down the footpath, right past the pharmacy across the street, and since the car was red, I could see it when I turned the corner. It was parked, and there were no other cars around,' Steven remembered. 'The driver *must* have seen you.'

Sarah's eyebrows furrowed. She had been tired yesterday and assumed the near accident had been her fault for not paying enough attention to the traffic. 'Maybe he was playing on his phone?' she offered, but Steven didn't seem convinced.

'To me, it almost looked as if he was waiting for you.'

Sarah shook her head in disbelief, sending her auburn curls flying. 'That's ridiculous, why would he do that?' she questioned. 'I'm a single woman in her early thirties who works in a coffee shop! I don't mean to disappoint you, Steven, but my life is hardly a James Bond movie. I don't have any enemies.'

But in the back of her mind, she remembered William's claim that she was in danger.

Steven shrugged. 'Just saying, I found the whole situation very strange.' He took a deep breath. 'Well, at least you are OK.'

'Yes,' Sarah said. 'Thanks to you.' She felt the constant

need to thank him, but he only smiled and made a dismissive gesture.

'It's OK, Sarah, I would have done that for anyone. You don't owe me anything and you don't have to thank me for the rest of your life every time you see me.'

Sarah left it at that for the moment, but she knew that she surely would express her gratitude again.

The rest of the day, Sarah busied herself with work. For a change, she was glad that the shop was bustling because that way she was distracted, and her thoughts couldn't stray. Her life had taken on a very strange feel. First the hallucinations, then William, and now the accident that probably hadn't been an accident after all. At least, not if Steven was correct. The most extraordinary thing that had happened to her up to this point in her life had been to receive an anonymous gift box full of very peculiar sex toys. It had turned out to be a prank from one of her childhood friends, a girl named Pamela whom she hadn't seen or spoken to in over eight years.

But now? Everything seemed sideways.

Not being alone with her thoughts was the main reason why she accepted Charlotte's invitation to go out with her and some of her friends later that day, including Camille and Stuart. Her acceptance was answered with a loud cheer from Charlotte that made some of their customers jump. Steven shot them a glance but didn't say anything, and they knew they weren't in trouble.

Sarah would have picked any other place but since Camille lived close to it, they ended up at the Pogues. Sarah's gaze was automatically drawn towards the table in the corner, and she halfway expected to see William sitting there but he wasn't and she couldn't see him among the customers either, something that filled her with relief. She didn't want to handle additional craziness. Not today and hopefully never again. For once fate seemed to grant her this wish because the evening turned out to be quite enjoyable with no unforeseen incidents. When she left the pub a few hours later, her mood was much better than it had been before, and she looked forward to curling up underneath her blankets with a good book. She had only been drinking water and root beer and was completely sober when the hallucinations returned with a bang. Her apartment house was already in her line of sight, and she began rummaging through the depths of her handbag for her keys when her vision changed. And this time not just for a few seconds.

She saw an old cobblestone road. The streetlamps illuminating the way looked old and picturesque, they were wrought-iron and old-fashioned. Sarah paused in her step and blinked but the hallucination remained. There were still houses lining the street, but they looked different too. Reed-covered roofs, smoke rising from the chimneys. Some windows were illuminated, while others were in darkness. The air smelled fresh and clean, and the sounds of the bustling city had died down. She took a tentative step forward, feeling the uneven cobblestones under the sole of her shoes when everything suddenly went back to normal. Her neighbour Judith walked past her, with her annoying little pooch on a leash. She greeted her casually, and Sarah gaped at her before she finally managed to fake a smile and lift her hand for a return greeting. Her surroundings were perfectly normal, and her fingertips touched the cold material of her keys in her handbag.

With her near-death accident and the peculiar encounters with William, she had almost forgotten about her hallucinations, but now they had made a grand return. She tried to convince herself that this was just her nerves acting up. She almost died the day before. That surely would cause anyone to feel or see weird things, wouldn't it? But a small voice in the back of her mind told her this was not normal. Something strange was happening, and it scared the living shit out of Sarah.

For the next four weeks nothing out of the ordinary happened, and her life slowly got back to normal. Dull shifts at work, no hallucinations during the day, more or less good sleep at night.

She worked, and she occasionally went out with Charlotte. She helped at the homeless shelter every Wednesday and even managed to visit her parents over one weekend, something she didn't do very often. Her mother stuffed her with food and her father gave her the father-daughter-talk about men. Again. It was his way of showing that he cared about her. As a single child, she received the whole attention of her parents and even though she enjoyed it now and then, she was glad when she was back home after a weekend in the countryside.

She hadn't seen William since the evening at the Pogues, and the entire episode with him faded away in her memory. She still had no idea what he had wanted from her, but most likely, he had been some crazy weirdo who had stumbled in and out of her life. Just one of those things that sometimes happened.

She had bought Steven a Lego-style cup that had 'Thank you' written in large letters on it.

That way, she didn't feel compelled to say it over and over again. Otherwise, things had evened out between Steven and her. Charlotte was having the time of her life. She was madly in love, seeing Camille regularly now, and she glowed with happiness, something that made Sarah very happy for her best friend. Everything was settling down after this crazy period in her life and for a change Sarah didn't mind that everything was a little dull. Dull was exactly what she needed and wanted.

Chapter 4

It was on a Tuesday when Sarah went to the supermarket after work since her fridge had reached a stage of emptiness she couldn't ignore any longer. Relaxed, she strolled through the aisles while trying to remember what she needed since, of course, she had forgotten her shopping list. She was packing a few apples into a plastic bag and was about to put them into her shopping trolley when the noises around her died down. She hadn't noticed the constant background chatter of the other people and the low music from the speakers before, but the sudden silence was deafening. The light was different too, and when Sarah looked up, she wasn't in the supermarket any longer. She was still in a shop of some sort, but everything was different and foreign, and Sarah's eyes widened in surprise and confusion. There were shelves around that appeared as if they were usually laden with fresh fruit and vegetables, similar to the produce department she had just been standing in, but the shelves were made of wood and not of metal and plastic, and they were empty. The place appeared like some abandoned food store, a bit like an empty corner shop in a small village, and not comparable to the large supermarket she was in. Her gaze dropped to her shopping trolley, but it was gone, replaced by a basket. But she was still holding the plastic bag with six green apples in her hand. Sarah's heart began to race within her chest, and she could feel the palms of her hands going sweaty. She blinked fiercely a few times because the other hallucinations had changed back when she did that, but this time, nothing happened.

She turned her head to look around and almost jumped when she saw a small woman standing a few steps behind her, studying her intently and with obvious surprise on her face. She was wearing old-fashioned clothes and seemed to be in her forties.

'Do you want to trade?' she asked, when her eyes fell on the apples in Sarah's hands. She spoke English but with a heavy accent, that reminded Sarah of something, but she couldn't put her finger on what.

'Trade what?' Sarah replied in lack of anything else to say. Even though she knew that this was another hallucination, everything about this encounter felt real. There even was a different scent in the air, it smelled a bit like the ground after it had rained. What was the word for that? Petrichor?

'What do you want for them?' the woman inquired, and there was a desperate expression in her eyes. Sarah studied the woman more closely and could see that she was skinny, her cheeks hollow. She looked hungry.

'Uhm... you can just have them,' Sarah answered, and held the apples out to the woman.

'Thank you!' the woman whispered, as she took the apples from her hands, and Sarah found herself standing in the vegetable department of her supermarket. There was soft music playing and she heard the chatter of the other people. The apples were gone. She couldn't breathe, fear and anxiety gripping her tightly and she felt like running, an old and useless instinct because where was she supposed to run to? There was no danger here. And things started slowly sinking in because there was only one rational explanation left. She was losing her mind. There was no way she could ignore what just had happened. She was seeing things that weren't there. Not only seeing but also hearing, smelling, and feeling things. She remembered the incident after she had visited the pub. It had been shorter then, but it had been the same nonetheless. She was seeing different versions of her reality. As if she was taking a glance into the past. She knew it wasn't a brain tumour because her physician had ruled that out after all the tests she had undergone. But something was seriously wrong with her and even though there were long and normal periods, it kept happening, and the hallucinations were getting longer and more real each time. But if she was going crazy, where had the apples gone? Had she been standing here staring into nothing and someone had taken them from her hands? Had she put them away without noticing it? But she couldn't see the bag anywhere around. While her brain rationally tried to explain what she had seen, her body was still full of adrenaline, enhancing her senses and she flinched violently when she heard the voice.

'Excuse me, dear,' a woman addressed her, and Sarah shot around, expecting to see the stranger from her hallucination but it was a different woman who wanted to reach past her for the bananas. Sarah stepped aside, and the woman studied her with concern. 'Are you alright, love? You look as if you've seen a ghost.'

'I'm fine,' she said, even though she wasn't. 'Thank you,' she added, her voice sounding far away.

Leaving the shopping trolley behind, she turned around and almost fled the supermarket until she found herself sitting on the wall that enclosed the parking lot. Her breathing and her heartbeat slowly calmed down, but her thoughts were racing and there was a deep fear running through her.

What was happening?

'You saw everything in an old-fashioned way?' Charlotte asked.

Sarah hadn't known where to go but she hadn't wanted to be at home on her own, so she had turned up at Charlotte's place. Her best friend was sharing a large apartment with three guys who were in a band. At least that's what they told everyone. The only thing Sarah ever saw them doing was hanging around in the apartment and smoking weed but Charlotte liked living with them because there was always chocolate around, she claimed. The women were in Charlotte's room, sitting comfortably on some large cushions on the floor.

'Yes, it was weird. The shelves were still there but they were made of wood as was the whole building. The ceilings were lower, the light was different, but I was still standing in the vegetable department, I think,' she tried to explain. The more she repeated it, the crazier it sounded, and she wasn't sure what she'd have done if their roles were reversed and Charlotte had come to her with a story like this. She would probably have assumed her friend had accidentally swallowed some pills from her flatmates. 'I know how crazy that sounds,' she admitted, hearing the desperation in her voice. 'I think I'm losing my mind, Charlie.' She felt like crying.

'You are not losing your mind,' Charlotte responded, and she sounded so sure that Sarah felt relief.

'But what's going on? Why is my life this crazy all of a sudden?' she demanded to know. 'Other than those strange hallucinations, I feel completely normal. But they're so real. I can hear, smell, and feel things, too, when I have those visions.'

'Hallucinations of all sorts can be caused by trauma or stress,' Charlotte explained, and Sarah nervously shifted around on her cushion. Sure, she had gone through a nasty break-up a few months ago but she thought that she had more or less recovered from that. A trauma was something different, wasn't it? Or was there something in her past she had forgotten about?

Charlotte got up, went over to her desk, and scribbled something down on a piece of paper before handing it to her. 'Dr Ballantyne,' it read. 'This is the shrink Camille is seeing.' Sarah felt surprised. She hadn't been aware that Charlotte's girlfriend was seeing a therapist or why. 'You can google his number. Camille says he's very good. Maybe he can help you to sort this out.'

A therapist? Sarah swallowed and studied the piece of paper in her hand. That would mean poking around her childhood, her memories, and everything that had ever happened in her life. At least that was what Sarah assumed, since she had never been to one.

'Just try it out,' Charlotte suggested, as if able to read her thoughts. 'You never know until you try. Camille says it's helped her a great deal.'

Sarah mustered the courage to look up at Charlotte

but there was no judgment in her best friend's eyes. Just love. And concern. 'Thank you,' she whispered, pocketing the slip of paper.

The next day at work passed without any incidents, and since it was Wednesday, she was due for her shift at the homeless shelter after work. As usual, Joe greeted her warmly when she walked in, and soon the two started working. This time, Sarah helped him out in the kitchen, something she usually enjoyed because Joe always entertained her with stories of his life. Today was no different.

'Did I tell you the story where I visited another time?' he asked, and Sarah shook her head.

'I had been living on the streets for a few years already and decided to expand my horizon a little, so I walked into a different part of the city, a part I had never been in before,' he began to speak.

They were going to hand out mashed potatoes, sausages and cabbage today, and Sarah stirred the cabbage while listening to Joe's deep and pleasant voice.

'And suddenly I stumbled into something that seemed like from another century.'

Sarah slowly turned her head to study Joe. 'What do you mean by another century?' she inquired cautiously.

Joe laughed. 'I was standing in the middle of a street. It was all cobblestones, the streetlamps were wrought iron and ornamental of some sort and the houses looked like that too. Brick, but old-fashioned in a way. I don't know anything about architecture and can't tell you the style, but it wasn't twenty-first century.' Sarah's entire focus was fixed on Joe now, the spoon in her hand forgotten.

'I walked down that street, which was a very strange feeling. As if walking through a different time. But I had been drinking and things were a little blurry around the edges. They always were, back then.'

His voice got quieter before he gave a hearty laugh. 'Turned out, I had stumbled right into a film set. They had rebuilt an entire street and when I reached the end of the street, I was back in the city.' He laughed again. 'It was like walking from one universe into another.'

Sarah's eyes were fixed on him, and she slowly released the breath she hadn't been aware of holding in. For a moment she had hoped that this would relate to her hallucinations. That this had happened to someone else too. That there was an explanation for everything she was experiencing.

'What's wrong?' Joe wanted to know, having noticed the expression on her face.

And even though Sarah had not intended to tell anyone about her problems, except Charlotte and any possible doctors or therapists, the whole story poured out of her. What had happened to her throughout the last few months, how the doctor hadn't found anything on her brain, and that she was considering seeing a therapist. '...and I'm scared,' she finished the story.

Joe was quiet for some time, and Sarah felt awkward. What if he started laughing, or worse, what if he thought her completely nuts?

But his voice was calm when he spoke. 'The one thing I know for sure is that even though I greatly appreciate therapists and what they do for people, you certainly don't need to see one.'

They had never before talked about personal things. Anytime it came close to being personal, Joe would make a witty remark and change the subject. He was a very withdrawn person, something she had never noticed before. Or maybe she had never paid enough attention to him because she had never cared enough to notice. There was a rare clarity in his voice when he continued to speak, and Sarah knew that she would get a real insight into his mind now.

'I can see you're scared,' he started, 'but if I've learned anything during my life,' a life that hadn't been easy, as she knew, 'it is to take things as they come. Fear won't get you anywhere. It only clouds your judgment. Never allow it to rule you.' His eyes wandered across her face as if he was seeing her properly for the first time. 'As for what you're seeing,' he fell quiet for a moment. 'I've seen things too, and to this day, I don't know if they were real or not.' He searched her gaze, a gentle expression in his eyes. 'Everything happens for a reason. You're a good woman. I've seen many people come and go here throughout the years, but you're special. You've never looked down on me or anyone here, despite our pasts or status. Whatever it is you're going through and experiencing, never doubt yourself. There is always a reason for everything.'

The fear that had gripped her for so long that it felt like a second skin lessened a little. It was still there, on the backburner, but it felt a little easier to breathe. Even if there was no real reason behind what was happening to her, Joe was right. Whatever this was, she would deal with it. She would handle it, and she would get through it. As she always had and always would. On impulse, she threw her arms around Joe's neck and pulled him into a hug. His arms went around her in return, and he held her tightly for a moment. 'Thank you,' Sarah said, and Joe smiled his warm smile at her. She didn't just mean the fact that he had listened to her and given her advice but also the fact that he had opened up to her, if only a little.

'Anytime,' he replied. 'And I mean that literally.' And with that, he got back to preparing the meal for the evening and an amicable silence settled over them.

Sarah left the shelter at her usual time, heading straight home. It was a clear night but there was the first hint of autumn in the air and the days were getting shorter. It was past 10pm and dark outside, but her path was illuminated by the streetlamps. Since that hallucination in the super-market, she felt an underlying tension, a fear that she would start seeing things again, but she was slightly better after having talked to Joe. It wasn't so much what he had said but the fact that he had taken her seriously, and that he believed in her.

She was so deeply caught up in her thoughts that she only noticed the shadow when it was too late. And for the first time in her life, she stared into the barrel of a gun. Her body froze instantly, immediately realizing what her mind wasn't able to grasp. Her eyes went up to see an unfamiliar male face peering out from the shadows of the hood of a black jacket, and her hands instinctively went up in front of her in a silly gesture of defence or defeat. Fear gripped her tightly and she broke out in sweat, despite feeling ice cold at the same time.

'I have some money and my phone is in my bag,' she offered but her voice only came out as a whisper. 'Take it. You can have it all but please don't hurt me.' Her thoughts were racing in her mind, but she wasn't able to grasp a single one of them. The man did not react to her words but the expression on his face darkened and something she only could describe as an evil grin appeared.

'I don't want your money or your phone,' he whispered, and the expression Sarah could read in his eyes caused her to open her mouth in an attempt to scream. The sound was lodged within her throat, and she only managed to release a pathetic wail. He wasn't here to rob her, he was here to shoot her, and there was nothing she could do about it. She could see how his index finger started to curl, he was less than a second away from pulling the trigger.

The club came out of nowhere, hitting the man forcefully against the side of his head and causing him to topple over. The sound of a gunshot rang out through the night and Sarah stayed frozen on the spot, convinced that she had been hit, her mouth falling open in another attempt to scream and finally, the sound managed to escape.

Loud, shrill, and full of panic.

The club, which was swung by another hooded figure, was coming down onto the man's head forcefully once more. This finally seemed to do the trick and the man collapsed to the ground, the gun slipping from his limp fingers. Sarah slowly glanced down her body, expecting to see blood seeping through a hole in her shirt but there was nothing. She didn't feel any pain either, but she had read somewhere that the pain was often postponed after being shot, and she expected it to set in at any moment, but there was nothing. To be absolutely sure, she ran her hands over her body, feeling the urgent need to physically convince herself that she still was in one piece. Deep relief set in when she realised that he had missed her. Sarah's ears were ringing from the shot when she looked up at the other figure. He wasn't holding a club but an actual thick branch from a tree, and his face was hidden in the shadows of his hood. When he moved, the streetlamp next to them illuminated parts of it. It was William.

'Are you hurt?' he asked, his voice sounding stressed.

'I don't know,' she replied, 'I don't think so.' She opened her mouth to ask a question, but her legs buckled underneath her, not able to carry her weight any longer and she dropped to her knees, knowing she could have been dead. Again. She felt the rough pavement underneath the palms of her hands, heard the blood rushing through her ears, and detected the smell of smoke in the air. All things she wouldn't have experienced any longer if it hadn't been for William.

'Why?' she wanted to know. 'Who is that?' She could hear the first signs of hysteria lying in her voice, but she didn't care, figuring that she was entitled to some hysteria.

William pushed the gun out of the reach of the unconscious man with his foot before kneeling next to her. 'We have to leave,' he urged her on, completely ignoring her questions. 'Someone has heard the shot and your screams.' He pointed towards the windows of the house to their left which had been dark before and were illuminated now, shadows of heads popping up everywhere. 'The police will be here soon.'

Sarah looked at him in confusion. Her thoughts were a viscous mass, and every thought needed a moment to rise to the surface. 'The police?' That was a good thing, wasn't it? Not that they had been successful in finding the driver of the red car that had almost killed her a few weeks ago but they would surely investigate properly when it came to someone shooting an unarmed woman on the street.

'So what?' she said and voiced her thoughts out loud. 'That's a good thing, isn't it? This man wanted to kill me!' She almost shouted now and this time the hysteria was audible. Besides, she didn't think that she was able to get up anyway.

William sighed. 'Make sure that he can't get to the gun if he wakes,' he instructed, got up, and disappeared in a nearby alley.

'William!' she shouted after him, but he had already become one with the shadows.

'Fuck!' she screamed in frustration and fear and because she was utterly fed up. The thought of her attacker waking up before the police arrived gave her some strength back and she slowly got up, shoving the gun further out of the man's reach. She didn't touch it, thinking that it wasn't a good thing to be caught with a gun in her hand by the police but if he would move so much as a muscle, she would be able to reach down and pick it up quickly.

She just stood there, staring at the unconscious man on the ground in front of her, anxiously checking for any signs that he would wake up and waiting for the police, all the while trying not to vomit.

At the police station, she gave a formal statement and was asked to help create a sketch of William's face because he was an important witness who had disappeared, and nothing had come up when they had run his name through their system. They had arrested the attacker – who luckily hadn't woken up before the police arrived – and he had been taken to the hospital with a fractured skull. Sarah told them that she'd be dead without William and that the attacker had wanted to kill her, but they didn't seem to believe her and filed it under armed robbery. Sarah was too exhausted to contradict them. She had no proof anyway, other than what her intuition had screamed at her while she had stared down that barrel.

Chapter 5

It was past midnight when they released her, at least offering to drive her either home or to a hospital nearby. Sarah decided to go home. She wasn't injured and all she wanted was to go to bed and sleep. Preferably for a few months.

During the ride home, she gazed out of the window of the police car without seeing much of her environment. Her life had become a mess, and she had no idea why, or how to stop this.

Everything had started with her first hallucination and by now Sarah felt as if she was sitting in the middle of a spider's web that had been woven around her without her being aware of it. And someone was pulling the strings, and she was tossed around, the helpless victim of something she didn't understand. Within the course of a few weeks, she had almost died twice, and twice she had been saved. Sarah dryly asked herself if she should order a dozen of those 'thank you' mugs.

Apparently, she needed them now. Not that she liked finding herself in the role of the damsel in distress.

She wasn't really surprised that William was waiting for her in front of her apartment door. She was more than exhausted, but she hesitated only for a moment before opening the door for him. After all, he had saved her life. Also, he seemed to know at least some of the things that were going on. And without him, she'd be dead, and if this didn't qualify him to enter her apartment, nothing ever would.

Inside, Sarah slumped down in her armchair. She craved a stiff drink but she was too exhausted to get up and stayed where she was, studying William who hesitantly entered the living room, having shoved his hands into the pockets of his jacket. His gaze nervously wandered around the room and towards the windows and the door, as if he was expecting to be attacked at any moment. And who knew, maybe he was. After almost being shot for a reason she still didn't know by a stranger, she was much more open to hearing William out than she had been the last time. And she needed answers.

'What is going on around me?' she asked, when she couldn't stand the silence any longer. 'Who are you, who was this man and why was he trying to kill me? And where did you come from? Have you been following me? And don't you tell me any stories again!' She wouldn't let him out of sight until she got some answers.

William sighed and ran his hand through his hair, revealing the entirety of the scar on his face before he sat down at the edge of her sofa, ready to jump up any time, and Sarah realised how tired he looked. It was a bone-deep tiredness and she wondered where he lived and how he slept. Or if he even slept at all. She somehow doubted it.

'Do you remember the story I told you in the pub?' he asked, 'about the other world, the slaughtering of the last Guardians, and what followed afterward?'

Sarah nodded.

'And I told you about the prophecy that shows how

the downfall of that world can be stopped, maybe even reversed?' Again, Sarah only nodded.

'The prophecy is about you.'

The silence that hung between them was heavy and Sarah watched him in absolute disbelief.

'Excuse me?' was all she managed to say, not quite sure if she had heard this correctly.

William studied her calmly, for once not nervously checking his surroundings. 'I know how crazy that must sound to you,' he said, 'but it's the truth.'

He appeared defeated and Sarah figured that he had anticipated her reaction.

'I wanted to tell you from the beginning, but I wasn't sure how to approach you, knowing that you wouldn't believe me. At the same time, I had to watch over you and make sure that Drake's men wouldn't get to you first. So I followed you.'

He looked really unhappy, but the words fell out of his mouth faster and faster, as if she'd stop listening if he didn't get it out all at once.

'But they had found you already. I'm sorry that I was too late when the car almost got you, but luckily your boss was there. But I managed to get to the sniper on the roof before he had the chance to shoot you.'

'The... sniper,' Sarah said.

Her thoughts couldn't catch up with her emotions any longer and she giggled, interrupting William's rambles. It didn't take long before she laughed hysterically, all the craziness she had endured tonight but also over the last few months making itself known in that laugh. She laughed until she cried, her sides cramping with pain, but she couldn't stop.

William stared at her in confusion as if she was losing her mind and maybe she was, and what a relief that would be. Her face was wet with tears when she finally managed to calm down, but she felt slightly better, some of the tension that had been building up during the events of the night having found a release.

She noticed that William held something in her direction. It was an old-fashioned handkerchief, made of fabric, but it was clean and she took it, surprised about the gentle gesture. She wiped the tears off her face and blew her nose before getting up and disappearing into the kitchen. When she returned, she had a bottle of Bailey's and two glasses with her. It was the only alcohol in the house, but she needed something now. She poured each of them a glass and handed one to William. She drank a large sip, only focusing on the sweet taste and the warmth of the booze in her throat.

'Sorry,' she apologised, 'but that was too much crazy for me to handle. What you are telling me is that there is another world, some sort of Stephen Hawking parallel world, that has magic and is going under because the last Guardians have been killed. But fear not because there is a prophecy about me that explains how I can save it.'

Now it was William's turn to nod at her. 'I don't know Stephen Hawking, but otherwise, yes.'

'And you're telling me that there is this evil guy named Drake trying to get me killed because why exactly? Oh yes, because I'm the only threat to his power because I theoretically could restore the magic in that world?'

Once again, William nodded.

'What kind of name is Drake for an alternate-magical villain, anyway?' she asked rhetorically, and continued to speak before he could reply to that. 'So, the incident with the car was no accident, the guy tonight was sent by Drake to kill me, and in addition there was a sniper I didn't even notice?' Sarah's voice had a slight hysterical undertone while she was clinging to her glass of Bailey's, deciding that it was a good time to take another long sip.

The really scary thing about William's story was that it explained a lot of the things that had happened to her over the last few months. Assuming that his story was the truth, everything fell into place and made sense. Even William's constant paranoia. In his logic, those people who tried to kill her had to be after him, too.

'You left me sitting at that pub the last time because the two men who came in belonged to Drake as well?'

'Yes.'

'And who are you? What do you have to do with all of this?' she demanded, wanting to understand his motivation for telling her this unbelievable story, his reason to be here.

For the first time since she had met him, he hesitated for a long time before he spoke. 'It's my world that's dying,' he stated. 'And I know about the prophecy, so what was I supposed to do? Watch everyone around me perish?'

Sarah had no answer to this. In his mind, he was obviously the hero. 'And what I'm seeing is this other world?'

Now it was William's turn to frown at her in confusion. 'What do you mean? What you're seeing?' he interrogated, leaning slightly forward.

'I'm having hallucinations,' Sarah admitted, not caring any longer. She didn't believe a word of William's story, but why not go along with it for a while? 'I'm seeing things that aren't there. One second, I'm walking down my street, and the next I'm somewhere else. It's like the same street, but it looks completely different. Old-fashioned in a way, more rural. The street lamps were wrought iron and decorated with these pretty ornaments. It also happened in the supermarket. There was even a woman who took my apples!'

William's frown deepened and was now accompanied by obvious surprise. 'You see those things? All of a sudden?'

'Yes,' Sarah replied, feeling more exhausted than she ever had felt in her entire life. She couldn't believe that she was discussing any of this with William. This was the weirdest story she had ever heard. Even considering it was nuts. At least she didn't feel crazy any longer when talking about her hallucinations, which was something, right? Because no one could match the craziness that William had unleashed on her. Compared to him, she was quite normal. But at the same time, she was at the end of her strength. The events of the last weeks, but mainly the attack tonight, were taking a toll on her body, and she noticed that her hands were shaking. She finished her Bailey's and put the empty glass down.

'I can't hear my thoughts any longer, and I haven't even gotten around to thanking you for saving my life tonight. I still don't know who you really are, what you want, or why you're telling me such a crazy story, but without you, I definitely would be dead now and for that, I'm grateful.'

She got up from the armchair, still shaking.

'I need a break from all of this, and I need some sleep.

Today was more than rough, and I'm going to bed.' She hesitated before adding, 'You can stay here and sleep on the sofa if you want.'

He looked almost as bad as she felt, and she didn't want to throw him out in the middle of the night. Also, and this was something she hated to admit to herself, she knew that she would feel safer with him around, despite the crazy story he just had told her.

'Thank you. I will stay,' he decided, and took a sip from his glass of Bailey's that he'd only been holding until now. 'That's not bad,' he stated, surprised, studying the drink in his glass.

'I'll be right back,' Sarah said, and left the living room to pick up a spare pillow and a blanket from her bedroom. She wasn't one hundred percent sure letting him stay was a good idea, but he surely hadn't saved her life just to kill her tonight, right? She was too exhausted to deal with these kinds of thoughts right now.

'The kitchen is over there,' she pointed towards a wall, 'if you're hungry or thirsty, take whatever you want. And the bathroom is over there,' she added, pointing at the opposite wall. 'Good night.'

And with those words, she left him, went straight into her room, and locked the door safely behind her. She was only able to take off her shoes before she collapsed onto the bed, falling asleep almost immediately.

She woke up because the sun was shining directly into her face, and she squinted against the light. She had obviously forgotten to close her curtains last night. The alarm clock on her nightstand told her that it was past nine am and Sarah yawned before the memory hit her full force and everything fell back into place. That attack last night. The time at the police station. William and his crazy story.

Fuck!

She shot up from the bed as if stung by a bee, reaching for her clothes before realising that she was still dressed from yesterday. It was Thursday and she was supposed to be at work. Where was her damn mobile phone? She found it in her jacket, and it showed numerous missed calls.

Some were from Steven but most of them were from Charlotte.

Shit.

She immediately called Steven's number and told him about the attack last night. He offered her a few days off, but she had to promise him in return to see a doctor today, a promise she already knew she was going to break. She felt bad when she ended the call. Steven's place was a small shop and anytime she couldn't work, Charlotte and Steven had to cover for her. Lately, Sarah had been missing quite often. But there was nothing she could do about it now. She sent a quick text to Charlotte, telling her that she was OK and that she would call her later. Sarah craved a shower and fresh clothes. And a coffee. In no particular order. But first, she would have to deal with the crazy man in her living room. She ran her hand through her unruly locks. Last night when she had been in shock, his story had sounded almost logical to her but in the light of the new morning, it was what it was. A crazy story by someone who seemed to be obsessed with her and had a very creative imagination. At least he hadn't tried to break into her bedroom last night. She carefully stepped out of the door, ready to deal with whatever was to come.

Her apartment was quiet and William was lying on the sofa, asleep. His face seemed younger like this, almost boyish and a strand of his hair had fallen across his forehead, concealing his prominent scar. While studying his sleeping figure, she realised that despite his weird behaviour and the strange stories, she had never felt threatened by him. He had scared her with his erratic behaviour but there had never been a sign that he was dangerous. He certainly seemed to believe in that story he had told her.

What was she supposed to do about him?

He surely wouldn't leave her alone, not if he believed his own tales. While she considered her options her eyes fell on the small coffee table. She always kept a few pens, some books, and empty paper there, where she scribbled down her shopping lists or notes during the day. William had drawn something on one of them. She stepped closer and picked the small piece of paper up to get a better look at it. When she realised what she was seeing, her blood ran cold, and she stumbled back in shock before sinking into her armchair. The world as she had known it crumbled and fell around her.

When she looked up after what seemed an eternity, William was awake. His eyes were open, and he studied her calmly. For once there was no nervous or desperate expression on his face. Instead, there almost was something like pity lying there.

'I knew it when you described your hallucinations, as you called them,' he said and slowly sat up.

Sarah couldn't move. Her hands were clenched around that little piece of paper while she stared at William. He slowly got up and approached her, kneeling in front of her, and gently pulling the paper out of her cramped hands.

'You aren't having hallucinations, and you aren't going crazy. I don't know how this is possible but what you are seeing,' he explained and smoothed out the paper, holding it up, 'is my world.'

His drawing showed the streetlamp Sarah had seen. Every detail was exact and there was no way on Earth that he could have known this because she hadn't told anyone about the details.

'My world is called Aphelia. And it was a beautiful place before the war started.'

Sarah studied William as if seeing him for the first time. She noticed that his eyes were green, his hair was black with a few first grey hairs at his temples, the scar wasn't as even as she had originally thought and he had pretty, soft lips. He returned her gaze calmly, kneeling on the floor in front of her, allowing her to deal with the shock of the revelation in her own way and at her own pace. She finally knew where his accent was coming from, and her eyes filled with tears. This was too big for her, too much. A part of her told her that this was crazy, that someone was playing an evil and sick prank on her. She even considered the option that all of this was just happening inside her head. Another thought crossed her mind. Maybe she was making William up and he wasn't here at all. Without having planned to do so she lifted her hand and grazed his cheek with the tips of her fingers. He blinked at her in surprise but held still otherwise, allowing her this exploration. His skin was warm, and the stubbles on his face scratched against her fingertips.

Nope, he was real.

She pulled her hand back and let it drop back into her lap. She thought about all the small things that had been inexplicable and they all added up now, leading to this revelation. Why her? There was nothing special about her. She wasn't overly talented in anything, she was pretty but not beautiful, and she certainly wasn't a scientist developing a cure for cancer or any other sort of hero. She was just a somewhat nerdy young-ish woman, who loved to read and who sold coffee.

This had to be some sort of mistake. But everything fit into William's story, down to the woman in her vision who had been hungry because apparently there was a war going on in her world. In William's world. Aphelia.

'Who are you?' The words tumbled from her lips. She didn't avert her eyes from his face and noticed the emotions that crossed it. There was surprise about her question, a flicker of unease, and then his expression turned blank, his face a mask, unable to be read any longer.

'No one special,' he answered. 'My name is William Lawrence, as you know. I found the prophecy and when I realised that there was a way to save my world from terror and despair, I knew I had to find you.'

The sadness in his face and voice seemed to be genuine but she still knew that he wasn't telling her the entire truth. She decided to let it lie, suspecting that she wouldn't be able to handle the whole truth right now anyway.

Her mobile phone rang, and Sarah almost jumped. It

was strange how something so mundane was still going on while the world as she had known it lay shattered at her feet. She didn't answer the call; she wasn't ready to face the world. She wasn't even able to get up from the armchair. Her thoughts seemed to be frozen and in overdrive at the same time. She had so many questions that she couldn't decide on which one to ask first but finally, a few words slipped out.

'The prophecy. What does it say?'

Chapter 6

William hesitated and by the expression on his face, Sarah knew that she wasn't going to like what she was going to hear. 'It doesn't say much,' William admitted slowly. 'But next to the prophecy was a letter, including a drawing of you and the mention of Earth, specifically Haleston in England. The letter said that there was only one way to save my world, and that you were the key to it. It also mentioned a second part of the prophecy, hidden in this world. And that you were going to be the one who finds it.' Silence filled the space between them.

'And it isn't, I don't know, a bit more specific?' Sarah asked, and William scratched his neck, suddenly appearing somewhat uncomfortable.

'I...' his voice trailed off. 'I never actually thought this far. Until now it was all about finding you and convincing you to listen to me and then it was about protecting you from Drake's men but when the prophecy claimed that you'd know how to find the second part of the prophecy, I just believed it.'

Sarah looked at him in absolute disbelief. 'I sell coffee!' she exclaimed. 'How am I supposed to find a hidden prophecy? I'm not a librarian, a clever scientist, or an archaeologist. I've never been out of this country in my entire life. I don't know anything about prophecies!'

She leaned back in her armchair, feeling drained. She

couldn't believe that she was discussing this with him. Parts of her mind were screaming at her that all of this was entirely crazy, while the rational part had accepted it as a logical explanation. She ran her hand through her hair and realised that she hadn't even brushed it yet.

'I don't think I ever can get up from this chair again,' she said.

'Do you need assistance?' William was up and at her side in an instant, and Sarah snorted. 'That's not what I meant.' She sighed deeply. 'Why have I been seeing your world randomly for the last few months?'

William shrugged. 'I don't know. I didn't even know that something like that was possible. I only learned that our tales about your world were true when I found the prophecy. Finding the secret passage here was quite difficult, and it took me a while. But once you realise that everything is true and you search for it, you can find a lot about your Earth in our history and art. The knowledge has just been forgotten, like the magic.'

Sarah thought about the wars on Earth, poverty, exploitation, climate change, and about capitalism in general. 'Maybe some things are supposed to be forgotten,' she stated.

William sat down on the sofa, leaning his elbows on his knees and folding his hands in front of him. 'Are you going to help me? Help us all?' he asked, and Sarah realised that he was holding his breath.

She knew that he wanted her to make a choice, but what did it mean? She wasn't even able to properly wrap her head around the whole story yet. How was she supposed to decide, especially because she had no clue what helping him would imply. Was she going to have to fight dragons? She knew nothing about his world or what the prophecy would require from her. The whole story was absurd, and Sarah lifted her hands in a helpless gesture.

'I don't even know what that means. I don't know anything any longer.'

'Allow me to show you my world and then you can make your decision,' William offered, and Sarah studied him, considering his request. She knew all of this was crazy but what did she have to lose? At least she would know once and for all if he was telling the truth. It would be the final proof.

'Are there dragons?' she wanted to know, and for the first time a smile flitted across his face, immediately turning him from average-looking into handsome.

'No,' he replied, and she could hear the amusement in his voice. 'No dragons.'

An hour later they stepped out of the front door. They had taken turns showering before having breakfast, which consisted only of coffee for Sarah because she wasn't hungry and hadn't been able to even eat a single slice of toast. William however had eaten a lot, nurturing her suspicion that he had no home here in this world. And how could he? If his story was true, he had no references any landlord would take.

William's demeanour changed completely as soon as they left the house. He was checking around nervously, and his jumpiness was contagious. Sarah felt the first bouts of paranoia herself, seeing danger in every shadow and around every corner. When he stopped her mid-step for the third time in a row to check something out, she finally addressed him.

'Would you please stop doing that? If you carry on like this, there doesn't need to be an ambush because I will die of a stress-induced heart attack.'

William ran his hand through his hair. 'Sorry,' he apologised. 'But they know I've been talking to you, and I'm afraid they'll intensify their efforts.'

'Their efforts to kill me,' Sarah said.

'Us,' he corrected her.

'Isn't that marvellous,' she mumbled to herself, now checking their surroundings nervously too before addressing William. 'Where are we going, anyway?'

William pulled out a plan of the public transport system and looked like a tourist who was going to ask for directions. He pointed at a spot in the countryside, just outside the city. 'We need to go there, by train and then by bus.'

'But why there?' Sarah inquired. 'What exactly is there?'

'The magic that once ruled our world isn't visible. You can't say a spell or use it to your liking in any way,' William tried to explain. 'It's just there, almost like a physical law, ensuring the balance of everything that is, and it's subject to fluctuations, always has been. Since the last Guardians are dead, it's disappearing from our world, but there are still some places where it remains. Places that have been able to store the magic in a way. It's fading there, too, but I found one of those spots just outside the city where the transition between our worlds is possible if you know how to do it. I don't know how long it'll still be possible.'

William fell silent and left Sarah pondering his words and everything else she had learned today.

About an hour later they stepped off the bus. Their journey had been uneventful, and they hadn't spoken much. Even though she had many questions, Sarah had kept to herself, not yet entirely convinced he was speaking the truth with his unbelievable story. She felt somewhat detached and surreal, and her mind was fighting with contradictory emotions and thoughts. One part of her screamed that she was crazy, and that even remotely considering anything William had told her qualified her for a nice long holiday in a mental hospital, while another part of her told her that it explained everything that had happened to her over the last couple of months. It all came down to the question of how William could possibly have known what the streetlamps in her hallucination had looked like. She settled down with the thought that she was about to find out once and for all. If William told the truth he would show her a different world.

And if there was no other world, she'd know he was crazy. As was she. Either way, it would be over soon.

They walked up a hill that overshadowed a small valley. There were meadows, some farmland and she could see cows and sheep grazing peacefully in the distance. A cluster of farm cottages appeared on the horizon, but they were small, and walking there surely would take at least half an hour. Sarah never had been out here before and she was surprised at how quiet and slow everything was, when only about an hour away, the madness of a large city waited.

They reached the top of the hill where a few trees were gathered. In the middle stood an ancient oak. Its trunk was huge, and the sweeping branches and leaves formed a natural roof, so thick that Sarah almost couldn't see the sky through it. A sense of peace washed over her when she stepped under the green canopy and Sarah wondered how old this tree was. It looked ancient to her, and the feeling of peace increased when she touched the rough bark. She sometimes felt like this when in the presence of old structures or things. Like that one time when she had visited a museum and there were artefacts on display, things that were so much older than her. Things that had seen different eras. She had felt small in their presence but not in a bad way. It was more comforting, a bit like watching the stars in the countryside when it was pitch dark. It was a soothing thought to be part of something large, powerful, and miraculous, and Sarah felt the same way when she touched the tree.

'What now?'

William, who had watched her silently, approached her. 'Take my hand and close your eyes.' He held out his hand. Sarah felt nervous when she took it. Now she would find out what this was all about. His skin was warm, his fingers calloused, and he held on to her tightly while Sarah closed her eyes as he had told her. And the world toppled. She couldn't describe it any better than that. She swiftly opened her eyes again and released her breath. Nothing had happened. Their surroundings looked exactly as they had before.

'What?' she said, not sure if she felt relieved or disappointed. 'Nothing happened!'

'Take a deep breath,' William suggested, releasing her hand and taking a step away from her.

Sarah obliged, and finally, it registered. The air smelled completely different. There was the scent of flowers in the air, wild herbs, and something she couldn't identify. Sarah's breath caught in her throat when they stepped out of the canopy of the old oak and into the open. The scent in the air intensified and in front of her she saw the same valley she had seen before, just that it had changed. There were no farmhouses, cows, or sheep. Instead, it was covered with a sea of blooming wildflowers, the source of the smell in the air. In the distance, trees were growing and even though she was no expert on trees, she was pretty sure that she never had seen these kinds of trees before.

She stood there, mouth open in surprise while she took in her surroundings. She had expected to be shocked, confused, or maybe scared. What she hadn't expected was the beauty of this place and the awe she felt at seeing it. It was just a hill in the countryside, but the colours of the flowers were much richer, the air smelled clean, and she knew that she wasn't on Earth any longer. She just knew. It was as scary as it was thrilling and she shivered, even though she wasn't cold.

'This is beautiful,' she finally whispered once she had recovered a bit, and her gaze fell on William. There was sadness lying in his eyes, but he quickly hid his expression and smiled at her.

'Welcome to Aphelia,' he said.

This was magical and utterly different from the

reality she had come to believe in as unchangeable. But as it turned out there was so much more out there than she had ever been able to fathom. She was torn between fear, because if something like this was possible, what else was, and relief because everything that had happened to her was finally explained and she knew for sure that she wasn't losing her mind.

She let her gaze wander over the valley, breathing in the foreign air and enjoying the peace this place radiated. Sarah felt the sudden urge to apologise to him for thinking that he was crazy.

But then, no one would have believed him.

'Turn around,' William whispered, and when Sarah did, she could see a dark column of smoke in the air on the horizon somewhere behind them.

'That's one of our villages, burning,' William explained.

'Oh…' she uttered. For a moment she had forgotten what he had told her about his world.

That there was a war going on here. To be fair, it was easy to forget in this peaceful scenery deep in the country-side, but Sarah was aware that he was still waiting for her decision.

'I want to see it,' she demanded, and William's expression darkened.

'It's too dangerous,' he denied her request.

'Do you want me to help you save this world?' she asked rhetorically. William nodded.

'Then you're going to show me what I'm saving it from.' She crossed her arms in front of her chest, not sure why she was insistent on seeing the burning village. It was not that she liked to see other people suffer, quite the opposite. She was quite squeamish when it came to seeing blood or any catastrophe. But she needed to know, needed to see for herself what was going on in this world.

'We're not prepared,' William tried to object. 'Look at your clothes.' Sarah studied herself. She was wearing jeans, her comfortable trainers that she usually wore for work, a plain green shirt, and a light brown jacket. She had no idea what the people in this world were wearing but when she thought back to the woman she had seen at the supermarket, she figured that she was supposed to wear something simpler.

'The people from Aphelia don't know about Earth. I told you that it is forgotten knowledge. They also don't know about magic and why things went downhill the way they did. All they know is that life turned miserable for them and that they're dying. If you turn up like this, it'll raise questions.'

Sarah's frown deepened. 'Just a little peek,' she insisted, standing her ground. 'We won't be seen if we take care. Please, William, I need to see it for myself.'

William studied her, clenching his jaw in annoyance but he gave in, not having much of a choice anyway. Not if he wanted her help. 'You stay close to me, and do whatever I say, understand? If I tell you to jump into a ditch, you will jump into a ditch.'

'Yes, sir!' Sarah yelled and saluted him, something that William didn't find funny in the least.

Aphelia resembled the rural parts of Earth, but she couldn't see any animals. When she asked William about them, he only pointed at his stomach and reminded Sarah about the fact that there was a famine going on. This was difficult to believe because everything seemed so peaceful. But then, she hadn't seen any cities yet, only the countryside. Funnily enough, this world was like a mirror of her own. During her visions, she had always found herself in the same place, just the setting had changed. She figured that if she returned to her world now, she'd be standing on the path that had led them to the old oak.

While they walked towards the smoke column in the distance, Sarah studied William. He had changed since they had appeared here. He seemed harder, broody, and even more withdrawn than he had been before, and Sarah wondered why. This was his world, but he was even more tense here, even though on Earth there had been people trying to kill them. Back there he had come across as desperate, nervous and headstrong. When she looked at him here, he seemed to be wearing an impenetrable mask, and she realised that she knew nothing about him. Who *was* he? What he had done for a living before finding the prophecy, and how had he found it anyway?

Things like this didn't happen coincidentally. She was about to ask him when he stopped and lifted his hand. She stopped, immediately studying their surroundings to find out what it was that had him alarmed. But she couldn't see or hear anything.

Without warning, William pulled her to the left and pushed her into the small ditch next to the path they had been walking down. Sarah did not resist, even though she landed ungracefully on all fours. And now, she could hear it, too – the sound of approaching horses. She had no idea how many, but it sounded like more than one. William had heard them way before she had, and now he was lying next to her on the ground, a silent warning in his eyes before he pressed his index finger to his lips. What was he thinking she was about to do? Break out into her favourite opera song? She was tempted to roll her eyes at him but held her breath instead because the horses had reached them. Sarah tried to make herself even smaller. She could feel the vibrations in the ground when they hurried past. It seemed to be at least twenty, and she could hear William releasing a deep breath when they were gone.

'Soldiers,' he explained, and there was a strange undertone to his voice. Was that anger? He ran his hand through his hair. 'I knew this was a bad idea. It's too dangerous. If they find you here, everything is lost. Let's go back,' he pleaded with her.

Sarah studied the horizon. The dark column was close, and she could already smell the smoke in the air. 'One short glance,' she insisted, not sure why it was so important for her to see the destruction of this world, but it was.

William sighed in defeat. 'Why are you so stubborn?' he questioned, but he didn't seem to expect a reply because he had already begun to climb back onto the path. Moments later, they were on their way to the village again.

When they reached the perimeter of the small town, Sarah wrinkled her nose. There was a stench lying in the air that made her want to gag, but she couldn't identify it. Nonetheless, she followed William, who led her toward a small patch of bushes they could hide behind. From here, they had a good view of the village. Or what was left of it.

The sight was worse than she had expected because beneath the destruction, the previous beauty of the village could be seen. There was not much of it left. Only devastation and piles of ashes, some of them still burning. Not one of the cute little houses was intact. But she didn't see anyone.

'Where are the people that used to live here?'

Wordlessly, William pointed towards his right, and shocked, Sarah realised that one of the piles burning somewhere in the distance was made entirely of bodies. She scrambled back, finally managed to get to her feet and she staggered away from the village, from the gruesome sight, from the horrible stench that now seemed to be etched to the insides of her nose forever.

William caught up with her after about a minute and wordlessly pulled her into his arms. At least he had the decency to not say something along the lines of, 'I told you so.' Instead, he only held her until she was able to breathe again. What had she been thinking? That the worst she would see here were some wounded people? William had told her that this world was at war and a dark place at the moment, but she hadn't been able to imagine how dark. And she didn't think that she had seen even half of it.

All those people. Slaughtered and left to burn with no one here to mourn them.

William slowly released her from his arms, and his face came into sight. 'Have you seen enough?' he wanted to know but there was no triumph lying in his voice. Just sadness.

'Yes,' Sarah whispered. This was entirely her fault. She had insisted. The stench in the air was still there and now, when she knew what it was, it was almost impossible to bear. It was one thing to hear about a war, but an entirely different thing to see some of its effects. 'What happened here?'

'Drake,' was William's only reply, and quietly they turned back in the direction they had come from and walked away from all the death and the destruction.

Until now everything had held a certain exciting quality for her – as if this was just a huge adventure – but she had landed back in harsh reality. This was real, it was dark, and it was dangerous, and Sarah had no idea why she had insisted on coming here in the first place. She wanted to go back home where everything was safe and familiar. Except that it wasn't. And for the first time, Sarah felt nothing but a wave of despair when she thought about her future. She knew that she had the choice whether to help William or not, but did she *really* have a choice? She didn't even know what helping him involved, or where she was supposed to find that second part of the prophecy but after what she had seen today, it certainly wouldn't be easy. It would be dangerous. But at least she would be able to help the people of Aphelia, wouldn't she? If she didn't help William, however, there would still be people after her, trying to kill her, and she had no idea how to escape them. If she wanted to return to her normal, and most of all safe, life she didn't have a choice. She somehow needed to fulfil that prophecy and hopefully be left alone by everyone afterwards. Her dull job at the coffee shop suddenly seemed like paradise.

She was very quiet on their way back, still able to smell the stench of death even though they had left the village behind, and the air was filled with the scent of wildflowers again. Sarah doubted that she would ever forget that smell. William left her to her thoughts, studying the surroundings carefully until they reached the hill and the old oak. He took her hand, as he had on the way here. 'Ready?' he asked, and Sarah nodded and closed her eyes, more than ready for the step back into her world.

Chapter 7

'Where the hell have you been?' Charlotte snapped at her. 'I was worried sick.' Sarah had called her after arriving back at her flat and realising that she had plenty of missed calls from Charlotte. And for once Sarah had no idea what to tell her. She hated the thought of lying to her best friend but what was she supposed to say? The more Charlie knew the more she'd be drawn into this mess, and Sarah wanted to protect her from all the craziness that recently had become her life. 'I was attacked last night and…' she started.

'I know,' Charlotte interrupted her, 'Steven told me, and that's why I've been trying to reach you the whole day. You said you'd call me!'

'I'm sorry,' Sarah said. 'I had my phone on mute and slept for most of the day. I didn't get much sleep last night.' That was barely a lie.

'What happened? Are you OK? Do you want me to come over?'

Sarah hesitated for a moment. She craved familiar and friendly company, but she didn't want to endanger Charlotte in any way. 'Thank you, but I'm just going back to sleep. I'll tell you everything tomorrow at work. I'm fine, really. I promise!' That was the biggest lie of all, but she knew that she couldn't allow Charlotte near her home for a while, it was too dangerous.

After the two women had finished the call, Sarah put her mobile phone down and stepped towards the windows, peering through the curtains. She felt anxious, expecting an attack of some sort every moment, something that made her very jumpy. While it had been William who was nervous on their way out of town, it was Sarah who had seen danger everywhere on their way back. Only when she had locked the door behind her, she had felt remotely safe, though not entirely. And now she was pacing restlessly through her small apartment, exhausted but too agitated to even sit down. Her whole life had been turned upside down in only twenty-four hours and she knew that nothing would ever be the same. Nothing *could* ever be the same. Her eyes fell on an open book she was currently reading lying on a table nearby. It was a great story that had drawn her in, but now it seemed shallow to her because nothing compared to what real life had thrown at her. In books, these kinds of things were always heroic, while in reality, everything was just dreadful and scary. She peered through the curtains and out the window again, dreading to see some shady figures while hoping to see William at the same time. He was the only connection to what was going on she had, the only person who was able to assure her that she wasn't losing her mind. And the only person she felt remotely safe with at the moment. He had mumbled something about things he had to do on delivering her home and making sure it was safe – for now – before he had rushed off, promising her he would return as fast as possible.

The street lay empty and still, and Sarah paced to the kitchen and looked into the fridge, remembering that she hadn't eaten the entire day, but even though her stomach gave an interested growl, the sight of food repelled her. The stench of the burning bodies still seemed to be attached to the inside of her nose. She closed the fridge without taking anything from it, just pouring herself a glass of water before she wandered restlessly back into her living room, where she sank onto the sofa and buried her head in her hands.

What was she supposed to do?

She felt more exhausted than ever when she woke up the next morning. Her mind hadn't allowed her to rest peacefully and every time she had fallen into a light sleep, she had dreamt utterly weird things, startling her awake. She was also worried about William. He had not returned yet, and deep down she had been listening and waiting for that knock on her door throughout the entire night. She felt grumpy and wondered if it was necessary to go to work today. With everything that was going on, working seemed so profane, but she knew that she couldn't leave Steven hanging, not after everything he had done for her. And she still needed the money and therefore the job. An hour and a half later, she walked into the coffee shop, where she was immediately greeted by Charlotte.

'Tell me what happened,' her best friend demanded to know, and Sarah launched into the story of the attack on her while she got ready for work. She didn't mention that William had waited for her after she had returned from the police or anything else that had happened since then. It wasn't that she didn't trust Charlotte with any of this, but she didn't want to pull her into this mess.

'And it happened in front of your house?' Charlotte inquired, and Sarah confirmed it with a nod.

Her best friend frowned at her while Sarah absent-mindedly wiped the counter clean since they would open in about ten minutes. 'There are a lot of strange things going on around you,' she observed, and studied her very closely.

Sarah had a hard time meeting her friend's gaze openly. If she only knew.

'Do you want to stay at my place for a few nights?' Charlotte offered and Sarah considered this for a moment. It was tempting because the bad guys couldn't find her there. But then, neither could William. Sarah mentally slapped herself. Of course, the bad guys would find her there, they had been watching her over the last couple of weeks or even months. They certainly knew who Charlotte was and where she lived. No, it was too dangerous for her friend.

'Greatly appreciated,' she answered, and meant it. 'But I'm only able to tolerate your flatmates in small doses. Also, I need to carry on normally with my life, otherwise, I allow my fears to get the better of me. You know how they say to get back into the saddle after falling off a horse? But thank you!' Out of an impulse she wrapped her arms around Charlotte and pulled her into a tight embrace. 'You know that I love you, don't you?' she asked, and heard Charlotte chuckle lightly.

'Love you too, doll.'

She released her friend, reached for her mug, and took a sip of coffee. That was when all hell broke loose.

It happened so fast that she couldn't even say what she noticed first. The blinding light that enveloped her, the earth-shattering noise that left her ears ringing for days, or the invisible force that hit her like an angry tsunami and blew her into the shelves behind like a rag doll, completely knocking the air from her lungs.

To her surprise, the impact when she landed on the floor wasn't really painful. The debris that rained down on her directly afterwards didn't hurt much either. Her mind, however, had a difficult time catching up with the events. Only seconds ago she had been standing behind the counter of the coffee shop she was working in, taking a sip from a silly Star Wars mug. And now she was face-down on the ground in a heap.

She still had the taste of coffee on her tongue when she slowly got back to her feet, a feat which was accompanied by a dull pain in her leg and her head. She didn't pay much attention to it right now, too shocked to feel properly.

The small, old-fashioned bell that usually announced the arrival of new customers was still hanging from the ceiling, ready to release its silvery sound as soon as the door was opened. The only problem was that there was no more door.

She stared right into the face of a stranger who was standing on the footpath on the other side of the street. His eyes were wide open, his mouth agape, and he was staring back at her as if she was a ghost. She could see that his lips were moving, but all she could hear was that loud ringing in her ears. She brought her hand to her face and when she looked at it, it was covered in dust and blood.

Her mind was finally able to catch up with what was going on and everything fell into place.

Sarah knew that life as she had come to know it was over. It had shattered into a thousand tiny pieces, just like the coffee shop around her. She heard something other than the ringing noise. A pathetic-sounding wail.

It took her a moment to realise that it was coming from her own mouth.

The bomb had exploded somewhere at the front of the shop, close to the door, and that was the only reason she and Charlotte were still alive. Their bodies had been sheltered by the counter and the blast itself hadn't managed to harm them much, but it had still sent them flying, debris had nicked their skin, and the air was filled with thick dust, making it difficult to breathe. Sarah's screams were mirrored by Charlotte's, and she reached blindly through the dust until her hand found the other woman. Charlotte's gaze found hers, her eyes wide in shock and fear, her face and hair covered in dust, a small trickle of blood running down the side of her cheek. When they looked around, they were greeted by the sight of destruction. The front door was gone. As were the shop windows. Glass was everywhere. The shelves, tables, and chairs were either destroyed or had fallen over. Everything was shattered or in disarray and they only noticed Steven when he came running towards them from his office.

'Are you hurt? What happened? Oh my God!' He gawked at the place and them in terror.

Sarah and Charlotte looked at each other and down at their bodies. They were dirty and covered in dust. There were some bleeding scratches where their skin hadn't been covered and Sarah felt a dull headache coming on. She had bumped her head when dropping to the floor and there was some blood on her face even though she had no idea where it came from, but other than that they were unharmed. Everything sounded a little dull, and there was a loud ringing in Sarah's ears.

'I'm OK,' she reassured him, but her voice was coming from far away. 'I think.'

But she wasn't. She was far from OK. They had planted a bomb right here where she worked. The explosion was her fault, and it was a miracle that no one had gotten hurt. Steven had been in the office, and it had been sheer luck that she and Charlotte had both been standing behind the counter and that no customers had been in yet. Tears started filling her eyes and silently ran down her face, leaving lines in her dusty face. A pool of people had gathered around, drawn in by the noise of the explosion and a pair of strong hands led her to a chair and pushed her down onto it. Someone else draped a blanket over her shoulders and she gripped it and pulled it tightly around herself. She never understood why people were given a blanket after an accident, always assuming that it had something to do with shock and body temperature, but she was grateful for the blanket now. It gave her the feeling of being comforted, of being safe. Charlotte was seated next to her, and Steven was running through the remains of his shop in shock, coming back to them to make sure that they were indeed OK before running around like a headless chicken again. Sarah studied the broken table on the floor in front of her. She wasn't sure if she was in shock, but her thoughts were surprisingly clear. This was her fault. She had drawn them here, endangered some of the most important people to her. This couldn't happen again. She needed to disappear, go undercover, and hide somewhere until she figured a way out of this mess. If she wasn't around people any longer, no one would get hurt.

She was more scared than ever, but deep down something else stirred within her, a strength she hadn't known she possessed. She wouldn't allow this to continue. She wouldn't hide and wait for things to come, and she definitely wouldn't wait to see anyone around her die for reasons she didn't even fully understand herself. Instead, she would get active, she would find this fucking prophecy, and William, and then she would end this and go back to her normal life. She had no idea how and where to start, and the enormity of everything was weighing down on her, but she would take it one step at a time. The first step was that she needed to disappear. Now.

She turned her head and glanced at Charlotte, who was studying her closely in return. Her best friend looked dishevelled and there was a deep scratch across her forehead that was bleeding, but her eyes were clear and observant. There were sirens in the distance, so there wasn't much time left.

'What's going on in your life?'

Sarah felt a rush of affection for her beautiful, warm-hearted, and perceptive Charlotte. She didn't know what she would do without this woman. Sarah leaned forward to only allow Charlotte to hear her words. 'I can't tell you now, but I need to disappear for a while,' she said. 'I'll explain everything to you when I can, I promise. Don't come searching for me, please.'

Charlotte studied Sarah for a few moments, deep concern lying in her friend's eyes but there was also faith.

'I knew you weren't crazy,' she only commented and at that, fresh tears were spilling from Sarah's eyes.

'I love you,' she whispered, and Charlotte smiled.

'I love you, too. And I'm here if you need me,' her best friend said in return, and Sarah felt more tears welling up. But she couldn't allow herself to drown in her emotions. It was time to leave. The sirens were close now, and Sarah got up and placed the blanket over the chair.

'Where are you going?' Steven was at her side immediately, his hands still fluttering around in shock and agitation.

'Bathroom,' Sarah replied and pointed towards the toilet signs.

'Be safe there,' he said after considering. At any other given moment, she would have found this remark funny, but she knew exactly where he was coming from.

The woman staring back at her in the mirror looked haunted, weary, and beyond tired.

Sarah turned the tap on and washed as much blood and dust as possible from her hair, face, and clothes. At least she wasn't bleeding openly any longer. Afterwards, she carefully opened the door and checked her surroundings. The police had arrived. If she wanted to leave, she would have to do it now. She caught Charlotte's eye, and her friend gave her the thumbs-up sign before getting up from her chair. 'Officers?' she said and approached two policemen blocking the hole where the door had been. 'I might have noticed something earlier...'

Her voice faded as she led the two men away, and by the time more police and the fire brigade turned up Sarah had slipped out of the destroyed shop and out of her old life.

Chapter 8

This time, Joe didn't greet her with his usual wide smile when he saw her. Instead, his eyes widened in surprise and worry, and he instantly came rushing towards her. Sarah hadn't dared going back to her apartment and she had nothing with her other than the things she was wearing. To say they looked battered would have been euphemistic. She knew she needed help, and she had waited at the homeless shelter, hidden behind one of the large dumpsters at the side of the road, just in case someone had followed her. The shelter would open in about two hours, but Joe was often there early. He enjoyed setting up everything in peace and solitude before any of the official employees came rushing in. His apartment was where he slept, but the shelter was his home.

'I need help,' Sarah admitted, and Joe raised his eyebrows while ushering her into the place, forcing her to sit down.

'I can see that.' He turned around to fumble with the coffee machine. Sarah was nervous but knew that Joe liked to do things in his own time, and she kept quiet until he finally turned around with two cups of coffee in his hands, placing them on the table before he sat down in front of her. 'How can I help you?'

He didn't even ask what happened, allowing her to

tell the story on her own accord. 'I can't go back home. There are people after me. Bad people, and I need to go into hiding,' Sarah explained, the words falling out of her faster and faster, while she wrapped her cold fingers around the warm mug with the coffee. 'But I don't know where to go. I need clothes and everything else. I can't come back here, either, because they know about this place, and I don't want to endanger anyone else. They bombed Steven's coffee shop to kill me.' She was crying now without being aware of it. 'And they could've killed Charlie and Steven and everyone else just because they want me dead. I'm so scared and...'

Joe placed a hand on her arm, a gesture that immediately calmed Sarah down, and she took a deep and shuddering breath. 'Drink your coffee,' he ordered gently, and Sarah obliged, focusing on the hot sensation in her throat.

'You were right,' she whispered before wiping some tears from her face. 'About things happening for a reason. But I have no control over anything, and everyone around me is in danger. I need to hide somewhere for a while.' She took another shuddering breath before glancing up at Joe.

The man studied her attentively. 'Are you hurt?'

'A few scratches but nothing bad,' Sarah answered. 'Just dusty and shaken and desperate and scared to the bones.'

Joe nodded. '35 Maple Street. An old friend of mine lives there. Gladys Hudman. She's a bit grumpy but has a heart of gold. If you tell her that I sent you, she'll let you stay for a few nights.'

Sarah was surprised about how deep the relief and

the gratitude she felt for Joe ran. He hadn't asked any questions, questions she wouldn't have been able to answer anyway, and he hadn't told her to go to the police. Instead, he had given her something she could hold on to, an outlook on how to survive the next few days.

'And now you go to our storeroom and pick some clean clothes for yourself. If you go back on the streets like this, you'll definitely attract attention.'

When she returned, Joe was rummaging through the kitchen. Sarah had changed her clothes and she appeared more or less ordinary again. Just a scratch at the side of her head and the expression in her eyes told her that things were far from normal. That and the dark circles underneath her eyes that almost looked like bruises. Joe wordlessly handed her a plastic bag that was filled with sandwiches, apples, crisps, bottles of water, and even a toothbrush and Sarah could feel tears stinging behind her eyes again.

'Thank you, Joe,' was all she was able to say. 'I'll try and let you know that I'm OK occasionally. Please don't tell anyone where I am, and if people come looking for me, pretend you don't know me well. Make sure you're safe. They're really dangerous.'

Joe put his hand gently onto her shoulder. 'I'll be fine. Just watch out for yourself, love.' The concern in his voice was enough to make her tear up, but Sarah swallowed her emotions down. She had cried enough for today.

Before she slipped out the door, she turned around. 'One more thing. Do you remember the stranger I had trouble with a few weeks ago? Dark hair, large scar across his forehead?'

Joe nodded.

'If he asks for me, tell him where to find me. He's the only one allowed to know.'

Joe seemed surprised about this, and he looked as if he was on the verge of asking a question, but he stayed silent, and Sarah slipped out and back onto the streets.

On her way to Maple Street, she stopped at a bank machine to get as much money as she could and at a local store where she bought some additional clothes she would need. She was nervous when she arrived at the address Joe had given her. Number 35 Maple Street was a normal-looking house in a row of normal-looking houses on an ordinary street. Sarah's heart was in her throat when she knocked on the door. After a few moments, an elderly woman regarded her sternly. 'Yes?' she asked.

'My name is Sarah O'Donoghue,' Sarah started. 'Joe from the homeless shelter told me that I could come here and stay for a few days. I'm in trouble.'

The woman studied her from head to toe before she opened the door further for her. 'Take off your shoes and meet me in the kitchen,' she ordered, and Sarah followed her inside, doing as the woman had said. A few moments later they were sitting at the kitchen table. Everything was old and worn but clean, and Gladys gave her a stern look before coming to her judgment. 'You're not like the others,' she stated, placing a hot cup of tea in front of Sarah.

Sarah wrapped her hand around the cup, soaking up the warmth. Since the bomb had exploded, she seemed to be constantly freezing. 'The others?'

Gladys nodded. 'The other girls Joe sends me. Usually, they're beaten up by their husbands, boyfriends, or pimps, and need a place to stay and hide for a few days until they get their life sorted out. Sadly, many of them just go back. But you're different. You're not running from a man.'

The last part hadn't been a question but a statement, and Sarah was surprised about how perceptive Gladys was. She took a sip from the tea to sort through her thoughts. It seemed as if Joe was up to much more than she had been aware of, but she had put only little effort into getting to know him properly before. If she survived the mess she was in, that would change.

'I'm running too,' Sarah finally confirmed Gladys's observation. 'But not from a man.' She fell quiet, not wanting to explain this further. 'And I very much appreciate your help. Yours and Joe's. Thank you. I promise to pay you back at some point in the future when I can.'

Gladys waved her off. 'I'm a bored old woman who has nothing better to do, anyway,' she responded, but Sarah didn't believe her. There seemed to be much more to Gladys than met the eye, and she smiled at the woman before taking another sip of her tea. It was hot and strong.

'You can stay in the room upstairs, first door to the left. There are fresh linens in the cupboard. Help yourself to anything in the kitchen. I cook one hot meal every day, usually dinner, and you're welcome to join me. The living room is mine. I enjoy watching my daily soaps. If you don't talk through them, you can join me in there too, but don't go into it on your own. It's my private area. Understood?'

'Yes,' Sarah agreed. 'Thank you,' she added.

She realised how exhausted she felt, and she wanted to take a bath to get rid of the dust from Steven's coffee shop that seemed to have engrained itself into her skin. As if Gladys had read her thoughts, she pointed up. 'And the bathroom for the guests is upstairs too, second door to the left.'

The hot water was finally able to drive the cold out of her bones, and she allowed herself to soak in the bathtub for a long time, relaxing her tense muscles with the hot water. Her thoughts, however, were dark. Even though she had found a place where she could take a breath and where she would be safe for a while, this didn't solve the actual problem. Sarah thought about her options but concluded that there was only one. She couldn't go back to her old life, not after what had happened today, and she had no idea where to look for William. Which only left one thing to do. She had to find the second part of the prophecy on her own. But how? There were no clues, no hints, and she had no idea where she was supposed to start her search. William had never told her how he had found the first part of the prophecy. It had to be something that was related to her, that was close to her. How was a prophecy even supposed to look? Was it something written on an old scroll she would find in a museum? Or was it something modern, like a code that she had to find and decipher? Or would someone on the streets start whispering cryptic messages to her like a crazy person?

After finishing her bath, she put on a fresh set of clothes and dried her hair before she returned to her room. She had no make-up with her, but she rarely used it anyway, and when she studied her reflection in the mirror, she was surprised about how normal she appeared. She had survived four attacks, and the life she had known was over, but she looked as if she was getting ready for a normal day at work.

Which reminded her that you should never judge a book by its cover. Like William. Sarah knew that there was way more to him than met the eye. She was worried about him. Where was he? Why hadn't he returned to her place like he promised he would? What if something had happened to him? What if he was dead?

She ran her hand through her hair, trying to distract herself by properly taking in her new surroundings for the first time. She was in a plain guest room with a single bed, a large wardrobe, a table, and a chair. It was minimalistic but even though the furniture was old, it wasn't shabby, and Gladys had tried to give it a homely feel by decorating the room with pillows, and a vase with fresh flowers. On the wall above the bed was a painting that showed a forest scene. It was supposed to have a calming effect on the viewer but for Sarah it did the opposite because it reminded her of the large oak that functioned as a portal to Aphelia.

She pulled her mobile phone out of her pocket and studied it. She had switched it off before starting her shift at the coffee shop in the morning and wasn't sure if it was a good idea to turn it back on. What if she could be tracked through it? She didn't even know if they had mobile phones in Aphelia but in the end, it was not worth the risk. Who was she supposed to call anyway? She didn't want to worry her parents and Charlotte knew that she was in hiding. Sarah probably had some missed calls from Steven, but she relied on Charlotte to come up with a story about where she had gone. And she wouldn't have to return to work anyway since the coffee shop was in pieces. The thought that Charlotte or her family could still be in danger crossed her mind.

What if they took one of them to force Sarah out of hiding? But that plan could only work if they knew where Sarah was. A residual risk remained but there was nothing she could do about this except for finding the prophecy and solving this clusterfuck that had become her life. She would have to live with the fear for her loved ones until then.

The next few days were the most uneventful, yet the most frustrating, she had experienced in a while. Sarah stayed clear of every spot in town that could be traced back to her. She didn't meet up with anyone she knew and didn't go close to her apartment, or any other place that was connected to her. Instead, she visited every museum in the city she could find because she had to start with the search for the prophecy somewhere, and a museum was a place as good to start as anywhere else. Even though she learned a lot about Greenwich, the art of the eighteenth century, the Tudors, and even the future of sustainability in packaging in an exhibition called *Reuse, Refill, Rethink*, there was nothing about prophecies in general or the one she was searching for specifically. She kept her eyes open when she was out on the streets, checking every graffiti for hidden messages. Her mind was going into overdrive, while she was always watching her back for followers too. She spent her evenings with Gladys in front of the television, where they watched old telenovelas in amicable silence, but Sarah grew more and more restless and frustrated with the lack of progress the more days passed. She hated the situation she was in, she hated feeling scared and helpless. She hadn't switched her mobile phone back on yet, deciding that it wasn't worth the risk, but she had been allowed onto Gladys' old computer. It was very slow but at least it was connected to the internet. Sarah had done extensive research about prophecies where she had stumbled over plenty of things, names, and places but none of it rang a bell. She was close to desperation when Gladys knocked on the door to her room the next day, shortly after breakfast.

'Joe called,' Gladys informed her after popping her head through the door. 'He wants to meet you at his place.' She handed Sarah a piece of paper with an address written on it. Sarah had never been to Joe's apartment before. 'He said it's urgent and that your friend's there.'

Sarah's heart leaped inside her chest. 'William?' she asked hopefully, but Gladys only shrugged, indicating that she didn't know more than that, and Sarah told herself to calm down. Technically, Joe could also be talking about Charlotte. Her best friend had visited the shelter a few times, picking Sarah up after her volunteer work, but she didn't think that Joe ever had met her. Also, Sarah had given Joe clear instructions only to tell William where she was and no one else.

Chapter 9

Impatiently, she rang the doorbell for the second time. What was taking him so long? Sarah nervously glanced over her shoulder, a habit she had picked up and perfected now. She used any reflective surface to check for followers, always waited after turning a corner to see if someone was after her, and the occasional peek over the shoulder had become a habit, too. There was nothing unusual to see but Sarah felt tense, anyway. In James Bond movies, stuff like this always seemed much fancier. She didn't like pulling Joe into her mess, but she didn't have a choice.

Besides, she never had been close to Joe so maybe her pursuers wouldn't look for her here.

She was relieved to hear the buzzer and almost ran up the stairs to the second floor of the apartment house where Joe lived.

He greeted her at the door. 'Is everything OK?' she asked breathlessly.

'I'm fine,' Joe responded, 'but your friend isn't.'

'What happened?' Sarah quickly followed Joe into his apartment.

'I don't know,' Joe answered. 'It's the door to your left,' he added, and Sarah rushed into what appeared to be the living room. It was small, clean, and comfortable. Two large sofas filled most of the space, the walls plastered with photographs. Usually, she would have taken a closer look at them, but Sarah only had eyes for the figure lying on the sofa. Her first thought was that William was dead. His face was the colour of ash, and his eyes were closed. There was a lot of blood on his clothes. She froze in her steps, she wasn't good with seeing blood, but right now her concern about William was stronger than that.

'He's asleep,' Joe explained, his reassuring voice instantly calming Sarah down. 'He wouldn't let me touch him.' He pointed towards the small coffee table where things from a first aid kit were lying around; plasters, iodine, dressing material, and much more. 'He stumbled down the street towards the shelter when I arrived there for work this morning. Luckily, I caught him before he could come near it, I think it's being watched.' He spoke in a neutral tone but for the first time, Sarah could hear something like curiosity in Joe's voice. This was probably even weird for him.

'At first, he didn't want to come with me, but when I told him that you had gone into hiding and that I knew where you were, he followed me. Only barely made it here. When I wanted to check his injuries, he freaked out on me, and he has been drifting in and out of sleep ever since. Every time I try to touch him, he resists me. I left him alone and called Gladys.'

Sarah slowly stepped towards William's lifeless body. His chest was moving, but he looked pretty dead other-wise. She knelt in front of the sofa and reached for the scissors that were lying on the table nearby. She hesitated for only a fraction of a moment before cutting up William's shirt. The blood had dried on it, making the fabric stiff and difficult to cut through but Sarah managed and when she pushed the remains of his shirt to the sides to get a closer view of his injuries, she realised that William was awake. His eyes were resting on her and he placed his hand above hers. His skin was dry and hot.

'You're alive,' he said, and she could hear the relief in his voice.

'And I seem to have managed way better than you,' she retorted lightly even though she felt like crying. William's chest looked horrible. There were bruises and cuts everywhere, some of them deep. He appeared to have been tortured.

'We need to call an ambulance for you,' she decided, because the wounds were nothing that could be fixed with a band-aid and some disinfectant. Immediately William's grip on her hand strengthened.

'No,' he objected, 'they would expect that. I'm sure they monitor the hospitals.'

They surely couldn't monitor all the hospitals in the city, but Sarah hesitated nonetheless, not wanting to make any mistakes. 'But you could have internal injuries, like bleeding. Something that could kill you.' Her voice was shaking, while she tried not to show how much the sight of him was affecting her.

'I've gotten through worse,' William informed her, but Sarah could see how exhausting even this little bit of conversation was for him. She was torn apart between respecting his wishes and calling for professional help. Maybe that decision could wait for another while.

'Could you get me some warm water to clean him up?' she asked over her shoulder at Joe who had been waiting by the door patiently.

'Just rest,' she said gently to William, 'you're safe here for now. I'll tend to your wounds.'

William's grip on her hand immediately went slack, and his eyes fell shut. He was out cold before she even could say *Whatthefuckactuallyhappenedtoyou*. Sarah felt like crying, but she swallowed down her emotions. She knew that it was stupid, but she couldn't help but feel guilty. He had endured this because of her. Her mind told her that none of this was her fault since she had not chosen it, but her hands wouldn't stop shaking. She used the scissors to cut open his trousers too, leaving his boxer shorts untouched. His legs looked better than his chest, but they were heavily bruised too. What had happened to him? It seemed as if he had been cut and smashed into a wall repeatedly. Joe returned with a pot of warm water, putting it on the floor next to her, then watched in silence as Sarah cleaned and bandaged William's wounds as well as she could.

'We could call Angela,' Joe broke the silence after a while, and Sarah immediately felt stupid for not thinking about it earlier. Angela Winters was a general practitioner. Once a week, she came to the shelter in the evening and treated the homeless for free. She was never there on Wednesdays though, so Sarah only knew her briefly.

'Yes,' she agreed, the relief audible in her voice. Angela would be able to tell how severe William's injuries were and if he needed to be taken to hospital. Because if he was at risk of dying, Sarah would call an ambulance for him, no matter the risk.

Joe left the room without another word and after a moment she could hear him talking on the phone before he returned. 'She is on her way,' he informed her and sat down on the other sofa while Sarah closed her eyes in relief.

'Looks to me as if you are neck-deep in something a bit too big for you,' he remarked, and Sarah paused for a moment before she continued to tend to William's wounds.

'I know,' she whispered, 'but I never wanted this or even had a choice.'

'There is always a choice,' Joe said, and Sarah held his gaze openly.

The next thirty minutes were the longest of her life. She watched over William as well as she could and anxiously watched him sleep until the doorbell rang. Sarah jumped, despite having eagerly anticipated it. 'Please make sure it's her,' she said to Joe, paranoid of being found by Drake's people.

A few moments later, Angela Winters was standing in the doorway. Since it wasn't difficult to figure out who the patient was, she immediately rushed to William's side. After putting on some medical gloves she started to examine him carefully. Sarah stood at the head of the sofa, out of the way, and watched how Angela paid special attention to William's torso and the large bruises underneath his skin.

'We need to wake him up,' she ordered. 'I want to give him something against the pain, and I have to ask him some questions.'

She glanced at Joe, assuming that William was his friend, but Joe nodded at Sarah, and she bent over to be in William's line of vision. 'William,' she said quietly. 'Will!' She carefully placed her hand against his bruised face. He awoke with a start but immediately calmed down when he saw her.

'Don't get upset,' she said, 'but we called a doctor. She isn't official,' she clarified hastily when sensing William's concern. 'I trust her, alright? She'll give you something for the pain, and then she'll take a closer look at you to see if you need further medical attention. Please.' William considered her words while his eyes wandered over to Angela.

'My name is Angela Winters,' the woman introduced herself. 'And you've taken a really good beating there.'

Fascinated, Sarah watched how William gradually relaxed while Angela kept talking to him. At the same time, she injected something into his veins, explaining that it was a pain medication. Afterwards, she carried on with her examination, only asking a few questions while her fingers gently assessed his injuries.

'Can you sit up?' she finally wanted to know, and William managed. The painkiller was obviously working already because he moved with more ease than he had before. His back was bruised like the front of his torso but that wasn't what made Sarah's breath hitch in her throat. There was a birthmark underneath his right shoulder blade. It was almost shaped like a star and Sarah stared at it in surprise. Not many people knew about this, but she had the same birthmark in the exact same place. She resisted the urge to reach out and run her fingers over it. How was this possible? Angela removed her medical gloves, obviously finished with the examination. William sank back onto the sofa with an exhausted sigh, the birthmark hidden again.

'You've been beaten up pretty badly,' Angela stated the obvious. 'And there are a few stab wounds too, but they are not deep. There are no broken bones, and I don't think that there's internal bleeding, either.'

Sarah released a breath, while the doctor continued to speak.

'From what I can tell, you have a concussion and there are numerous cuts and bruises across your whole body. Those will heal in time, but you must take care of that concussion, which is the reason you're so sleepy.' Her words were meant to be for Sarah and Joe but directed at William. 'Don't move for at least three days. Sleep as much as you can. If you experience nausea or feel worse otherwise, go to hospital immediately. I would prefer for you to be monitored in one but since Joe has called me, I don't think this is an option.' This had been a statement and not a question.

She turned around, this time directing her words at Sarah whom she had identified as the person who was with William. 'I'll leave you some strong painkillers. Don't give him more than three a day for no longer than three days. If his condition gets worse, if he isn't responsive or not able to talk properly any longer, take him to a hospital immediately!'

Sarah accepted the pills that were placed into the palms of her hands. 'Thank you,' she said, realising that all she did these days was thank people for their help. She put the doctor on her mental list for a 'thank you' mug, right underneath Joe and Gladys.

Joe walked Angela out and she could hear them murmuring for a moment before the front door was closed, and Joe returned to the living room.

'As soon as he's a little better, I'll book a hotel room for us,' Sarah informed Joe. 'We won't be here for much longer.'

She didn't have much money in the bank for a long hotel stay, but she couldn't take William to Gladys' and didn't want to be an additional burden to Joe. He had done more for her than she ever could have imagined.

Joe placed a hand on her shoulder. 'He can stay here until he's better, and so can you. I'll give Gladys a call so she won't worry. And now sit down, you're barely holding it together. I'll get us a coffee.' With those words, he left the living room and Sarah sank onto the other sofa, feeling drained.

For the next three days, William slept most of the time. The cuts started to heal, and the bruises slowly began to take on another colour, but he was barely awake and when he was, he was suffering from a tremendous headache. Sarah and Joe mainly left him alone to sleep and Sarah made sure that he took his pills and drank some water anytime he woke. She even prepared some soup and light food for him but other than that there wasn't much to do. She slept on the other sofa in Joe's living room, and when she woke up on the fourth day, William was awake and sitting upright, his eyes clear for the first time.

'Good morning,' he greeted her, and Sarah was immediately wide awake.

'Good morning,' she replied, and sat up while trying to smooth out her hair which was standing in every direction, as usual in the mornings. 'Do you feel better?'

William smiled. 'I feel like a used punch bag and am

barely able to move without something hurting, but my head feels much better, and I'm not that tired anymore.'

'Are you hungry?' Sarah inquired, standing up, ready to get him whatever he wanted.

'Yes, but it can wait. Please sit down, we should talk first.'

Sarah sank back down onto the sofa, pulling her legs up, hugging her knees, and placing her chin on top of them. 'What happened to you? Where have you been?'

William studied her. 'I walked into a trap,' he admitted. 'I wanted to get some of my things and return to you the same night after we came back from Aphelia, but they waited for me.

Turns out they found the abandoned house where I used to sleep.'

Sarah quietly asked the question she had been dreading to ask. 'What did they do to you?'

His green eyes met hers shortly before he averted them. 'At first, they only held me captive, but when their plan with the bomb didn't work out, they came back.' His voice was flat, entirely void of emotion. 'They tried to find out your whereabouts, but I didn't know where you were. You hid well. Not that I would have told them, anyway.' There was a grim satisfaction in his voice, if only for a moment. 'At some point, I managed to escape. I wasn't of use to them any longer and I knew that they were about to kill me.'

Sarah knew that he had left out large parts of his story, but she didn't probe him for more information. Instead, she felt the urge to reach out and console him, but she didn't know how he would react, so she stayed rooted to the spot.

'What about you?' he asked into the heavy silence. 'What happened?'

'When you didn't come back, I went to work like every day, but they blew up the shop. After the explosion, I realised that I had to disappear. That bomb could have killed someone else. It could have killed Charlotte.' Her voice almost broke but she pushed her emotions aside. 'Joe helped me. He gave me the address of a friend and I was at her place until he called me here.'

'Any news about the prophecy?' The hope in his voice was painful for Sarah.

She licked her lips and pushed a strand of hair behind her ear to win some time before she replied. 'No,' she admitted, quickly summarizing everything she had tried over the last couple of days. 'But when Dr Winters was here and examined you, I saw the birthmark you have on your right shoulder. I have the same one.' She placed her feet back on the floor, turned her upper body around, and pushed her loose shirt down until her shoulder blade with the birthmark was visible. 'I don't know what it means, but...' she hesitated before saying what she was thinking. 'What if *you* are the second part of the prophecy?'

William's eyes were fixed on the small mark on her shoulder, staring at it with a burning intensity Sarah could almost physically feel. She pulled her shirt back up and crossed her arms in front of her chest.

'It's peculiar, isn't it?' she interrupted the silence between them. 'You said that I would recognise the second prophecy as soon as I saw it, and I immediately spotted you in that nightclub a few months ago, between all those other people.'

Sure, he had been sticking out of the crowd like a sore

thumb, which was why she had paid special attention to him in the first place, but their matching birthmarks were more than just a strange coincidence, and Sarah never really believed in coincidences anyway.

'Besides, I have no idea where else to search for the prophecy anymore.'

'But if I was the second part of the prophecy, what would that mean?' he asked slowly. 'What are we supposed to do?'

Sarah shook her head. 'I have no idea, it's your world.' She suddenly felt annoyed.

She hated feeling clueless and she hated feeling responsible even more. 'Maybe it means that we must find the prophecy together or maybe it doesn't mean anything at all. How am I supposed to know? Why am I the only one that can find it anyway?' Frustrated she ran her hand through her curly hair. 'I have no idea where to look,' she admitted. 'I can't go back home, I can't go anywhere, and I can't even check back with Charlotte or any of my other friends because I have to protect them. Charlotte and Steven almost died because of this. Because of me. I hate this, OK? I never asked for this, and I don't know anything about that damn prophecy!'

Sarah hadn't realised how loud she had gotten until Joe popped his head through the door. 'Everything alright in here?'

She had entirely forgotten that they were in his flat, and she wondered how much he had been able to overhear from their conversation.

'It's all good,' she answered tiredly, and Joe's head disappeared again. She sighed in frustration before meeting William's gaze.

'It's OK,' he tried to comfort her, but Sarah could see the disappointment in his eyes. He had probably imagined this part to be easier, but at least he knew what he was fighting for. She seemed to stumble from one catastrophe into the next, only following the events that unfolded around her instead of being ahead of them for once.

William looked as frustrated as she felt, and a tense silence settled over the room while both were lost in their own thoughts.

Joe surprised them by walking back into the living room. He was carrying a tray with breakfast rolls, marmalade, butter, cheese, and two pots of freshly brewed coffee. The smell was fantastic, and even William lifted his head. Wordlessly, Joe put the tray down on the table and handed them each a mug. Obviously, his go-to comfort drink was coffee, and Sarah accepted the hot and strong brew, gratefully taking a long sip. They ate in silence, the tension slowly lifting from the room, and when Sarah brushed some breadcrumbs from her shirt, she felt much better.

'I don't know what is going on with the two of you,' Joe spoke up, 'and by what I have been able to hear, I don't want to know either.' He took a sip of his coffee and for the first time, Sarah realised how old Joe looked. She knew that he was somewhere in his fifties but the long years on the streets hadn't done his body any favours.

'But when you're searching for something that's only for you to find, maybe you should search where only you can look,' he advised.

'What do you mean?' Sarah questioned.

'Look inside of you,' Joe answered, before getting up. 'I'm off to the shelter now, leaving the mess for you two to clean up.' He pointed at the dirty dishes. 'It has to have at least one advantage to have you occupying my living room.' And with those words he was gone, leaving them alone.

Sarah leaned comfortably against the backrest of the sofa while she thought about Joe's words. In a way, they made sense. If she was searching for something that was only for her to find, maybe she could only find it inside herself. She took a long sip of her coffee before she noticed that William was studying her.

'He has a point,' he admitted.

'I know,' Sarah agreed, 'but that doesn't make it any easier.'

For a while, they sat in silence while Sarah was wracking her brain about Joe's words. 'That birthmark isn't the only thing that makes you special, you know?' William interrupted the silence.

'Oh, you are surely hinting at my exquisite looks, my super brain, and my utterly charming personality,' Sarah replied dryly, something that elicited a chuckle from William.

'Yes, of course,' he said, 'but there is also something else.' He took a sip of his coffee before putting the mug down. 'You see, every person in my world has a counterpart, some sort of twin in this world. They resemble each other greatly when it comes to appearance and personality.'

Sarah let that information sink in. 'What is mine like?' she wanted to know.

'I don't think you have one,' he answered. 'And this is what makes you special. I mean, I tried to find her upon seeing the prophecy. I figured that I could learn something about you by meeting her. That would have made it easier to approach you in this world, but I didn't find her. And I am pretty good at finding people.'

'Maybe she doesn't want to be found?' Sarah guessed. It was a strange thought to have some sort of doppelgänger in another world. It reminded her of Stephen Hawking's theory about parallel universes once more.

'Maybe,' William replied slowly, 'but I don't think so. I think part of why there is a prophecy about you and no one else, is that you probably don't have a counterpart. You could be the only one there is. But it is just a theory.'

Sarah shrugged. 'How did you actually find me here?' She had been wondering this for quite some time.

'It was easier than I thought,' William explained. 'Our worlds are very similar, almost alike. We have more or less the same flora and fauna, the same ways of living, the same system with school and work. It's not that we are aliens on a strange world where physics don't work the way you are used to. Aphelia is almost the same as Earth, which made it easy for me to navigate here. After finding the prophecy I also found a lot of books describing Earth and your way of living in great detail. This knowledge was hidden by the Guardians, along with the knowledge of magic, so there must have been a time where my people knew about Earth. At least a few.' He reached for his mug and took a sip of his coffee before continuing to speak. 'And as I said, I already knew the city you'd be in, Haleston. Once I had settled in here, I went to the public library and checked the pictures in the yearbooks of the nearby schools. But I couldn't find your face there, so I assume you didn't grow up here?'

Sarah confirmed that with a nod, thinking about the small village she had grown up in.

There had been a school in the next larger town. A bus had picked her up every morning.

'But then I got lucky,' William continued his story. 'I skimmed over some local newspapers in the archive because I couldn't think of anything else to do when I saw your face on a picture in an article. Next to a pig.'

'The Farmers Market,' Sarah and William said in unison. It was the only time in her life when she had been in a newspaper.

'I won that damn pig,' Sarah laughed.

Shortly after she had moved to Haleston, she had gone shopping at the Farmers Market for some fresh eggs. Out of an impulse she had participated in a raffle there. What she hadn't realised was that the first prize was a living pig. Of course, the only time in her life she ever had won anything, it was a damn pig.

'It was at a raffle, and they took a picture of me and the pig since the animal was the main prize.' She laughed again at the memory. 'For a moment I freaked out, thinking I had to share my tiny apartment with a pig, but in the end, one of the farmers was kind enough to buy it from me so at least I got some money out of it. And some newspaper fame. My dad still has that article on his wall at home.'

William grinned at her story, clearly amused by it. 'Well, your name was underneath the picture, and finding you after that was easy.' He finished his explanation and leaned back on the sofa, clearly exhausted. 'Anyway, would you help me to get up?' he asked. 'I would like to help with those dishes and then have a shower, but I'm not sure if I can trust my body yet.' At those words, Sarah's gaze fell on his chest. Bruises in different stages of healing peeked out from underneath the bandages, displaying almost all colours of the rainbow. He had to be in pain, but he hadn't complained once.

Sarah put her cup aside and got up to help him. William's body was warm and heavy against hers, and he smelled faintly of herbs, but it was obvious that he needed a shower, too.

After a few tentative steps, he was stable on his feet. 'Go and take that shower,' she said. 'I'll take care of the dishes; you can do them the next time.'

'Thank you,' he said, 'I won't lock the bathroom door, so I can call if I need you.'

Sarah watched him leave the room, allowing her eyes to roam freely across his body. He was muscular with broad shoulders, radiating strength even though he was clearly in pain when walking. He was quite handsome, she decided before averting her eyes. Other than that, she couldn't read William at all. He was very withdrawn, and she didn't think that she had seen much of his true personality so far. He always seemed to be surrounded by a wall. What he was trying to protect himself from, Sarah didn't know.

A few moments later she heard the shower running and went back to sit down on the sofa with her coffee, mulling over Joe's words. The prophecy was inside her. What was that supposed to mean? She still pondered over this while clearing their stuff from breakfast, making a few trips to the kitchen, and suddenly she remembered something. She slowly closed the door to the fridge, her brows furrowing.

Could it be? Was it really that simple?

When William returned to the living room, only a towel slung around his hips, he found Sarah pacing the room in excitement. 'I think I might've found it,' she blurted out. 'The prophecy, I mean I know where to find it. Probably. I'm not one hundred percent sure, but...' Her eyes fell on his almost naked form, and she stopped pacing and talking. Without the bandages around his chest, she could see every bruise. The cuts were healing nicely, and he seemed much better than he had two days ago. Sarah swallowed when she realised that she was staring openly at William's chiselled, muscular chest.

'The prophecy?' There was disbelief but also excitement in William's voice.

'Yes,' Sarah responded, finally able to avert her eyes from his chest, bringing her gaze back to his eyes. 'Years ago, long before I moved here, I had this phase.' She was embarrassed to admit this and cringed inwardly while she continued to speak. 'I wrote poetry. No, let me rephrase that, I attempted to write poetry. It was the opposite of good, but for a while, I was obsessed with it. I filled journal after journal with it. When I moved here, I threw all of them away, except for this one journal even though it was as badly written as the rest of it. To this day I don't know why I kept it.'

William stepped toward her, radiating excitement, and Sarah continued to speak. 'I figured it was a phase, like the aftermath of my angsty puberty. Of course, back then I fancied myself to be an overly talented writer, when in reality most of it was really cringe-worthy stuff.' She realised that she had begun to ramble and cut herself short. 'But what if it wasn't? At least not all of it. What if I wrote the prophecy down myself at some point? What if it is hidden somewhere in there?'

'But what makes you think that?' William asked.

Sarah tilted her head slightly before she answered him. 'I don't remember much of what I wrote, and I haven't read it in years, probably to protect myself from the embarrassment, but I remember clearly that I wrote about a large old tree, like the one that functions as the portal. I don't know,' she hesitated, 'maybe I'm wrong, and it's just awful poetry, but when Joe said that it probably was inside me...' Her voice trailed off and she felt insecure.

William was standing close to her and she could feel the heat his body was radiating. For the first time in days his eyes were gleaming with hope and excitement while he considered this idea.

'And why are you naked?' she finally inquired. 'Joe gave you some clothes, didn't he?'

William looked down at his chest as if he had forgotten. 'Oh, that. I need help with the bandages.'

'Yes. Of course.' She blushed while ushering him to the sofa and retrieving the spare bandages Joe had organized. They sat down and she started covering his cuts, as she had already done a few times over the last few days. She was getting quite skilled at it even though he had been more or less asleep the previous times. When she was done with his chest, she tended to his back, her eyes once again falling on the birthmark, and she couldn't resist running her fingers over it lightly.

'This is weird, don't you think?' she asked, but William pulled away from her hastily.

'Yes,' he mumbled while getting up swiftly, or as

swiftly as he could in his state. 'Thanks for the help,' he added stiffly before going back into the bathroom to retrieve his clothes.

Sarah followed him with her eyes. Had he just *flinched* from her?

'We need to go to my apartment to get the journal,' Sarah announced when William returned from the bathroom, this time fully dressed, his hair slightly damp.

He leaned against the door frame, and she noticed that he still moved carefully but already was way more mobile than he had been before. 'I know,' he said, 'and I don't like it. They are definitely watching it, hoping you'll return.'

'What if we send someone else there to get it for us?' Sarah suggested but immediately discarded the idea the moment she had spoken it out loud. William shook his head.

'They'll know you sent them. Trust me, you don't want any of your friends and acquaintances to suffer from the same fate I did.'

Sarah shuddered when she thought about that. 'You're right, that was a bad idea.' She felt the irrational urge to apologise for what had happened to him, even though none of it had been her fault. Why did she feel so responsible?

'We need a good plan,' she finally said, 'but first, more coffee!'

Chapter 10

It was pitch dark three nights later, the only light coming from the streetlamps since the moon was hidden behind thick clouds. It was raining lightly when Sarah and William arrived at the street where she lived. Used to live, she corrected herself, and where she was going to live again as soon as this nightmare was over. She needed to believe in this, needed to have faith that things would get back to normal for her, otherwise she would go crazy. They were dressed completely in black, the hoods of their jackets drawn tightly over their faces. For a while, they stayed hidden in the shadows of a bus stop, watching the street nervously. They were hoping that whoever watched her place was tired or not too attentive.

Neither of them detected anything unusual, and after a while, William suggested getting a bit closer. Soon after, they were sneaking through her neighbours' backyards. Sarah had to suppress a nervous giggle on seeing one of them, Grace, dancing funnily to some music Sarah wasn't able to hear in her well-lit kitchen. At the same time, she felt uncomfortable, not wanting to pry on the privacy of her neighbours like this. William quickly pulled her along, and Grace was out of sight again. The rain stopped while they were hiding behind the fence that separated her direct neighbour's garden from hers. There was no movement, and nothing seemed out of place. When William deemed it to be safe, Sarah took the lead since she was more familiar with the surroundings. She knew that the fence was broken in one place so they wouldn't have to climb it and a few moments later they slipped through the opening. It was very dark and there was only a little bit of light coming from one of the windows on the top floor, and the two stood there for a moment, letting their eyes adjust to the darkness.

Maybe it was something she heard, but Sarah sensed the danger before it became apparent. Out of instinct, she grabbed William by his jacket sleeve and pulled him back just in time. The figure came out of nowhere and just for a second the scarce light was reflected on a metallic surface.

'Knife,' she muttered, though she wasn't sure. It was too dark to see properly. William was gone from her grasp in an instant and in the dim light, she could see two silhouettes fighting somewhere in the shadows in front of her. She pressed her hand against her mouth to suppress the scream that was lodged in her throat. The fight was eerily quiet, too, as if the figures were trying to avoid alarming the neighbourhood. Sarah had rarely felt as helpless as in this moment. She looked around to see if there was anything she could use as a weapon when one of the shadows dropped to the ground.

'William?' she whispered in alarm.

'I'm OK,' the figure still standing said, and Sarah's shoulders sagged in relief.

The feeling was short-lived because Sarah witnessed in horror how William knelt next to their attacker. She saw a swift move and heard a horrible cracking sound, one that would haunt her in her dreams. William had broken the other man's neck without hesitation.

Sarah felt shaken to the core. 'Why did you do that?' she whispered, her fingernails biting deep into the palms of her hand, drawing blood without her noticing. 'What did you do that for?' She repeated her question while staring at the dead lump on the ground. It was too dark to read the expression on William's face and he only grabbed her by the arm and pulled her along, towards the house.

'Hurry up,' his voice was entirely void of emotions, 'he probably wasn't alone.' Numbly Sarah followed along, but she was horrified. Even though she had almost been killed a couple of times, the dead man in the backyard of her house made all of this more real than anything else could have. She fumbled for her keys, but her hands were shaking so badly that she dropped them by the back door. William picked them up and handed them back to her. His face was illuminated faintly, and it was a stoic mask, entirely unreadable. She finally managed to slip the key in, and they quietly stepped into the house, taking the stairs without turning on the lights until they stood in front of her apartment. There was a lot of mail lying on the floor, but Sarah ignored it, carefully opening the door to her flat halfway, expecting another bomb to go off, but she was only greeted by an eerie silence. William went in first, making sure that no one was waiting inside the apartment for them, returning a few moments later.

'It's clear,' he informed her, and Sarah walked inside. She couldn't remember where exactly she had put the journal with the possible prophecy. It was most likely in one of the cluttered drawers that she used to store all the things in that had no other place. She didn't hesitate and went right into her living room, which was illuminated by the light of the streetlamps falling through the windows. Sarah pulled out the first drawer and spilled its contents onto the carpet quietly but carelessly. Old letters, piles of papers, a few books, her sewing kit that she had been searching for, and some other things gathered at her feet, and she rummaged through the pile, quickly realising that the journal wasn't here. She was successful with the third drawer and finally held the small book in her hand. It looked old, tattered, and so cheap, and it seemed unlikely that this should hold something as powerful as a prophecy that her heart sank. Nonetheless, she turned around to glance at William who had been waiting impatiently in the background, always keeping the door in sight.

'Did you find it?' he asked.

'Yes,' Sarah replied, her voice calmer than she felt.

'Good, let's go.' Once again, he reached for her arm to pull her along but this time Sarah saw it coming and stepped aside.

'Why did you have to kill the man out there?' she requested to know again.

The expression on William's face darkened. 'Would you have liked it better if he had killed us?' he retorted sharply.

'No,' Sarah responded. 'But he was down on the ground and unconscious. We could have, I don't know, tied him up or something like that.'

William laughed at her words and the sound cut right into her soul. 'Don't be naive, Sarah,' he spat at her. 'It's us or them. Come on, now!' Sarah reluctantly followed and while she peered at his broad shoulders in the dim twilight, she painfully realised again that she knew nothing about William. She probably didn't even like him much, either.

No one followed them on their way back to Joe's apartment, but Sarah was quiet and withdrawn, repeatedly checking for her journal but not taking a look inside yet. She wanted to do that back in the safety of Joe's place. She felt uncomfortable in William's presence. He had killed someone in cold blood, and that wasn't something she could just ignore. So far Sarah had seen him as an ally, as someone who would help her along the way, someone who would be able to guide her, but now she was questioning everything. What kind of person was he? Anytime she asked a personal question, he evaded answering.

William didn't speak either, and the two stepped into Joe's apartment in icy silence. Sarah hung her black jacket on the clothes rack before she ventured into the kitchen to grab a cold beer from the fridge. It was around 3am, but there was no way that she would be able to sleep now anyway. When she returned to the living room, she found William sitting in darkness on the sofa. He was staring out of the window studying the moon that finally was showing itself. She didn't switch on the light but sat down on the other sofa in silence, occasionally sipping at her beer. The journal was lying next to her, but she wasn't ready to open it yet. She knew that they needed to talk about what had happened, for this adventure to even have a remote chance of being successful.

'Why did you do it?' she questioned him again, and this time William didn't get angry. He released a deep breath and leaned his head against the backrest of the sofa. The moonlight illuminated his profile, and Sarah could see that he had his eyes closed.

'You don't know anything about me,' he voiced out loud what Sarah had been thinking earlier.

'Then tell me about you.' Her voice was soft. William opened his eyes and turned his head to study her.

'It's not a pretty story,' he warned her.

'I don't need pretty, I need true,' she said, and William turned his head to look out of the window. For a long time, he didn't say a word, and Sarah wondered if he had fallen asleep, but then his voice came out of the shadows.

'I was orphaned at a very young age. My parents were murdered when I was eight years old. After that, my aunt took me in, but she died not too much later. By the time I was ten years old, I had no one left to care for me.'

Sarah listened quietly.

'I did what I had to do to survive; I begged, I stole and when I got a bit older, I joined a group of young men. In this world, you probably would call them a gang. We each had no one else, and for a while, things went well. I had a family again, people who cared, and we had each other's backs. We stole to survive, but no one was harmed.'

William fell silent and Sarah noticed that her beer was empty, but she just set the bottle on the floor. She didn't want to interrupt the moment. William had never been this open before, and she instinctively felt he would close down again quickly if she even did so much as move a muscle.

'But things turned bad. Gareth joined our group. He was older than we were, and he soon became our leader. We admired him and looked up to him. He seemed strong and invincible, and he always protected us. But after a while, he sent us to do his dirty work for him. Small things in the beginning but it turned worse quickly. I killed the first man when I was seventeen years old. He was from an opposing gang, and it was either me or him. I was just faster.'

William had spoken without audible emotions and almost sounded like a robot. 'I still remember his face and the expression on it when he realised what I was about to do. It haunts me every night.'

Sarah didn't dare to breathe.

'I left Gareth and the boys when I was twenty-three. Everything I am guilty of, I've done to survive, but I couldn't do it any longer. Since then, I've been trying to forget. Forget who I was, who I am, and what I've done.'

Sarah intently observed the quiet figure on the other sofa. Her mouth was dry, and she wasn't sure what she felt. A part of her was horrified, repelled, and disgusted by what she had learned, and another part wanted to walk over and comfort him. She did neither, and when William spoke again there was almost something like relief lying in his voice. Sarah didn't think that he ever had told this story to anyone before, ever.

'And when the man was lying there at my feet tonight, all I could think of was how he would come after us and how he would kill us or worse, and I did it. I didn't even think about it twice.'

Silence settled over the room, but it was not an icy silence any longer. Sarah got up. Her leg had fallen asleep and it was all pins and needles when she hobbled into the kitchen and grabbed two bottles of beer from the fridge. William hadn't moved when she returned to the living room, and she sat down, this time on the sofa next to him before she handed him a beer. He took it and turned his head to look at her. The expression in his eyes was unreadable, and his face was a mask again.

'I remember something someone told me not long ago,' Sarah said. 'There always is a choice.' She took a long sip of her beer. 'Maybe you shouldn't focus on who you have been and what you have done but on who you want to be and what you are going to do from now on.'

He held her gaze for a moment before glancing down at the beer in his hand. 'I can't forget,' he said, his thumb fiddling with the label of the bottle.

'Then don't,' Sarah replied. 'Just don't let your memories dictate who you are any longer.' She felt really tired. She was still having mixed feelings towards William, but her initial shock and horror had abated. His story was as complicated as he was but at least he finally allowed her a glimpse behind the mask he wore all the time. Even though this had made things more difficult. At least for her.

She sighed deeply and briefly placed her hand on his arm. It was warm underneath her touch. 'The sun will be rising soon. I'm going to try to catch a few hours of sleep. You should, too. Tomorrow, we are going to look at the prophecy. If it is the prophecy and not just some embarrassing gibberish I wrote.'

With those words, she was about to get up to leave for the bathroom, but he reached for her hand and held it for a moment. It seemed as if he was going to say something but after a moment of silence, he let go of her again. 'Good night,' he said. 'Thank you,' he added, almost like an afterthought when she was already halfway out of the door.

Sarah had never been able to cope very well with lack of sleep, and she woke up three hours later, entirely grumpy and irritated. The sun was shining through the windows, and William was sitting on the other sofa, studying her.

'That's creepy,' Sarah said and pulled the blankets closer around her body, but she said it without verve. 'Did you sleep at all?' she wanted to know.

William shook his head. 'I couldn't, but I prepared breakfast.'

Sarah's eyes fell on the coffee table that was serving them as a dining table and saw it filled with everything that was needed for a hearty breakfast. Her mood improved, if only slightly. She was still somewhat shocked by what William had revealed about himself last night. He seemed more calm and less driven than before, but maybe she was only seeing him differently now. She slowly sat up, rubbing the sleep from her face.

'I'll get you a coffee,' William got up, and Sarah noticed that he seemed to have showered at some point too. He was wearing fresh clothes. She must have been out of it pretty badly, her body and mind urgently needing that rest.

'Joe's gone,' William called over his shoulder from the kitchen. 'He mentioned something about grocery shopping.' Sarah immediately felt guilty. They had been living there for almost a week, eating Joe's food and occupying his living room. It was time to find another solution now that William was on the mend.

When he returned with a mug of hot coffee for her, she studied him. He was moving normally again so whatever pain was left, he seemed capable of dealing with it.

'Thanks,' she said, taking the coffee from him. 'Maybe it's time to find another place to stay. Joe has been more than kind to us, but I don't want to take advantage of him for much longer. I owe him a lot.'

William nodded and sat down, reaching for a slice of toast, but Sarah lost her appetite when her eyes fell on the small journal that was lying on the floor in front of the sofa. She had slept with it, and it must have fallen at some point. She was scared to pick it up. If there was nothing in there, they would have to start all over again, while still having no idea where to search for the prophecy next. But if it was in there, things would be taken a step further, something she dreaded too. She sighed, took a sip of coffee, and picked the small book up. There was no reason to postpone this. It was as bad as she remembered, and she cringed when she read her attempts at what she had thought to be great poetry at that time. There was nothing more than her badly written drivel on the first few pages but when she skimmed over a few more pages, her eyes widened, and she forgot to breathe. She had found the poem about the tree, the one she had remembered in the first place. Her written words weren't what had her utterly excited all of a sudden, but the sketch she had done next to the poem. She had never been any good at drawing, but the picture roughly depicted the tree where they had switched over to William's world. And next to it was a sketch of the birthmark they both shared. She glanced up and saw that William was staring at her intently, the toast untouched in his hand. She didn't say a word but turned the book around to show him the drawing and the sketch.

The amount of relief that flooded his face was almost

comical to watch and he released a deep breath, his eyes lighting up. 'You found it,' he announced, and for a moment he looked as if he was about to jump up and down on the sofa, but instead he took a hearty bite from his toast and grinned at her.

'Looks like,' Sarah replied. 'It is horribly written though. I don't know how I ever got the idea I was great at poetry.'

She took a sip of her coffee and finally reached for a plain slice of toast too. It would take some time to read through the journal and find out what there was of the actual prophecy.

She finished the little book about twenty minutes later. William's gaze had not left her face. His intense stare had been unnerving, but she hadn't told him off, almost feeling as nervous about this as he did. The question that was written all over his face was undeniable when she lowered the journal.

'I'm not sure,' she said. 'There are a few passages that could be a prophecy.'

No matter how much she disliked the thought of allowing William to read anything from her journal, she knew that she had no other choice, because she didn't have enough knowledge of his world to differentiate the fiction within her poetry from something more. The poem about the tree mentioned a portal, but she never would have believed it to be true if she hadn't experienced it first-hand.

Reluctantly, she handed the small book to William. 'I marked the pages that could possibly be it,' she informed him but didn't let go when he reached for it. 'Don't laugh. I know it's terrible.'

'I would never,' William promised, but he wasn't entirely successful in hiding his amusement from her.

'Whatever,' she grumbled, 'I'm going to shower.' There was no way she'd stick around to see his reactions to her work.

She took her time in the bathroom, paying special attention to her hair-do instead of just putting it into a ponytail, and her red locks framed her face nicely when she was done. She also put an effort into her choice of clothing instead of slipping back into her regular sweatpants. Not that she had much to choose from. She had planned to get some more things from her apartment, but she had forgotten to do so because of the events of that night. All in all, she did everything to postpone having to go back into the living room. When she ran out of things to do in the bathroom, she took a deep breath, braced herself, and walked back to William. But there was no amusement, hidden or not. Instead, she instantly knew that he had found it. The excitement was plastered all over his face and he confirmed her thoughts by presenting a page to her.

'This is it.'

Sarah sat down, feeling tense, while William read out loud.

Hidden from mankind's eyes, where time and space are frozen. Is where the dragon sleeps.

Together you will rise to the break of a new dawn and banish the darkness forever.

Silence hung in the air between them and slowly Sarah released her breath. 'That's it?' she asked. 'That sounds like a badly written mix of *Lord of the Rings* and *Twilight*.'

'What?' William had no idea what she was talking about since he was not familiar with the books or the culture of her world.

'Doesn't matter,' she waved him off. 'What does it mean? Didn't you say there were no dragons in your world?'

'There are no dragons. Where the dragon sleeps refers to a mountain range in Aphelia. It looks like a sleeping dragon.'

Sarah felt disappointed. She had expected something different and more precise, hoping for clear instructions and now she saw herself stumbling around a massive mountain in a foreign world with William while searching for a place where *Time and space were frozen*. What was that supposed to mean? Also, *Together you will rise*? In any case, they would have to go back to Aphelia for the next step, and she was having mixed feelings about that too.

William read the disappointment that was obvious on her face correctly. 'It's a prophecy, not an instruction manual,' he explained, and shrugged. 'Trust me, it took me ages to figure out the first part of it and to find you. But I did, in the end. We'll figure this one out, too.'

Sarah sighed before she reached for her coffee mug. The brew was lukewarm, but she finished it nonetheless before pouring herself another cup, figuring that she would need it.

Chapter 11

The next two weeks went by in a blur while they prepared for the upcoming trip. William left to skip back to Aphelia to get some appropriate clothing for her. Despite the fact that she knew where he had gone, Sarah worried about him constantly until he finally returned, his backpack filled with the latest fashion from his world. They also gathered what Sarah teasingly called the adventure standard equipment. The people of Aphelia probably weren't using bright neon orange reflecting tents, so they searched for a pretty basic camouflage tent, sleeping bags, matches, knives, a rope, and some supplies. Stuff you would take for camping, except that it was all pretty basic. When they were not busy gathering supplies or equipment, William attempted to teach Sarah some self-defence moves. They gave it up again soon after destroying Joe's favourite vase during one of Sarah's futile attempts to get out of a headlock.

Ever since finding the prophecy, William was in some sort of frenzy, organizing things and bouncing around so fast that Sarah almost got dizzy watching him. He was excited to get back to his world and when she glanced at him, there was new found hope in his eyes. Sarah however, felt herself getting quieter and more withdrawn the closer the time for their journey came. It was one thing to be forced to live in hiding, but at least she was doing it in her world, a place that was familiar to her and where she had a social network to fall back on. It was an entirely different story to be in another world, especially one that was at war, and she was scared. Besides, she still had no idea what she was supposed to do there.

She had written a long letter to Joe, in which she explained everything. She gave it to him after receiving his promise that he would only read it if she didn't return within three months. She hoped that this was enough time. Not that Joe would be able to do anything to help her if she didn't return, but she also enclosed some farewell letters to her parents, Charlotte, and some other people she cared about. In case she never returned, she didn't want to leave them wondering about her fate for the rest of their lives. Of course, she hadn't written down the entire truth for them, but enough to understand that she wouldn't be able to return.

And while William had a new spring to his step, her heart was heavy when they approached the old oak on the hill.

'I know that it might be necessary,' she interrupted the silence at some point. 'But can you try and not kill anyone?'

William turned his head to catch her eye. She couldn't read his expression, but he nodded. 'And you're going to show me how to use the portal, right?' she added. They had talked about it before. She didn't want to be stuck in his world without knowing her way back home if something happened to William.

He confirmed her question with a nod but Sarah realised that he was mainly focused on their surroundings again, trying to spot a trap or anything that seemed odd to him. This behaviour was already familiar to her, and she wondered if she'd ever see him relaxed. It was quiet, and they reached the old oak without any interruptions. Again, Sarah immediately felt humble in the presence of the tree, and she circled the large trunk once, running her fingers gently over the cracked, thick bark.

'You can feel it, can you?' William studied her curiously. 'Places like this radiate power. Not everyone notices it, but a lot of people are either drawn to or repelled by these kinds of places.'

'I find it peaceful here,' Sarah said, before she turned around to face William. 'It reminds me of my grandmother's garden.' As a child, she had visited her Granny often and the backyard behind her grandparents' cottage had always been her favourite place. There had been a weeping willow and underneath its branches and hidden from the world, Sarah had felt safe and protected.

'I'll show you how you can switch from one world to the other,' William said. 'But let me go first and see if the air's clear on the other side.'

'OK,' Sarah took a step back and watched with fascination how he touched the tree and simply disappeared. There was no fading away or anything like that. One second he was there, the next he wasn't. She pulled the rough jacket closer around her body and studied the belongings he had left behind. It took her a moment to realise that she felt vulnerable when William wasn't around, and she was relieved when he returned a few minutes later, slightly out of breath but unharmed. She always fancied herself to be an independent woman and disliked feeling vulnerable without him. But then, her situation wasn't exactly normal, wasn't it?

'There was a guard,' he reported and smiled shortly when he saw the question that was lying in her eyes. 'I only knocked him out.'

Sarah returned his smile.

'Alright, come here. I'll show you how to flip over. It's quite simple. Just close your eyes and touch the tree. This also works with the other portals. There aren't many around these days, but some. Just in case you can't make it back to this one. You'll feel it when something is a portal, like you feel it here.'

Sarah nodded, closing her eyes and focusing on his voice. The bark felt warm underneath her fingers.

'Now feel the tree, feel its power, and follow it.'

Sarah's eyebrows furrowed. She had no clue what he meant by this, but when she focused, she felt something. There was a hum of power and a slight pull as if something was tugging at her, she couldn't describe it any better than that.

'It'll take you some time to figure it out. When I tried the first time…' his voice was cut off and she felt like being pulled forward and falling at the same time.

The scent in the air was exactly as she remembered, and when she opened her eyes there was a silent figure on the ground, right next to the tree. Sarah stepped closer, noticing blood on the man's head but he was breathing regularly, and Sarah released a deep breath.

'Told you I only knocked him out,' William startled her. Changing worlds apparently didn't create any noise. She gave him a quick smile, but she was still amazed at how easy it had been for her to switch to this place. It filled her with a sense of reverence.

She walked out from underneath the canopy of the

tree and stood on the hill. And for the first time, she *saw.*

During her first visit, she had been too agitated; the impressions washing over her and drowning her but now she was calm and collected. She watched the scenery in front of her, noticing how the landscape very much resembled the one in her world. This one was more rural though, at least at first glance. The first time she had seen farms and fields for crops, and stables for livestock. But when she thought about it, she wasn't sure any longer if this was just a rural world. Because at second glance Sarah had seen electric lights in some places. There were no visible power lines so maybe there was some technology underground, something she didn't see. It was probably best to ask William about it and not draw any quick conclusions about this world.

William appeared at her side, carrying their baggage. 'You managed fast,' he commented on her switch to the other world. 'It took me days.'

'I think I've been doing it before,' Sarah said slowly. 'Unconsciously. You know, all those visions and hallucinations I had. When my street suddenly changed and what happened in that supermarket.' Her voice trailed off.

'That's impossible,' William explained, 'you need a place with a concentration of magic for that and I doubt that a supermarket is one of them.'

Sarah gave him a side-eye. 'You tell me that there's magic and then say that something is impossible at the same time?' She laughed shortly. 'But you're right. I don't think that I stepped into this world before, it was more like... looking at it through a window.'

But her thoughts wandered back to the woman who had taken her apples. There had been some sort of connection between their worlds.

So much had happened in her life in such a short amount of time that she never fully realised what her hallucinations had been. After almost being killed, being on the run, and venturing into a different world, her previous problems had been pushed to the back of her mind. But when she thought about it, it was obvious. She had never suffered from visions or hallucinations, there had never been a brain tumour and she certainly hadn't gone crazy. She had simply caught glimpses into a different world; into this world. And it had happened even before she had met William. If she needed more proof that she was somehow connected to this crazy story, this was the one. Everything had led her here, to this moment, to this world. And suddenly she felt a little better about what was going on, her fears lifting a little. Maybe she needed to have faith that everything was going to be alright in the end.

'OK,' she said and rubbed her hands together. 'Let me hop worlds a couple of times to practice. I want to make sure that I know how to return on my own if anything unplanned happens.' Such as him being killed or her getting lost, but she said neither of those things out loud.

Twenty minutes later Sarah was satisfied, and the two were on their way. They took the same route they had taken a few weeks back, but this time Sarah paid more attention to her surroundings, taking everything in. After they had walked in silence for a while, Sarah inquired how everything worked in this world. She hadn't seen any signs of technology or a sewer system or anything that would explain how things were run here and she was curious. William immediately began a long explanation about how Aphelia had once resembled Earth but that the overexploitation of resources and the pollution of the soil, water, and sky had become too much. A radical change had taken place, coupled with some amazing inventions, and since then the inhabitants of Aphelia were living in harmony with their world, without having to miss the comfort that modern technologies brought. He explained how they generated power from natural resources like wind, sun, and water, and that the power lines were underground, as was the rest of the infrastructure. The surface was only used for farming, at least in the countryside.

Sarah was impressed, wondering if those technologies and inventions he had mentioned could possibly work on Earth too and another thought crossed her mind. 'Do you have money or something like it?' The question elicited a smile from William.

'No, we are long past that stage,' he explained. 'We work for the community; everyone has what they need and sometimes we exchange things for other things but money is a thing of the past.' His face darkened and he suddenly looked broody and withdrawn. 'At least it was like that before the war. Now those who have or want more than others gain power again.'

After that, they walked in silence while Sarah pondered on William's words. The people here had created a perfect environment to live in, and Sarah felt ashamed of her own world. The craving for profit that was valued way above human life, the exploitation and pollution of nature, the cruel industrial livestock farming, all of it was barbaric in comparison, and she wondered how William had seen Earth. He never said anything about it. Ashamed, she realised that she had ignorantly and arrogantly assumed that Aphelia was retrogressive compared with Earth, when it was the other way around. At least before this world had gone to war, that was. Living in a perfect environment apparently didn't prevent people like Drake from craving power. Maybe it was in human nature, after all.

'How come no one knows about magic in this world any longer?' she asked. 'Especially because it seems crucial for Aphelia. The story you told me about the last Guardians for example. Drake was only able to rise to power because that happened, right? How could it come to this? Because otherwise, you seem to be living in a perfect balance with each other and the nature around you here.'

William spoke slowly when he replied, something that told Sarah that he was carefully choosing his words. 'It was a deliberate decision from the founding fathers and mothers of the League of the Guardians to keep magic hidden,' he explained. 'Back when things started to change in Aphelia centuries ago. The knowledge of magic brought immense power and some people tried to use it to their advantage, resisting the changes to our world. Changes that everyone benefited from. So magic was gradually hidden by the most honourable and honest members of our society, the Guardians. It took a long time, but the old tales fell into oblivion, and you know the result.'

Sarah pondered his words. 'But what does magic do? Is it like in Harry Potter?'

William's brows furrowed, and Sarah realised once again that cultural references were lost on him.

'Like, can you use magic for spells or, you know, influence your surroundings in any way?' she specified.

'There are no direct spells,' he explained. 'It's more like rituals? I am not sure how it works myself. I wasn't one of the Guardians, I only...' he stopped speaking abruptly. 'I only found the prophecy,' he continued. 'Before that, I didn't know about magic, either. But I began to do some research, and consulted some of the old books the Guardians left behind, but as you can imagine, none of it was specific. What I learned is that when you finally understand the magic of this world, you'll grow to be very powerful. That's all I know. Other than that, I stumble around in the dark just as everyone else does, which explains why I'm just a regular guy. See?' He spun around playfully and offered her a grin.

'But powerful enough to convince a random woman from another world to follow you into yours,' she observed, glad that the mood between them was light for a change.

'The most random woman who writes horrible poetry,' William added helpfully, his grin deepening.

'Says the broody one who wouldn't recognise a great poem even if it was staring him right in the face.' She swatted at his arm lightly, and he laughed.

They continued to banter like that and the last resentments she had felt towards him after he had killed the man in her backyard mellowed out. He was the only person in this new and foreign world she could trust, and she did, she realised with surprise.

Not much happened, but the next few days were still very eventful for Sarah since everything was new. She learned so much about this world, its continents, countries, inhabitants, and its flora and fauna that her head was bursting with information. At the same time, they were quiet days, characterized by a comfortable routine William and Sarah settled into. They rose with the sun and retired when it got dark, sharing a tent during the nights and getting more and more comfortable in each other's presence. They stayed off the main roads, hid whenever someone crossed their path, avoided large cities, and when they passed through one of the small villages, they had the hoods of their jackets drawn tight over their heads, hiding their faces in the shadows.

By now, Sarah could detect lots of telltale signs of the famine that was wrecking this world.

They only saw a few animals or wildlife but a lot of empty traps during their hike. At the same time people were collecting anything edible from nature. Berries, fruits, nuts, whatever was available was plucked, often before it was ripe, and Sarah was glad that William had packed many supplies for them. Even though it was tedious to eat plain rice and dried fruit every day, Sarah never got too hungry. She fantasised about the Irish stew her mother made or the pizza she sometimes got from the little shop at the corner of her street, but she never said it out loud. She was aware that people of this world were dying from lack of food, and it would have been more than disrespectful to complain.

A few days later she would learn just how hungry the people of Aphelia had become. She and William were walking through a village that appeared deserted when they heard voices.

William immediately pulled her behind a thick hedge where they cowered down on the ground, making themselves as small and invisible as possible. Moments later, a man and a woman came out of one of the barns adjoining a farmhouse. The woman was carrying a small, skinny chicken and both were beaming. This probably equalled a feast for them, or maybe they wanted to keep the chicken for the eggs. In any case, Sarah couldn't help but smile at their joy.

Before she could relax, since there didn't seem to be any danger coming from the couple, she felt William's touch against her arm. When she looked at him, he pressed a finger to his lips, his eyes giving her a silent warning. Through the leaves of the hedge, she noticed a group of three men approaching the couple quietly from behind. She hadn't seen them, so they must have been hiding in one of the farmhouses. The couple hadn't noticed them yet, and even though Sarah felt the urge to shout out a warning, she kept quiet, because William's grasp around her arm had gotten stronger. Sometimes, he seemed to be able to read her mind.

The attack was quick and brutal. It couldn't have taken more than a minute before the man and the woman were on the ground. Once the group had run off with the stolen chicken, Sarah crawled out of her hiding place and ran over toward the couple. Maybe she could still help.

Again, the grip of William's hand was strong around her arm when he caught up with her. 'It's too late,' he said. 'Look.'

Sarah stopped, realising with horror that he was right. Even from the distance, she could tell that they were dead, their heads bashed in, their lifeless bodies left carelessly right where they had fallen.

'They killed two people over a chicken.' Her voice was flat.

'Come on,' William said gently, leading her away from the gruesome sight and back into the woods.

After that, they stayed in the countryside and gave a wide berth to all the larger accumulations of people and cities, but even so, the signs of destruction and war were everywhere. They passed through destroyed villages, burned-out forests, and vandalised fields. William explained that there were no real parties in this conflict but that everyone had started attacking their neighbours, desperate for resources, fuelled by Drake and his men who took what they wanted and killed everyone resenting his status as the new leader of Aphelia. The public order had collapsed, and everyone was just struggling to survive, ruled by the terror of Drake.

Luckily, most advanced weapons, such as guns and bombs, had been disassembled and destroyed during the changes to society in Aphelia, so the damage could have been worse, even though it was still bad enough. But William was convinced that the knowledge of how to use a gun or assemble a bomb was still out there somewhere and that Drake was researching it right now. The fact that his men had sent a sniper after Sarah was proof enough of that for him.

At the same time, William never seemed to tire of painting the picture of how wonderful this world had been before the dark time, as he called it, and she gladly listened and learned as much as she could. Only when their talk strayed too far into his personal life did he sidetrack her with something, still unwilling to talk about himself. Sarah sometimes wondered if she had only been imagining him telling her his life story in the darkness of the night in Joe's living room because now he was as withdrawn and close-lipped as ever.

They made good progress, but during their second week, they were about to turn the corner of the small path leading through the forest when William stopped suddenly. Only seconds later, a group of what looked like soldiers came in sight, and there was no more time to hide. 'Run,' William ordered while he reached for her hand, and before the soldiers could react, they were crashing through the underbrush.

Branches were whipping into their faces, leaving cuts and bruises while thorns clawed at their clothes. William did not let go of her hand, pulling her after him relentlessly. Sarah didn't need to look over her shoulder, she could hear the soldiers following them, but they were putting more and more distance between them.

'Up there,' William hissed and before she knew what was happening, she was pushed up a huge tree with wide branches. Sarah had never been the best at climbing, but adrenaline gave her extra strength, and soon they were clinging to a large branch at least three metres above the ground.

Sarah's heart was racing, and she was still very much out of breath when the group of soldiers ran past their tree and vanished in the underbrush, not even slowing down. This time William didn't need to give her a warning. Sarah stayed as quiet as she could and only after what felt like a very long time did William finally speak.

'Those were soldiers, Drake's men.'

'I kind of figured,' Sarah replied dryly. 'Are they gone?'

'I can't hear them anymore, so for now we should be safe. Also, look,' he pointed at the horizon. From up here, a mountain massif was to be seen in the distance. 'That's the Sleeping Dragon,' he announced. Sarah squinted her eyes against the sun. She had to admit that it indeed looked a bit like a sleeping dragon.

'How long until we get there?' she wanted to know.

William studied the mountains in the distance. 'Maybe two more weeks,' he guessed. 'Since we have to stay off the main roads, it's taking us at least twice as long as it usually would.'

Sarah sighed deeply. She understood why they couldn't use main roads but there was something else she had been meaning to ask for a while. 'Why do we have to walk all the time, anyway? I mean, this is a highly developed world, you surely have means of transport, don't you?'

'Of course we have,' William laughed. 'But we can't use them, it's not safe. You need identification, and the system is monitored closely. In addition, most of them aren't running right now with the war and the lack of resources.'

And with that, he began to climb down the tree, and Sarah followed. Back on the ground, she realised how exhausted she was. Even though seeing the Sleeping Dragon for the first time had given her a boost of energy, her feet hurt. She was used to standing and walking a lot because of her job, but she wasn't used to hiking this much in such a short amount of time. And she wasn't used to running through the woods and climbing trees. She had tried to ignore the growing sores on the soles of her feet, but she didn't want to walk any further. She needed a break. Sinking onto a fallen tree she groaned.

'My feet are killing me. I'm sorry, but I need a break, and I'm not talking about a few minutes.' She assumed that he would prefer to keep going, but surprisingly, William sank next to her and gave her a lop-sided smile.

'Mine are killing me too, I am not used to this, either,' he admitted, and Sarah laughed.

'Let's put up the tent somewhere, take the day off from walking, and see if we feel better tomorrow.'

Chapter 12

They found a small clearing hidden by thick underbrush, next to a small stream, and decided to stay there for the rest of the day. They put up the tent, and William placed a few rabbit snares on the ground at each side of the clearing, though neither of them had much hope of catching anything. They had put out the snares every night but never caught anything. Once everything was set up, they plopped down on the ground next to the stream, removed their shoes and socks, and cooled their hurting feet in the water, allowing a comfortable silence to settle over them.

Sarah lay back and watched the sky, enjoying the unexpected peace. She even nodded off for a while, but woke up again when her feet got uncomfortably cold. She sat up and pulled them out of the stream to study them. Surprisingly enough there were no open blisters, but the soles of her feet were painful when she pressed them, feeling very overused. To her surprise, William reached out and took one of her feet into his hands. 'Let me see this,' he said, and Sarah's eyebrows rose. Even though they were around each other all the time there had been little to no touch between them.

William examined her foot before he gently started running his thumbs over the sensitive skin of her soles, not hard enough to cause any pain, but with enough pressure that it would loosen up some of the tension. Sarah certainly hadn't anticipated receiving a foot massage from 'Mr I'm So Withdrawn And Stoic It Hurts', but what she had anticipated even less was her physical reaction to his innocent touch. His fingers were warm, his touch tender, and the nerve endings of her feet felt as if on fire. A very pleasant shiver crept up her spine, and she realised that she had temporarily stopped breathing. She drew in a deep breath while staring at him as if seeing him for the first time. Why did she suddenly feel as if she was walking on very thin ice?

William didn't notice her inner turmoil. His eyes were on her foot, the muscles of his arms shifting underneath his skin while his moves were gentle and consistent, sending more shivers across her spine. Sarah tried hard to push the mental picture aside, but she couldn't help wondering how his touch would feel on other parts of her body.

He looked up at her and when their eyes met the world spun to a halt around her. There was a new expression in his gaze that made her feel as if someone had punched her in the stomach. Neither of them averted their eyes. Instead, they were staring at each other for way too long to pretend that this was a regular exchange. William had stopped massaging her foot, but he still held it between his hands while Sarah's mind was entirely blank. She knew that she was supposed to say something – anything – to ease the sudden tension between them, to laugh this off, to move her foot out of his reach, or to get up, but she did none of that.

Instead, she watched how he let go of her foot and slipped towards her, not once averting his eyes from hers.

Her heart skipped a beat as he got closer, and she felt almost hypnotized by the intensity of his gaze. Had his eyes always been this green?

She knew that she was seeing the real William. His façade had cracked, and she was getting another glimpse of what he thought and felt. It was desire. For her. And he made no attempt to hide it. She had been running from him and then running with him, but there was nowhere to run right now.

His face was only inches away, and she could feel his warm breath caressing her face. She lifted her chin and closed her eyes, her lips parting slightly to receive his kiss. Her heart was threatening to explode, beating so hard that she could almost hear it. She wanted this. Badly.

A loud, cracking sound to their left made them both flinch, and Sarah's eyes shot open.

William jumped to his feet but stayed in a crouch, while he intently stared into the direction of the sound. She released one deep breath, then another, while she tried to calm down. She glanced in the direction of the sound, but her thoughts were miles away. What had just happened? They had been about to kiss, and she had wanted it. She *still* wanted it. What the hell?

William exchanged a quick look with her, but his expression was distanced again. The moment between them was over, and Sarah felt a mixture of relief and disappointment. William gestured for her to keep quiet before he got up, crossed the small stream, and disappeared into the forest.

She released another deep and shaky breath and ran her hand through her hair. She was only mildly concerned about the noise in the woods since it was likely just an animal. This clearing was well-hidden, and the soldiers surely were long gone. It was very unlikely that there was a real threat around. Nonetheless, when her eyes fell on the set of knives they had brought along for cooking, she grabbed one and put it into the waistband of her pants. She was pretty sure that she wouldn't be able to use it because the mere thought of her stabbing anyone was ridiculous. But it was better to be armed after all.

While she waited for William's return, she wondered how she was supposed to act once he came back. Should she pretend the moment between them hadn't happened? Or would they continue where they had stopped? She felt nervous. Kissing him was a bad idea. It would complicate everything, but at the same time, there was no doubt that she had wanted it. As had he.

When she had thought about William, it all had been about surviving and getting back to her old life. He was an ally, a means to an end, someone she needed for help, and someone who needed her help in return. A weird twist of fate had tossed them together, and they had been stuck with each other ever since.

But now?

There was no denying that she felt drawn to him, at least on a physical level. But other than physical? She had no idea. There was no time for something like this. Surviving should be her first and main interest. Surviving and getting back to her old life. Then, and only then, she could allow herself to think about kissing someone. Every-thing else would be a distraction she couldn't afford.

She sighed. Once William returned, she would tell him that something like this was not going to happen again, and she would keep her distance from him now, which would be difficult with only one tent.

It was very quiet in the clearing, and it dawned on Sarah that William had been gone for quite a long time already. There had been no more noises, and it was peculiar that he wasn't back yet. Too late, the thought entered her mind that if this indeed was an attack, it was the most logical thing to have someone make a noise somewhere while sneaking up from behind. She hadn't even finished this thought when a rough bag was slipped over her head and a couple of strong hands gripped her tightly.

Sarah screamed and struggled against the arms holding her but immediately went still when she felt cold steel against her throat. It didn't take much imagination to realise that it was a blade. An unfamiliar voice whispered into her ear, 'Be quiet if you want to live.' Sarah allowed the hands on her arms to hold her steady, not even daring to breathe any longer.

'Good girl,' the man whispered, and she felt the sting of a needle in her arm. She tried to fight the sudden dizziness, but her limbs went heavy, and a few moments later the world went dark.

She slowly rose back to the surface of consciousness. She felt dizzy and disoriented, and for a short merciful timespan didn't remember what happened. There was a dirty light bulb above her head, and she squinted against the brightness. A glance around told her that she was in some sort of prison cell, lying on a stretcher that was screwed to the wall, and covered by a thin mattress. The walls were made of concrete stone, darkened through the ages. She slowly sat up and took in more details. There was a thin and scratchy-looking blanket lying by her feet, neatly folded. Her head was pounding with every move she made, and she groaned. She was indeed in some sort of cell, but the door stood slightly ajar. At least she wasn't locked in. Where the hell was she?

'Fuck,' she whispered, when her memories came crashing back. She remembered the clearing, and William, but mainly how stupid she had been. She buried her head in her hands as if she could undo what had happened simply by hiding from the world as she had done as a child.

She had been abducted, almost certainly by Drake's men, but at least she was alive and in one piece. She could still feel the effects of the drug running through her system. She was dizzy, slightly queasy, and had trouble focusing. And then there was the headache. Sarah quickly checked the waistband of her pants but wasn't surprised to find her knife gone.

She put her feet on the ground and waited for the bout of dizziness to pass before she carefully got up to take a better look around. But whoever had put her in this cell, had made sure to check it thoroughly. There was nothing in here she could use as a weapon, not even a rusty nail or an old piece of plywood. After taking a few tentative steps and realising she could walk, she made her way to the door. It creaked lightly when she opened it, and she carefully stuck her head out. She had expected a guard or something but instead, she was greeted by a deserted corridor with plenty of cells similar to hers. To her right, there was a concrete brick wall, and Sarah turned left. The other cells were empty and the scent of mould and dust in the air told her that they hadn't been in use for a while. The building was quiet and felt entirely devoid of life. She had hoped to find William, but there was no one around. Maybe he had managed to escape.

The hallway took a sharp turn left, and she could see that it ended in a room. She could hear voices. Male voices. More than two. She couldn't make out what they were saying but she was pretty sure that one of the voices belonged to the man who had captured her at the clearing. Carefully, she peered around the corner. The corridor opened into a large room built from the same darkened stone. Since there were no windows here either, she figured that she was in some sort of basement or underground bunker. The room was sparsely furnished, and there was a fire burning brightly in a large fireplace to her right. Six large round tables were standing in the room, which appeared to have functioned as a common room for guards at some point. Only one of the tables was occupied by five men, playing cards. They were wearing uniforms and appeared to be soldiers.

She withdrew again and considered her options. There was no other way out of here but the chances of her getting through this room unnoticed were slim. Still, she had to try. She inhaled deeply and held her breath while slowly pushing herself around the corner, trying to blend into the wall. She took a few quiet steps before ducking behind the first of the tables. She slowly released her breath, pleased with herself. This had gone surprisingly well. She quickly crawled forward and bridged the open space to the next table where she paused again.

Now she could make out what the men were saying.

'...wife?'

Sarah rolled her eyes. No matter which world she was in, men seemed to be the same everywhere. But the next words proved her wrong, and she felt embarrassed for drawing quick conclusions.

'I don't know.' There was sadness in his voice. 'I don't know where she is. After he took her.'

Sarah was distracted by these words, and her foot hit an empty chair. It made a small scraping noise against the stone floor. It became quiet in the room, and Sarah held her breath, trying to make herself as small and invisible as possible.

'Did you hear that?' More silence.

'That was nothing. Just the fire crackling.'

'Shouldn't we take a look?'

'It was the fire!' This was the man who had abducted her. He seemed to hold some authority over the others because they fell quiet immediately. 'The dose I gave her was enough to knock out an elephant, she won't wake up for a while.' And with that, the conversation at the table resumed, but Sarah couldn't make out a single word any longer because her blood was rushing loudly through her ears. It felt like an eternity before her heartbeat calmed down, and she found the courage to move forward again. Pushing the strange conversation she had witnessed to the back of her mind, she focused on her way out. Only one table was left between her and the exit. She slowly crept forward; her eyes fixed on her path to freedom when she felt a hand on her shoulder. For a man his size, he was extremely light-footed.

'Look at that, our princess is awake,' he said, and Sarah slowly got up from her crouch.

Four heads had turned to study her, and she kept her posture straight, not wanting to show them her fear. She also felt annoyed. She almost had made it.

Almost.

The soldiers looked rough and slightly unkempt, but at the same time, there was a discipline about them. Sarah felt embarrassed about being caught now and about how stupid she had been at the clearing. But after all, she was a barista and not a superhero. No one had ever taught her what to do in these kinds of situations.

'Where am I and what do you want with me?' she questioned, surprised about how confident her voice sounded.

'Drake wants to see you,' the man beside her said.

'He could have asked nicely, you know?' she snapped, wondering where this sudden bout of bravery, or maybe stupidity, came from.

The men exchanged surprised glances and broke into laughter.

'Well, princess,' the man mimicked a small bow. 'Drake would like to talk to you, are you coming?'

'How could I resist such a nice invitation?' Sarah responded dryly and immediately told herself to shut up. She wasn't sure if it was the drugs that made her feel this way but buried underneath all the fear was real anger. These men were the ones who had been trying to kill her back on Earth. And they had tortured William. Sarah hadn't forgotten what he had looked like, the bruises almost entirely covering his body, and the pain he had been in.

They walked through a few similar, deserted corridors, up a few flights of stairs, and finally reached an iron gate that separated the cell block from the rest of the building. They seemed to be in a castle of some sort. Obviously, there were equivalents here in Aphelia. She realised how little she actually knew about this world. Sarah had seen skylines of larger cities that looked similar to those on Earth in the distance, but William had always made sure to stay clear of them. She had assumed that it was because the impact of the famine and the war were much worse in the cities than they were in the countryside. She couldn't even begin to imagine what living in a city with many other hungry humans would be like. Again, she wondered where William was. Had he been brought somewhere else? Or had he managed to escape? Maybe he had since he was so much better at this. He surely was fine. He had to be.

Too late, Sarah realised that she probably should have paid more attention to her surroundings and where they were going. If there was even the slightest chance to escape, every little thing she knew about this place was going to help. But then, who was she kidding? How was she supposed to escape as long as those men were guarding her? She wasn't even sure what she was doing here. In her world, Drake's men had tried to kill her more than once, and now he wanted to talk to her? About what? Why not kill her directly and save him the bother? There had been plenty of opportunities for the soldiers in the woods. She thought about all those movies where the villain messed up because instead of killing the other person, they bragged about their plan and in the end failed because of it. Her heart grew heavy, and the short stint of bravery she had felt earlier was gone when she thought about facing Drake, the man who had tried to kill her ever since learning about her existence.

He was nothing like she had expected. The fact was that he was remarkably handsome. He seemed only a few years older than Sarah, and he was tall and slim. His brown locks framed his pretty face perfectly and enhanced the warmth in his chocolate-brown eyes. They were accompanied by an even nose, full lips, and perfect teeth. When he smiled at her warmly, two dimples appeared. He seemed the equivalent of a cute puppy, and Sarah looked at him in surprise.

This was the mass-murdering, power-hungry, and utterly evil Drake?

'Sarah,' he greeted her warmly, 'I'm sorry for how we had to take you, but we didn't see any other way.'

'Are you also sorry for trying to kill me numerous times, back in my world?' Sarah retaliated before thinking about it.

Drake's grin deepened.

'Nothing personal,' he retorted, and waved at a servant who was waiting in the corner. The man bowed and approached with a tray holding a carafe and wine glasses. They looked heavy and expensive. He put the tray down on a nearby table and started filling the glasses with what seemed to be red wine before offering one to Sarah. She shook her head. She definitely wouldn't be drinking any wine with Drake. Or anything else.

Drake accepted a glass and sipped from it before he stepped closer. 'You probably understand that trying to kill you was a necessary precaution,' he explained, 'even though I'm glad that I didn't succeed. What a waste that would have been.' He circled her slowly as if studying a trinket, he was deciding whether to purchase.

'They told me you were pretty, but not *how* pretty.'

Sarah clenched her jaw. He had turned from a cute puppy into a creep in less than ten seconds.

'I was curious to see you, you know?' he continued to speak. 'An ordinary girl from the other world, defying my men and making it as far as you have.'

He came to a halt in front of her and despite looking like an angel, there was something within his gaze that made her feel very, very scared and she averted her eyes from his, not wanting him to be able to read hers any longer.

'Where is William?' she demanded to know, surprised about how confident she sounded.

'Our mutual friend,' Drake said and smiled, but there was no warmth in it. 'He escaped my men, but don't worry. I'm sure he'll come looking for you soon, and you'll be reunited in no time.'

Sarah suppressed a sigh of relief, not wanting to show Drake how much she had worried. 'Where am I?'

'In my castle,' Drake confirmed her earlier suspicion. 'You are my guest. Of course, I can't allow you to leave, but no harm shall come upon you while you are here.'

This sentence caused Sarah to frown at him. She was getting tired of his games. 'I thought I was such a risk to you and your plans, why don't you just kill me?'

Drake laughed as if she had said the funniest thing in the world. 'I might,' he admitted as if talking about the weather, and a cold shiver crept up Sarah's spine. 'But not now. I need to know some things first.'

The cold shiver reached Sarah's neck, and she could feel the fine hairs rising there.

'I'm curious. What is it that makes you so special?'

Without warning, he leaned in on her, and for a moment, she had the absurd idea that he was going to kiss her, but he only took a deep breath, inhaling her scent. Sarah froze while he continued to speak, still way too close for her liking.

'There is something about you, and I would like to know what it is.'

'There's nothing special about me,' Sarah answered while trying not to flinch away from him. She made the attempt to sound calm, but she felt desperate, remembering what his men had done to William when they had wanted answers. She knew exactly what Drake wanted to know. He wanted to learn about the prophecy, he wanted to know where they had been heading and what they had planned to do there.

Drake tilted his head while he studied her but finally took a step back, immediately making it easier for her to breathe again. 'I think you are underestimating yourself. But whatever.' He suddenly seemed to have lost interest in her and turned around to walk back towards a large desk he had been sitting behind when she had entered.

'You will keep me company for dinner later on.' That was not a question. 'Dress nicely.'

And with those words, he waved his hand as if shaking off an irksome fly and immediately the servant came forward and beckoned her to follow him. Sarah shot a last glance at Drake, but he was already focused on the papers on his desk.

The servant took her to a spacious room, and she heard the lock of the door snapping shut behind him. She tried the handle only to confirm that she was now officially a prisoner in a very luxurious room with its own bathroom. There was a large double four-poster bed and tasteful furniture. When she looked out the huge window, the view was breathtaking. The castle was located on a low mountain overlooking a large city and it was beautiful, at least at first glance. The houses were snuggled against each other, pretty and clean. She could see public parks that were groomed, plenty of trees, and even a few small lakes. At second sight, she could see that things weren't as good as they appeared. A few of the houses had been burned down and she could see more than one column of smoke rising towards the sky in the distance. There weren't many people. A few were roaming the streets, like tiny ants from her point of view, and she wondered why there weren't more of them. Maybe most of the population had left after the lack of food?

The chances in the countryside were probably better, but William and Sarah hadn't seen many people there, either. Maybe Aphelia didn't have as many inhabitants as Earth?

She turned around and her eyes fell on a dress lying on the bed. It was beautiful, and she understood what Drake had meant when he had told her to dress nicely. 'Ugh.' She groaned in annoyance. Did he expect her to wear this? For him? This was like in a bad movie, just that in her case the bad guy definitely wouldn't turn into the kind prince. She didn't *want* to dress up for Drake, but she hesitated. She knew that she needed to be clever to survive this for as long as possible. Being stubborn wouldn't get her far, no matter how much she wanted to. As much as she disliked the thought of William coming to her rescue, she had no clue how she'd be able to escape otherwise. It was not like she had any experience in all of this. She sank onto the bed and ran her hand over the green silk of the dress. It looked and felt amazing, and she didn't doubt for a second that she'd be stunning in it.

Without any warning, tears started to fill her eyes and before she knew it, she was crying, releasing all the tension that had built up over the last few weeks. She hadn't cried since the bombing of Steven's shop. And she couldn't stop, finally allowing herself to feel the tremendous fear that had settled deep into her bones. Her utter loneliness. Her life had spun out of her control. Fate was tossing her around, and now here she was, about to put on a beautiful dress to have dinner with someone who wanted to kill her, in a world she didn't understand, and without her only ally. When she managed to calm down, her head was pounding but this time it was because she had been crying so much. She felt slightly better and took a shuddering breath, knowing she couldn't allow herself to wallow in self-pity any longer. It wouldn't get her anywhere. She got up and walked into the bathroom, which was luxurious and spacious too, and decided to take a shower. During their hike, she had only been able to wash herself with cold water, and if she was locked in here, she might as well make the best of it. Her eyes took in her reflection in the mirror above the sink, and she looked like a mess. Dark circles underneath her red-rimmed eyes, her hair bushy and straggly, her skin pale.

'Let's do this,' she whispered to herself, and soon she was soaking under the hot water of the shower. Drake had promised that no harm would come to her while she was here, and she clung to his words, not daring to paint her options because that would have been a very bleak picture.

Chapter 13

The dinner table was set beautifully, with crystal glasses and candleholders, fresh flowers, and more cutlery than she had ever used in one meal, and she wondered again what game Drake was playing. His eyes were resting on her since she had entered, accompanied by the servant who had picked her up at her room earlier. She didn't like the way Drake looked at her but pretended not to notice that he was there at all. The servant pulled out a chair for her and she quickly sat down opposite Drake, relieved that she was able to hide most of herself from his prying eyes.

'You look beautiful,' he commented, and she knew that he was telling the truth. The dress clung to her curves perfectly, its colour emphasizing the colour of her hair and her eyes. Since she usually wore jeans and a nerdy T-shirt, she didn't feel too comfortable in it, even less so knowing who she was wearing it for. She wondered if he had picked it out himself.

'Tell me about yourself,' he requested while the servant poured them some wine and brought a plate with mushroom soup. The thought crossed her mind that the food could be poisoned, but it didn't make much sense. He could have killed her, why an elaborate plot to poison her soup now? Also, he wanted to know things from her, things she wouldn't be able to tell him if she was dead.

And, last but not least, she was starving, and the soup smelled delicious.

'What do you want to know?' she asked before trying a spoonful of soup. It was as good as it smelled.

'I don't care,' he said and started eating as well.

'I work in a coffee shop,' she began. 'Worked. Before your men blew it up.' She glanced at him, wondering if he would get angry at her remark, but it only elicited a small chuckle from Drake. 'I live alone, as you already know, I like to read as you know as well and I help out in a homeless shelter once a week, something you're aware of, too.'

She leaned back in her chair, the spoon forgotten in her hand.

'What's this charade about? You know all there is to know about me. What do you really want from me?'

Despite her lingering fear, she grew more and more annoyed at him and his antics. Why couldn't he simply tell her what he wanted?

'That already told me a lot,' Drake let her know and wiped his mouth with a napkin. 'You're fearless.'

Sarah's eyebrows rose. 'Hardly,' she muttered.

'Straightforward and fierce, if needed,' Drake added, ignoring her remark.

'Listen,' she interrupted. 'All I want is to go home and for this to be over. I never wanted or choose this.'

Drake took a sip of his wine before he put the glass back down on the table. 'Oh, but you did,' he stated. 'And do you think I wanted this?' he asked. 'Do you think I like to see my people starve and suffer? Ever since our mutual friend William killed the last two Guardians, I've been trying to...' He fell quiet upon seeing the expression on

Sarah's face, and a sly smile crossed his lips.

'You didn't know that, did you? Of course, he wouldn't have told you.'

The spoon sank down to the table as Sarah tried to play it cool.

'Tell me, how well do you know him?' Drake asked, and leaned back in his chair, taking another sip of wine.

Her silence said it all.

'He didn't just kill them, he *slaughtered* them,' Drake elaborated. 'They were unarmed. You should have seen it. It was a bloodbath.'

Sarah knew that Drake was playing her, that he had intended to drop this bomb on her all along, knowing that it was going to shock her, even though she didn't know to what end. Could this be true? Why would William kill the last Guardians and then go to find her to reverse what he had set in motion? That didn't make any sense, but it explained how he had gotten to the prophecy in the first place. And it would be typical for William to not tell her something like this. He had hardly told her anything. Her thoughts were spinning, and she felt played and helpless. She was the centre of the game between these two men, without having a clue what was going on, and she was very tired of it.

She grabbed her glass of wine and took a long sip. When she put it down, her face was an unreadable mask. 'Of course, I knew that,' she pretended before picking up the spoon and eating some more of her soup. 'I wasn't aware that you knew.'

Drake's handsome face darkened, the smug expression flickering, and he leaned forward. 'I know everything.'

'Do you?' Sarah retorted. 'Good for you.' She was

utterly fed up with him and took another sip of wine. Like the soup, it tasted delicious, and she hadn't had anything fancy in a while.

Drake leaned against the backrest of his chair and studied her. But then he shrugged, and the tension lifted from the room. 'Doesn't matter,' he said. 'Let's enjoy the meal for now. We can talk about this again, once William joins us. I'm sure he'll be here soon.'

The rest of the dinner was surprisingly uneventful. Just like William, Drake liked to talk about Aphelia, and he filled most of the time with small talk about his world while they had meat, potatoes, and roasted vegetables as the main course and fruit salad for dessert. Sarah finished her glass of wine but didn't accept another one. She didn't want to be drunk around Drake. When the servant brought her back to her chambers after they had finished eating, Sarah was more confused than ever, not sure what to make of the evening.

Back in her room, she replayed the whole situation in her head, trying to make sense of it. Drake hadn't asked about the prophecy nor where they had been going. Did he know? He had said that he wanted answers, but there had been no questions. Why these games? Her head was swimming, and the wine had made her drowsy, so she sat down on her bed. What was Drake planning? He had wanted to tell her the story about William, there was no doubt about that.

Probably to divide them, to make her distrust William. Sarah wasn't sure how she felt about this revelation. She had hidden her shock about it well – or so she hoped – but now she was alone in her room, she allowed the realisation to settle in. She believed Drake and wasn't surprised that William had been keeping even more things from her. He had done that from the very beginning. If she ever saw him again, they needed to have a long and proper talk about this. No more secrets, no more hidden agendas. She needed to know what happened, and why it had happened. She knew that there were always two sides to a story, and she was willing to give William the benefit of the doubt, but she needed answers. Honest answers.

A small bird flew past her window, resembling a hummingbird. Everything in this world resembled something from Earth but was a little different at the same time. The bird seemed to glimpse and wink at her, its tiny wings fluttering, and Sarah giggled. Her hand shot to her mouth, and she stifled her laugh. She wasn't the type to giggle, never had been, never wanted to be. The drowsy feeling got stronger and was now accompanied by a light-headed feeling. She had tried some pot with her first boyfriend behind the neighbours' barn when they were seventeen years old, and this felt somewhat similar. Minus the craving for chocolate and cheese, or the dry mouth.

Alarmed, she tried to sit up, because something was clearly wrong, but her urge to laugh and her dizziness were accompanied by a heavy feeling, and she found it difficult to move her limbs. She gathered herself and managed to get up with a huge effort, but her legs wouldn't hold her, and she sank back down onto the bed. She was angry with herself. Her initial thought that the food could be poisoned had probably been right and she cursed herself for her stupidity. She was making one mistake after another. Her upper body felt very heavy too and she sank back into the pillows, now lying on the bed.

It was an enormous effort to even lift as much as a hand but at the same time, she felt deeply relaxed, almost giddy. Whatever he had given her, it would make billions if sold as a drug on Earth.

She wasn't surprised when Drake stood next to her bed, seemingly appearing out of thin air. Maybe she had even slept a little, she couldn't tell. The room was spinning around her, but her body felt warm, relaxed, and just great. 'I hoped I wouldn't see you ever again,' she announced. At least she still was able to talk.

Drake sat down next to her and smiled but there was no warmth in his eyes or on his face.

'You look like a cute puppy but underneath you're a rotten fruit,' she heard herself say and wondered why she couldn't keep her mouth shut. She giggled, finding herself very funny.

'Truth serum,' Drake informed her coldly. 'It was in the wine. I figured that your face was too pretty to be beaten up like William's. This way, you will tell me everything I want to know, and no one will get hurt. At least, not much.'

The giggles got stuck in her throat when Drake ran his index finger gently across her cheek.

Sarah tried to recoil but couldn't move.

'It also paralyses you to some degree,' he informed her, the sly smile back on his face and Sarah felt like throwing up. This was worse than anything she could have imagined.

'Now tell me what the second part of the prophecy is.'

Despite her will to remain silent, her words came out. *'Hidden from mankind's eyes, where time and space are frozen. Is where the dragon sleeps. Together you will rise, to the break of a new dawn, and banish the darkness forever,'* she quoted from her memory, her voice sounding stiff.

'This is where you were heading to? The Sleeping Dragon?' he questioned, and Sarah nodded weakly despite her best efforts not to.

'What were you going to do there?'

'I don't know,' she answered. 'We have no idea what it means.'

For a second he appeared surprised, but then Drake laughed, and the sound cut into her like a knife. 'It's amazing that you two came as far as you did. You have no idea. About anything.' His fingers played with a strand of her hair.

'Don't touch me,' she spat out, but somehow her words didn't seem to have a connection to her body any longer, which felt heavy, warm, and good. In a way, she never had felt better, but there were these voices in her head, screaming.

'You have no idea how special you are, do you? Because I think I've found out what it is,' he said almost gently, his fingers running through her hair now. Sarah turned her head away from him as much as she could.

'You've been having strange visions?' he asked. 'Hallucinations? Finding yourself in other places all of a sudden?'

Slowly, and despite herself, Sarah's eyes sought out his.

Drake smiled, interpreting the silent question in them correctly. 'You can switch between worlds, Sarah,' he explained, 'because you have no counterpart in this one.

And as far as I'm aware, you are the *only* person in both of our worlds who is without a counterpart. Which, in return, means that you can exist in both. In a way, you do. This, my dear, makes you incredibly powerful.'

He leaned down, his face hovering only inches above hers, his breath grazing her face.

Sarah wanted to get away from him with everything she had, but she still couldn't move. 'And that's why I haven't killed you. Yet.'

His fingers ran down her cheek, stopping at the soft skin of her throat. 'With you at my side, nothing will be able to stop me.' His eyes were gleaming with something that came close to insanity. And rage, there was so much rage inside him.

All she wanted was to scream, but the only sound that escaped her throat was a pathetic whimper. She wasn't sure what he was about to do to her, but she knew that he loved this. He loved having power. Over everyone and everything. And over her.

'You're way too pretty to be wasted,' he remarked. 'Especially in this dress.'

He let his hand run across her naked shoulder, and Sarah felt like throwing up. She wanted to punch him in the face, kick, and fight, but she still couldn't move. She squeezed her eyes shut, trying to blank out the reality, and his touch. At the same time, she felt disgust and hate surging inside. Disgust about his fingers on her skin, and hate about her helplessness. No matter how hard she tried to move, her body wouldn't react to her efforts, lying there useless, even relaxed. In the frantic mess that was in her mind, one voice stood out. It sounded remarkably like Charlotte's.

You are not going to let this happen, the voice said matter-of-factly. *I know you better than that.*

Sarah's eyes shot open, and a rush of hope gripped her tightly. Of course! She willed herself to relax, ignoring the sickening presence of Drake next to her, while mentally bringing herself back to the magic tree. She remembered how it had felt to change worlds. She had done it before, and she could do it again. Drake had admitted it himself, she was able to walk between worlds. She had done this when giving the apples to the woman. She felt triumphant when there was the familiar pull, and her eyes sought out Drake's.

'Burn in hell, asshole!'

The echoes of her words faded into the distance of the abandoned building she found herself in only a fraction of a second later. She couldn't move, the effects of the poison still running through her veins, but she was on her own. Drake was gone. Sarah released a deep breath of relief, tears pooling in the corners of her eyes while she still felt Drake's fingers on her skin. She wasn't sure what he had been about to do, but she was very glad that she hadn't been around long enough to find out. The scent in the air told her that she was back on Earth, lying on the cold and hard stone floor of what seemed to be an abandoned hospital. It had a gloomy atmosphere and fit the fact that this was Drake's headquarters in the other world. Even though the castle had been pretty like Drake, inside it had been rotten and dark.

It took a while until the effects of the truth serum began to wear off. She was tense the entire time, expecting Drake's men to come for her, but apparently, there was no portal close by. First, the control over her hands and arms returned, then over her legs and when she was finally able to sit up, she felt stiff. The cold from the stone floor had seeped into her bones, and she was shaking. The pretty but flimsy dress did nothing to warm her. At the same time, she felt triumphant. She had managed to find a way to escape him. He would be furious.

She staggered to her feet. She felt dizzy and weak, but her legs held her as she took some tentative steps to explore her surroundings. Her first assumption had been right, this was an old hospital. It had closed a long time ago, and rubbish and dust was gathering in the corners everywhere. The wind was blowing coldly through open doors and graffiti covered the walls. It was abandoned, and she didn't think that anyone had been here in a while. She walked towards one of the barricaded windows and peered through a hole. She saw some trees and realised that she'd need to leave the building to figure out where she was exactly.

Still a little weak on her feet, she stumbled through the property. She noticed the litter on the floor, empty plastic bottles, and remains of a picnic. There was an old camping chair and a few dirty mattresses lying on the ground. She even saw the remnants of a small fire. This was probably used as a meeting point for teenagers but was long deserted. She was shivering with the cold. The old and tattered blanket she spotted in one of the corners looked like something she usually wouldn't touch with a stick, but she picked it up and wrapped it around her shoulders nonetheless. She felt warmer immediately while trying not to think about what the stains on the fabric could possibly be.

Feeling slightly better, Sarah rushed past all the rubble and stepped out into the evening twilight, taking a deep breath and enjoying the fact that she was alive and unharmed. She was somewhere in a forest but there was the sound of traffic in the distance and the sky was illuminated, indicating a large city nearby, as it had been in Aphelia. The path leading away from the hospital was overgrown, but she was in her world and knew that it would eventually lead to a street, which would eventually lead to people. She walked down the path, eager to be back to some sort of civilization but then she slowed down. She wasn't looking for people, she was looking for William, wasn't she? Maybe she should think things through now before making any rash decisions. If Drake had told her the truth, William was on the run and very likely searching for her at his castle. If he had lied, he was probably imprisoned somewhere or dead. In any case, the castle was where she needed to be if she wanted to find out about William's fate.

She still couldn't just go back to her old life, and running wasn't an option either. Because where was she supposed to go? There was only one logical thing to do. She turned around and studied the building she had escaped from in the distance, an idea beginning to form in her head.

Chapter 14

Her heart was hammering so fiercely in her chest that she was convinced she'd have a heart attack at any moment. Her plan was as simple as it was risky. She knew that Drake would be out and searching for her, but there was one place he certainly wouldn't expect her. His own castle. It was huge and almost deserted, there were enough supplies for months, and if he was still alive, William would look for her there. Right now, she was hiding directly underneath Drake's nose, specifically, behind a dusty curtain in the entrance hall of his castle. The plan had sounded great in her head, and she had snuck back into the building like a thief in the night. Here, the memories of Drake's hands on her body, and the insanity in his eyes were much more palpable, and she wondered if her idea was great or just crazy.

She took a deep breath, trying to convince herself that she could always flip back to Earth if she was in danger. That thought calmed her down some, but she still wondered what she was doing here. Before all of this had begun, the most exciting thing she ever had done was a bungee jump on her seventeenth birthday. She was selling coffee, for God's sake, and now she was hiding in the home of a megalomaniac leader who wanted to kill her. Or use her abilities for his own benefit. She pulled herself together, took a deep breath, and pushed all those useless and distracting thoughts aside while she focused on her surroundings. She had slipped back to Aphelia outside, in the woods, shortly wondering what would happen if there was a tree when she switched over. Would she merge with it and die? She hoped that she'd never have to figure this out.

The castle had been lying quiet and still, and no one was around when she had tiptoed inside. The entrance hall was empty too, had been ever since her arrival, but she still hid behind the dusty curtain for another twenty minutes. Not because she thought that it would bring her any advantage but because she needed the time to gather her courage. Everything told her to call it a day, go back to Earth, and move to another continent. Africa wasn't bad, was it? But she stuck around, and as soon as she mustered up the courage to move, she left her hiding place and snuck as quietly as she could towards a corridor to her left. She picked it at random because it was closest to the curtain. Not that she needed to be silent. The place was eerily quiet, and she would hear anyone approaching for miles. Still, sneaking somehow felt mandatory and she couldn't bring herself to walk normally.

The castle was large, but Sarah quickly figured out the basic architecture and decided that she needed to find a hiding place rather than explore the building further. She wasn't here to take unnecessary risks. She found a storage room with supplies, where she took some dried meat and fruit. Next to it was a second storage room that appeared as if no one had stepped inside for at least a year. It contained blankets, pillows, and cleaning supplies but everything was covered by a thick layer of dust, and she arranged some of the blankets into a makeshift bed in the most remote corner before she settled down and hungrily ate the supplies. Even though she was still nervous, she was quite sure that she was safe in here for now and that no one would find her, at least for a while. She would probably be able to stay here for weeks before someone found her.

She just hoped that she wouldn't have to.

For the next three days, nothing happened. The castle was quieter than Disneyland on a closed night. Sarah hid during the day and explored the premises when it was dark. She noticed that there were very few servants which told her that Drake didn't trust anyone, or that no one wanted to work for him. Either way, she had no idea about how loyal his servants were to him, so Sarah made sure to stay in the shadows. She knew her way around by now, slipping from hiding place to hiding place. She had even ventured down into the cell block where she had woken up during her first visit, but it was deserted, and William wasn't there. On the second day, she had stolen some clean plain clothes to be able to get rid of the frilly green dress Drake had forced her to wear. It felt great to push it deep into one of the large bins that were used in the kitchen.

On the morning of the third day, she heard noises outside coming from the entrance hall. This was irregular since the place was usually eerily quiet and she silently snuck out of her storage room and towards the commotion. The relief she felt when she peered around the corner and saw William kneeling on the ground was bottomless. Drake was towering over him, and William had a bloody nose but appeared unharmed apart from that. He was dirty and the dark circles underneath his eyes indicated that he hadn't slept in a while, but his jaw was stubbornly set, and he held himself upright, despite the kneeling position.

'Here looking for the girl, are you?' Drake asked, and slowly circled William, who didn't respond but stared ahead of him at the curtain she had been hiding behind only a few days ago. 'She was a fierce little thing, biting and scratching when I took her.'

Again, William remained quiet, but Sarah could see the tiny twitch of the muscles in his jaw.

Drake laughed. 'Her blood ran warm over my hands when I was done with her, before I let my servants have a go at her, too.'

William seemed unperturbed, but his hands, clenched into tight fists gave him away.

'I killed her myself, afterwards,' Drake finally said, and all the fight left William's body. His shoulders sagged and he appeared smaller, his chin dropping down onto his chest. Sarah's heart went out to him, and she wanted to let him know that she was right here, and alive, but that would have been stupid, and she had done enough stupid things for a lifetime over the last few weeks.

'But you know what I liked best?' Drake was about to deliver the final blow. 'Telling her all about you killing the last Guardians.'

William's eyes shot up to Drake, and when Sarah saw the defeated look on his face, she knew for sure that Drake had been telling her the truth. At a silent command from their leader, the two soldiers behind William grabbed him underneath the armpits and dragged him off in the direction of the cell block.

After everyone had gone, Sarah returned to her hidey-hole but she couldn't sit still for longer than five minutes. She wanted to go down to the cell block and see William, tell him that she was alive, but she knew that it was safer to wait for the night. Also, at least one warden was surely going to be around, and she needed a plan. But her thoughts also circled around the conversation she had overheard about the killings of the last Guardians. Frustrated, she ran her hand through her frizzy hair that was in desperate need of a wash, feeling a sharp bout of annoyance about basically everything. She wanted a coffee, a pizza, different clothes, a hot shower, and some conditioner. And most of all she wanted William to be honest and open with her. How was she supposed to do all of this if she was being left in the dark all the time? How was she supposed to trust him? What happened? Why had he killed the last Guardians? It didn't make sense.

It was dark outside and had been for a long time when she tiptoed through the quiet castle towards the cell block. She was nervous about having to sneak past the guards but also about seeing William again. The last time they had seen each other, they had been about to kiss, but a lot of things had happened since then. At least for her. She kept her body pressed against the wall and stayed in the shadows when she arrived at the large room that eventually led into the corridor with the cells. She was pretty sure there would be at least one guard around but since it was dark in there, she couldn't see anyone. Despite feeling anxious to see William, she waited patiently until she heard it. Deep and even breathing, interrupted by some light snoring coming from the other corner of the room. Sarah raised her eyebrows. Was she incredibly lucky, or was this some sort of trap?

Her eyes slowly adjusted to the darkness in the room, and when she carefully ventured deeper into it, staying close to the walls, she could detect two figures slumped over at one of the tables in the corner, seemingly deep asleep. To make sure, she waited for another eternity before she mustered up the courage to sneak through the room quietly and slowly past the two men. She released a deep breath once she made it safely inside.

William was in the same cell she had been in, and when she peered through the hole in the door that was used to deliver food, she could make out his silhouette on the small stretcher mounted to the wall. She also heard his breathing, even and slow. She tried the door handle but was not surprised to find it locked.

'William,' she whispered. He didn't move and she tried again, this time a little louder.

'Will!'

He stirred, his head turning in her direction, while he slowly sat up. 'William,' she repeated a third time. 'It's me.'

'Sarah?' he asked, sleepiness and disbelief in his voice. He got up, swiftly approached her, and bent down to look through the hole in the door, too.

'You're alive,' he stated, his voice thick with emotion.

'Of course, I am.' She reached through the hole, and he immediately grasped her hand. His fingers were cold.

'Drake said...'

'Drake is an asshole,' Sarah interrupted him. 'And a liar. I'm fine.'

'But, how... what are you doing here? How did you get here?' William wanted to know, his mind trying to catch up.

'What does it look like?' she replied and grinned. 'I'm rescuing you. For once, you're the damsel in distress, and I wouldn't miss this opportunity for anything in the world.'

William shifted from one foot to the other, his eyes darting nervously over her shoulder. 'It's not worth it,' he commented quietly, and Sarah had to refrain from rolling her eyes at him.

'Just shut up, and don't let go of my hand,' she ordered, and interlaced her fingers with his, holding on to him tightly. She wasn't sure if this was going to work but when they had gone to Aphelia for the first time, he had taken her along, so why shouldn't it work the other way around, too?

'What are you...' she heard William ask but there was already the familiar pull and the world turned.

'...doing?' William's voice finished the sentence before an almost comic expression of utter surprise appeared on his features. They were at the abandoned hospital on Earth, standing underneath a doorframe that separated two rooms. Thankfully there was no door. She didn't know what would have happened to them otherwise.

'We need to leave quickly,' she urged him on while releasing his hand. 'It's possible that Drake has some men around here.' Of course, she couldn't be sure, but that's what she'd have done, had she been him.

'How did you do that?' William wanted to know,

completely ignoring her remark about Drake's men.

'I just can,' she tried to explain what she didn't even understand herself. 'I told you that my visions were feeling very real. I think it was because a part of me has travelled to this world many times before, and back. Drake explained that it's because I have no counterpart in Aphelia, so I can switch between both worlds with ease. He didn't elaborate much more than that.'

William gazed at her as if she was something from a dream. 'Is this real?'

'Yes, very.' Sarah replied. 'And if we don't go now, we could be back in the grasp of Drake's men or dead soon, and I really would like to avoid that. Also, this place is giving me the creeps.'

She reached for William's hand to pull him with her, but he flinched away from her touch and Sarah let her hand sink again. 'The last time on Earth when they had me,' he said, and there was distrust lying in his eyes, 'they gave me something. A poison. It made me see things, hear things, believe things. None of it was real. They tortured me. I saw you dying over and over again, and with you, every hope that I had left.'

His eyes were growing large with terror, not seeing her any longer but looking at something that had happened in the past, and Sarah's heart sank at his words. She knew that he hadn't told her the entire truth about what had happened back then, but this was horrible.

'I'm here,' Sarah reassured him gently but with growing despair. 'And I'm real. You need to trust me. I don't think it's safe for us here.' She couldn't tell what it was, but the sense of impending danger got stronger with every second that passed.

'Please, William,' she pleaded, but he once again flinched at her attempt to reach for him, and she did the only thing she could think of. She launched herself at him and pressed her lips against his. He froze at first, but gradually relaxed and his mouth softened against hers. Before the kiss could deepen or turn into something else, Sarah pulled away.

'It's me,' she confirmed, her lips tingling from the brief impact with his, but she didn't linger in the moment. William finally seemed to snap out of it. He allowed her to take his hand, and she pulled him after her, out of the building.

For once, her instincts had been working correctly, or maybe she had finally learned to listen to them, because they detected Drake's men in an adjoining building that looked like a garage or a storage space. It was night, and there was a small fire burning inside the building, a few people gathered around it. Most likely, there were more around, patrolling the area. William pulled her with him, and a moment later, they were crouched behind a bush, studying the scene. She had no idea what they were looking for exactly, because she saw or heard nothing unusual, but she gladly let William take the lead. He usually knew what he was doing, while she had stupidly walked into almost every trap along their way. After a while, he indicated she should move, and they quietly walked past the building with the fire. When Sarah managed to take a short peek through one of the broken windows, she saw that the building was empty, the silhouettes of the people she had seen were a pile of branches and leaves, leaving humanlike shadows. Another trap. Drake's men were hiding somewhere else.

William seemed to either have figured out where, or he had taken an educated guess, but he stayed clear of any paths and led them deeper into the woods instead. Slowly they left the abandoned building and the fire behind them. Sarah made sure to follow in William's exact footsteps and to make as little noise as possible, and she was surprisingly successful. The trees were growing thickly here and the moonlight had little hope of reaching them. After a while, they were entirely swallowed by darkness, yet William seemed to know where he was going and Sarah followed in his path, clinging to his hand like a lifeline. They didn't speak, and after a while, it was oddly peaceful. Sarah allowed her thoughts to drift. Her life had been nothing short of a whirlwind for the last few months, but she knew that the reason she had agreed to take on this adventure wasn't valid any longer. She had agreed to come with William because she had been scared and because she hadn't seen any other chance to go back to a normal life. But now she realised that she would never be able to simply go back to her old life. Not after everything that had happened. Too much had changed. She had changed, and her new knowledge of the world would never allow her to see things the same. But this thought didn't scare her any longer. Of course, she craved safety and normalcy, but she didn't think that she would ever be able to return to her quiet life and her books, that she would ever be selling coffee with Charlotte again. There was much more to everything now. Thinking about her, Sarah became aware of how much she missed her best friend. Her open-minded, funny, and loyal Charlotte. Now that they were back on Earth, she would have to find a way to contact her to let her know that she was OK. There surely was someone who would lend her a mobile phone for a short call, once they were out of the forest.

All of these thoughts were going through her mind while William's hand was warm in hers, leading her safely through the dark woods and Sarah still had no idea how he was able to see anything. Occasionally, some rays of moonlight managed to slip between the treetops but mostly it was dark, and she almost ran into him when he suddenly stopped and turned around. Her eyes had adjusted a little to the darkness, but she only could see the outline of his face.

'I think it's safe now,' he murmured, and Sarah released a deep breath, partly out of relief and partly because she was exhausted. It was the middle of the night, and she was tired from everything that had happened, the tension and the adrenaline slowly leaving her body. All she wanted was to sit down somewhere and rest. At the same time, she felt more alive than she ever had. William was standing close to her, and she became aware that she was still holding his hand and the silence between them got tense. There was so much she wanted to ask him, so much she needed to know.

'Is it true that you were the one that killed the last Guardians?'

She could feel his fingers tightening around hers before he tried to withdraw them, but Sarah held on to him tightly. She wouldn't allow him to retreat into his silence. Not this time.

He seemed to sense her determination because he fell still. 'Yes,' he whispered and there was tremendous pain in this one syllable that she almost took a step closer.

At the same time, the impact of his confession hit her hard.

'Why?'

This time the silence was long, and she didn't think that he would answer but then she could hear his haunted voice, only a whisper in the dark.

'Drake,' he almost spat out the name. 'He manipulated me into doing it. I knew he wasn't my friend, but his words were powerful, and he told me what I wanted to hear. I didn't see that... I should have...' his voice trailed off. 'I'll never forgive myself.'

He pulled his hand away from hers, and this time, she allowed it to happen.

'I understand if you don't want to be around me any longer. But please, fulfil the prophecy.' He sounded desperate. 'Not for me, but for all the people in this world. They suffer because of me. They suffer because of what I've done, and I need to fix this. I need to...'

His voice broke, and Sarah suddenly understood. She understood the urgency that always had been there within William. The desperation he had often radiated. The willingness to sacrifice everything for this mission, for this task. The pain she could see on his face when he didn't think she was looking.

'Please, help me, Sarah?'

His face was covered in darkness, but she could feel his gaze resting on her. His pain was palpable, and his regret genuine, but there was no easy answer to his request. She had been thrown into this situation and everything had changed because of what he had done. He had started this, and then he had gone searching for her, wanting her to fix his mess and drawing the lethal attention of Drake's men towards her. She had almost been killed, her friends had almost been killed, she had lost her job, her life, her home, and on top of it she had been assaulted. And they hadn't even reached the end of their journey yet. And William had not been honest with her. She stood there, her hand that had been warm in his only moments before going cold, and she was glad of the darkness because William couldn't see the emotional struggle on her face.

'Sarah?' his voice was a whisper, and he reached for her in the darkness, but she took a step back, not wanting any physical contact with him. The silence between them was heavy with unspoken things.

'I will fulfil the prophecy if I can,' she finally announced, surprised about how calm she sounded. 'But I'm not going to do it for you. I'm going to do it for myself. And for the people of Aphelia.'

Chapter 15

The next few days and weeks were the most difficult ones of their journey. The frustration and fear they had felt before didn't compare to the icy silence that had settled over them now.

After that night, they hadn't talked again, not really. They had been discussing practical things, like the decision to stay on Earth while travelling, since it was less dangerous. Not needing a place of concentrated magic anymore to return to Aphelia because Sarah could switch back everywhere made things a lot easier. They also decided to avoid large cities.

Everything they had owned, their equipment, supplies, and spare clothes had been left behind in Aphelia, and Sarah had neither her passport, nor her bank card any longer. There was no other choice than to steal the things they needed, no matter how much she disliked doing this.

They took some spare clothing from a washing line in the backyard of a house in one of the villages they passed through. At some point, they found a house with an unlocked door and snuck inside to take a shower and steal some food and other supplies. They did some hitchhiking which saved them at least three days of walking and brought them a lot closer to the mountains that were the equivalent to the Sleeping Dragon Mountain massif in

William's world.

Sarah made sure to write down all the houses and places they had stolen things from, intending to return everything or send some anonymous money later. She was also allowed to use a stranger's phone to make short phone calls to Charlotte and Joe, letting them know that she was alright. Her parents hadn't even realised that she had gone missing since they were used to the fact that Sarah only called them sporadically. Nonetheless, she placed a short call to them, assuring her mum that she was very busy but fine and that she would come to visit them soon. Her heart felt a lot lighter after those calls, and that day they found a friendly farmer who allowed them to stay in his barn overnight. He even invited them to eat with him and his family, and they accepted gratefully.

Later in the evening, he gave them some sleeping bags, pretending that they were old and not needed any longer and Sarah made sure to place him on her ever-growing list of people to thank later. It was a clear and cold night, and Sarah and William placed their sleeping bags on a pile of straw in the corner of the barn. From there, they could see the cold beauty of the stars through the open door. Sarah was almost asleep when William's voice interrupted the silence.

'I told you that my parents were murdered when I was eight.'

Sarah was immediately wide awake. She didn't move, knowing that it was easier for William to talk when he could pretend that no one else was around.

'What I didn't tell you was that I tried to find the killers of my parents ever since it happened. Only in my fantasy when I was a child, but when I joined the gang, I really started looking into it. It was a very strange story, you know. My parents were killed, but nothing was stolen, and to this day, I don't know why it happened.' He sighed. 'Or who did it.'

It was dark outside, and the sky was beautiful, but Sarah didn't even notice it. She was solely focused on William's voice.

'I don't know how Drake learned of my desire for revenge. But then, I never really made a secret out of it either. I was working with Gareth at the time he approached me, and all of us were what you could consider hired help, so we had a certain reputation. And trust me, we lived up to our reputation.'

Sarah couldn't lie still any longer and sat up in her sleeping bag. 'Why are you telling me this now?'

'Because I want you to know what happened. I want you to know my side of the story.' William sounded tired but determined, and Sarah hugged her knees and rested her chin on them while she listened to him.

'Drake and I became friends. It took a long time for me to trust him, but he has a way with words and he can be very charming. He helped me out of a difficult situation more than once. When I finally left Gareth and the group, Drake encouraged me, and even helped me find some work, so I could be a valuable member of society again. I trusted him, not seeing that other side of him. He was hiding it well, back then.'

He fell silent, caught in his memories, and Sarah allowed him to tell his story at his own pace.

'We were close for a while, but eventually grew apart, and I didn't hear from him for a while. But he turned up at my door one night, telling me he'd found my parents' murderers. The story he told me was logical and every little detail fit. He had never given me a reason to distrust him before, quite the opposite, and I believed him.'

Sarah's heart grew heavy, knowing how this story was going to end, but she wanted to hear it from William nonetheless.

'Even though I had sworn off my old lifestyle, I set out to finally get my revenge, the one thing I had promised to my eight-year-old self.'

William's voice was very quiet, and he finally sat up in his sleeping bag as well.

'I created a bloodbath, Sarah. I attacked and slaughtered two innocent people. Their blood is sticking to my hands more than any other blood I have ever spilled, and when they were dead, I found the prophecy. It was lying there right next to them as if I was destined to find it. As if everything was following a great scheme I couldn't see. And I don't know why I picked up the parchment and the other papers and read them, but as soon as I had, everything fell into place. I realised who the people were I had killed. I knew that Drake had manipulated me but at that time I didn't know why. I wanted to kill myself that day. I walked to a nearby cliff, standing at the edge for ages, ready to take my own life, but I realised that it was going to be the easy way out and that I didn't deserve it. I needed to fix what I had done, I needed to make up for my mistake, and that's when I started looking into everything and investigating. That's when I started to look for you.'

He was studying her intently, and despite the twilight in the room, she could see the anguish on his face.

'I will never forgive myself for what I've done. I know I was manipulated, but that doesn't take away my responsibility in it. It didn't take Drake much to convince me. Everything that has happened to my world, everything the people suffer from, it's all my fault. All I can do now is try to fix it.' He took a deep breath before continuing. 'I've never told you the words of the first prophecy, Sarah. Do you want to hear them?'

'Yes,' Sarah whispered, not trusting her voice to speak louder.

William leaned forward. 'When I opened the parchment there was a picture of you, and next to it were the words:

> *The darkness who slays needs to find the light that heals.*
> *A woman, pure of heart, from the other world.*
> *Unite what has been broken before to stop the world from falling.*
> *She has the part that is missing, hidden in the pockets of her life.*

Silence hung between them while Sarah pondered everything she had learned. She knew what it must have taken William to confess all of this to her, and her heart softened. She was also tired of the awkward tension between them.

'If I, for whatever reason, ever have to write a prophecy again, you are officially allowed to hit me over the head if I write confusing stuff like this,' she quipped, trying to lift the heavy mood in the room. There was nothing she could say about what he had told her that would make any of it easier, anyway.

'I mean, what's wrong with these people? Why can't they give instructions or a user's manual instead of this ambiguous verse? Something like, *Throw the ring into Mount Doom and things are peachy again*? I mean, we still don't even know what we have to do when we reach the Sleeping Dragon!'

The words of the first prophecy made a little more sense than the ones from the second. The darkness that slayed was very likely William, which left her to be the light that healed. What the hell was that supposed to mean?

'And pure of heart? Not very likely,' she added loudly. Whoever had written that, had never been inside her mind. At all.

'Yes, you are,' William said. 'You decided to help me no matter what the personal cost, that's a choice you made. Even after finding out I wasn't honest with you, you stuck with your decision.'

'It's not like I had many alternatives, did I?' Sarah remarked.

'You did,' William sounded very sure. 'There's always a choice. You could've run. You could've worked with Drake. I'm sure he would have spared your life and even offered you whatever you desired for your cooperation. But you didn't.'

Sarah was dumbstruck. She hadn't even considered this, not even realising that it was an option since it had been so far out of the range of what she was willing to do.

'I would be lying if I said that I didn't care what you think of me,' William continued to speak, and her gaze was drawn back to his exhausted face. 'I know that I messed everything up. I should have told you all of this much earlier, maybe then you'd still trust me. I'm sorry, Sarah.'

Sarah sighed, feeling tired. Tired of not being able to sleep in her bed, tired of constantly having to look over her shoulder, tired of being hungry all the time but mainly tired of being angry at William. The guilt he carried around like a flaming torch was burning hot, and he was right. If he had told her all of this from the beginning, the rift between them wouldn't be there. But he hadn't, and it was there. She couldn't bring herself to forgive him yet, but she understood what his motives were, and that was a start.

'Did Drake hurt you?' he asked out of the blue, and the only thing that gave his tension away was the fact that he kept plucking little straws out of their makeshift bed, rolling them between his fingers fiercely. Sarah realised that they had never talked about what happened while they had been separated. His question surprised her. She thought that he'd ask something regarding the prophecy first. Hard facts before feelings. That kind of thing.

'Not really,' she answered after a short moment of hesitation, not sure if she wanted to talk about it in detail. She involuntarily shuddered at the memory of Drake's probing hands across her throat. 'I think he was about to,' she felt queasy at the memory. 'But I made a narrow escape.'

William stayed quiet but she could feel his gaze resting upon her, his fingers still playing with the straw.

'He drugged me,' she told him, 'and made me tell him the second part of the prophecy.' She lowered her head. 'I'm sorry.'

'Don't be,' William's voice was gentle. 'Don't you ever

be sorry for something like that. It wasn't your fault.'

For a moment, it appeared as if he was about to reach out to her and touch her, but his hand fell back to his side, and after a moment, he lay back down in the straw. Sarah felt a deep tiredness, which wasn't entirely physical. Wordlessly, she moved closer to him and lay down by his side, resting her head against his shoulder, and slipping her arm across his stomach. She could sense his surprise, but then his hand came to rest gently on her arm in return.

'This doesn't mean that I'm not mad anymore,' she told him, but she said it without emphasis.

They settled into a comfortable silence, and it wasn't long before the warmth of his body and the gentle rise and fall of his chest lulled her to sleep.

She slept better than she had in ages, feeling warm and protected at William's side, and when she blinked back into consciousness the next morning, she found him looking down at her. The deep lines that had been all over his face during the last few days had softened, and he almost looked boyish, if it weren't for the stubble on his face. Suddenly feeling self-conscious about their physical closeness, she withdrew from his arms and sat up, as usual trying to tame her hair that was sticking out in every direction.

'Good morning. Did you sleep well?' It was a polite question to lighten up the tension she felt.

'No,' he answered with a smile, and Sarah raised an eyebrow in surprise.

'My shoulder fell asleep, and I couldn't move,' he complained, but there was a twinkle in his eyes and she knew he wasn't serious.

'Tough,' she replied and was about to slap him play-fully when he continued to speak. 'Also, the night was too precious for sleep.'

It took a few moments until his words sank in.

'Oh,' she answered, not knowing where to look all of a sudden.

She was saved by the farmer who appeared in the doorframe of the barn. 'Good morning, you two. We have breakfast on the table, and you can take a shower after, if you want?'

Sarah broke into a large smile at that offer. 'I would die for a shower,' she announced, grabbing the few spare clothes she had. And for the first time in a long time, she felt light, almost happy, despite everything. William studied her quietly, an amused glint in his eyes, and she smiled at him, his words still ringing in her ears, and she wondered if the prospect of a shower was the only cause of her happiness.

About two hours later, they were on their way, together with a ton of new possessions.

They had backpacks, sleeping bags, and supplies for a couple of days. Sarah had refused to accept the money the farmer had offered them but when they took a break at some point later, she found it in one of the side pockets of her backpack, together with a bar of chocolate, something that brought tears to her eyes.

'You know,' she admitted after sharing the chocolate bar with William. 'At times, I don't like my world very much. But some people are making up for a lot,' she added, letting a piece of chocolate melt on her tongue.

The atmosphere between them was relaxed again. They were still treading lightly around each other, almost careful, but it felt much better after the heavy tension of the last few days.

Sarah had chosen to not put too much thought into what he had said this morning. Surely he had only been glad that they were on more or less good terms again. She reached for the money and counted it.

'Come on!' She beamed at him. 'We're taking the train.'

Chapter 16

Two days later Sarah and William were standing in front of the mountains on Earth that mirrored the Sleeping Dragon. They knew they would have to return to Aphelia soon, and since Drake knew where they were going, he would be there, too. With plenty of his men. They still didn't have a plan to restore the magic and heal Aphelia. They had talked a lot about the words of the prophecy over the last days of their journey but hadn't made much progress. Just one thing was obvious: they had to be there together. Sarah thought about the first line.

Unite what has been broken before to stop the world from falling.

What did that mean? What had been broken and needed to be united? This couldn't refer to her and William since she never had seen him before the club, she was sure of it. And upon asking him, he had confirmed this. Maybe this simply meant the magic?

And in the second prophecy, it said:

Together you will rise, to the break of a new dawn, and banish the darkness forever.

She was pretty sure that this was referring to her and William because who else could it refer to? When she had written the little paragraph into her journal, she had found it mysterious and intriguing, now it was only annoying.

And then:

Hidden from mankind's eyes, where time and space are frozen.

What was this supposed to mean?

Maybe things would get clearer when they were in Aphelia again.

Sarah, who had been studying the mountains ahead of them, joined William on a bench where he'd stopped to tie his shoelaces. It was a quiet place, very rural, and surrounded by trees. They hadn't seen many living souls outside for the last two days.

'Do you want to cross over here?' Willam asked, and Sarah looked at him. 'This place is as good as any, I suppose.'

Truth was, she was scared to go back to Aphelia. No matter how miserable their life on the road was, this was her world, and everything was familiar to her. She took a deep breath, held out her hand, and he took it. They hadn't touched since that night in the barn. His hand was warm, and she held onto it tightly. 'We don't know what to expect on the other side,' she said. 'Drake's men surely will be there somewhere, and I don't know if I'll get the opportunity to say this later, so I'll say it now.' She took a deep breath. 'Despite everything that has happened and everything that still might happen, I'm glad that you came into my life.'

William's brows rose in surprise and the expression on his face softened. 'And I'm very sorry for completely messing up yours,' he responded. 'I never wanted to endanger you.'

Sarah smiled at him. 'You know, I usually don't believe in fate and that kind of stuff, but maybe this was bound to happen. All of it. Only you could find the prophecy because you were the one that killed the Guardians. Maybe the path was always set for us.'

William's fingers tightened around hers, squeezing her hand almost painfully and Sarah closed her eyes. The pull was strong here, maybe because there was something special about those mountains. She jumped easily to Aphelia, taking William with her. The scenery was quite like the one they just had left. A quiet landscape and the mountains close by. Thankfully, there was no one around.

Sarah released a breath, reluctantly letting go of William's hand. Despite the things he had done in his life and the things he was capable of doing, he made her feel safe. She turned around and allowed herself to enjoy the scent in the air. No matter what state this world was in, it still smelled fantastic to her. Of wildflowers and something else she couldn't describe in words.

'Have you been here, to the Sleeping Dragon, before?' she wanted to know, hoping that William knew what to do, and where to go. 'We need to find the place that's *Hidden from mankind's eyes, where time and space are frozen,*' she quoted, but William only shook his head.

'I still have no idea what that means,' he admitted, and ran his hand through his hair before shouldering his backpack. 'But I suggest staying off the roads and even paths to avoid Drake's men for as long as we can. We need to stick together closely and make our way up onto the mountain. I hope that we'll detect something there that will give us an idea about what to do.'

Sarah nodded and tightened the straps of her backpack as well. She wondered if Drake had found out what the prophecy meant. In that case, he wouldn't have many men around, because it would be sufficient to catch them at the place they were supposed to go, wherever that was.

Four days later, Sarah was completely and utterly frustrated. The weather had changed the moment they had set foot onto the Sleeping Dragon, and since then it was almost constantly raining, making her miserable and cold. They were sleeping in small caves, or sometimes even underneath some naturally occurring ledges, huddled together for warmth. But despite this, Sarah's clothes never seemed to be dry anymore. She was cold, wet, and miserable all the time.

Additionally, the energy of these mountains started taking a toll on her. She couldn't describe what it was, but it seemed as if the rocks themselves were radiating a certain energy. Magic maybe? She had found the feeling exhilarating in the beginning, but the constant stream of energy was wearing her down. It didn't help that they were stumbling around like idiots, having no idea where they were going, and even William, who was usually the calmer of them, became irritable and snapped at her a few times, something he had never done before. Things escalated when she accidentally dropped one of their sleeping bags into a puddle and William had a go at her. She finally had enough.

'Do you think I did that on purpose?' she shouted,

her hair clinging to her face, frizzy and wet from the rain, her eyes glistening with anger and frustration. 'Do you think I want to be here, stumbling around this damn mountain in the pouring rain, while we're running out of supplies? Do you think I'm doing this for fun? I'm hungry, I'm soaked, and I've never felt so cold in my entire life. I want a pizza and a hot cup of coffee, a roof over my head, and a fire. And I want my bed, I didn't even know that a hip could feel sore like this.'

Sarah could feel the first tears of anger and frustration stinging behind her eyes, and she didn't hold them back. They began rolling down her face, mixing with the rain.

'I'm scared all the time that Drake's men are going to jump us, I haven't slept properly in days, I'm exhausted, and I'm freezing.' She didn't mention that she was also soaked down to her underwear. She was crying heavily now, the tension of the last few weeks finding relief.

The silence between them was deafening before William stepped towards her. 'I'm sorry,' he apologised, and wordlessly pulled her into his arms. Sarah rested her head against his broad chest and cried, her whole body shaking from the sobs.

After she felt somewhat better, she withdrew from his arms, immediately shivering from the cold. She straightened her posture nonetheless and wiped her face with her sleeve. 'Sorry,' she took a shaky breath. 'I'm OK, I think we can move on.' She was slightly embarrassed at her outburst.

'No,' William stated, and took her by the hand. 'I think we both need a break. We passed a small cabin about half an hour ago. It looked deserted, and maybe we could break in and spend the night there, dry our clothes, sleep in a proper bed, and take a rest. We haven't seen any of Drake's men, so I suspect that they're going to meet us at the end of our journey. But we're going to have a break in the meantime.' And with that, he marched down the path they had just climbed up, pulling her along, not even waiting for her reply. Not that she was going to object anyway.

The cabin was locked but it was no match for William, who picked the lock in under a minute. The door opened, and they were greeted by a dusty but otherwise clean and completely furnished cabin. There was one large room with a double bed in the corner, a fireplace, and a few cupboards of different sizes. A small kitchen held no supplies but there was running water, and it was warm. A small bathroom with a tiny shower completed the interior. William closed the curtains to hide them from the world outside. The room immediately fell into comfortable twilight and Sarah sank on the bed in exhaustion, too tired to even remove her shoes.

'I'll be right back,' William announced, before he stepped out of the cabin. When he returned, he smiled brightly, his arms full of logs. 'I found a shed with dry wood behind the house,' he informed her as he started a fire.

'Isn't that dangerous?' Sarah inquired.

'With the rain, the smoke won't be visible too far,' he replied. 'Besides, I don't care right now. We need to get warm.'

Sarah smiled tiredly and finally managed to walk into the small bathroom, where she wriggled out of her wet clothes. She was frozen to the bones and when she tried the tap of the shower, she didn't expect too much, but the water was warm, and Sarah immediately stepped underneath the stream and soaked in it. The lukewarm water didn't entirely manage to get rid of the cold in her bones, but it was a start.

She hung her soaked clothes over the towel rack and only put her wet shirt and panties back on to keep up a minimum of modesty before returning to the main room. William's gaze followed her when she walked over to the bed where she sat down cross-legged, wrapping herself tightly in the blanket. It was a bit dusty but otherwise clean and she didn't care anyway. It was warm and soft and that was what mattered. The fire was burning brightly, throwing dancing shadows on the walls while slowly filling the room with warmth.

William disappeared to the bathroom as well, and Sarah just sat there, staring into the flames, slowly feeling the heat return to her body. She was tired on a deep level, knowing that they couldn't continue like this. It didn't make sense to stumble through the mountains without having any idea where to look and what to look for. She was also worried because they hadn't seen any of Drake's men. It was peculiar and felt like the calm before the storm. When she was slightly warmer, she got up to check out their supplies. There wasn't much left, but they still had some apples, dry bread, and even a package of cookies. She gathered everything and returned to the bed, not wanting to leave the warmth of it for long. Placing their supplies on the small nightstand she wrapped herself back up in the blanket.

William was only wearing boxer shorts when he returned, and Sarah watched him walk across the room. He had brought all of their clothes with him, hanging them up over every surface he could find. They would dry much faster in here where the fire was heating the room. He was perfect. Tall, lean, and muscular, but Sarah mainly noticed the many scars covering his skin. They were more prominent now when his body wasn't covered in bruises. If he hadn't told her his story before, his body would have given it away right now. When he had hung up their clothes, he came straight over to the bed, and she could see the goosebumps on his skin. He sat down next to her and grabbed the second blanket to wrap around him.

For a long time, they sat there in silence, gathering some of their strength while allowing the fire to chase away the remains of the cold from their bones. Sarah was hungry, and she had been waiting for William to start eating, but when she turned her head to ask him about it her eyes fell on his face. His hair was still wet from the shower, sticking to the sides of his skull, and revealing the prominent scar on his forehead. Without thinking about it she removed one arm from her blanket, reached out, and ran her fingers across its whole length. He didn't flinch away from her touch as he had done so often but returned her gaze openly.

'I got that when I was seventeen,' he offered voluntarily, and Sarah realised how much he had changed around her. She remembered the withdrawn and desperate man he had been when she first met him. Her heart did a flip when their eyes locked and after a few seconds, Sarah leaned forward and kissed him.

He froze in surprise, but his lips quickly softened against hers and he cupped her face with his hands, returning the kiss with a passion that completely swept Sarah off her feet. There were many unspoken words and emotions in it, and she allowed it to last and deepen while falling into it. Everything that mattered was right here, and the hunger in that kiss was so strong that even the last of her thoughts came to a halt.

When they broke apart, her heart was racing, her skin flushed with desire, and she was breathless. She caught his gaze and saw her longing mirrored in his eyes. She threw off her blanket, letting it carelessly drop to the floor while he opened his arms to welcome her, and Sarah sat down on his lap, straddling him. His skin was warm against hers, and she wanted to feel more of it, she wanted to feel all of it. There was a mixture of longing and surprise in his eyes, but he didn't hesitate, his strong arms wrapping around her body, pulling her closer.

'I've been wanting to do this from the first time I laid eyes on you,' he whispered, before placing a trail of soft kisses across the sensitive skin of her neck. Sarah leaned her head back to give him better access. She felt like she was floating and falling at the same time, and even though a part of her was surprised about what was going on, another, much bigger part of her knew that this was just right. It felt perfect. He felt perfect. Everything had been leading to this point, from the moment William had tried to kiss her at that clearing, maybe even before that, and she had never been so sure of something in her whole life. She wanted this. Her body was burning for him and when his hands started exploring her skin, she couldn't hold it together any longer.

'But this is much better than anything I ever dreamt...' he continued to speak but Sarah cut him short by grabbing the hem of her shirt, pulling it over her head, and dropping it to the floor before she closed his mouth with

another kiss. After that, he didn't speak anymore. Neither
of them did.

Chapter 17

The fire had burned down, the remaining glow casting a dark red light against the wooden walls, when Sarah and William returned to reality. His strong arms were wrapped around her, holding her close to his body while she rested her head on his bare chest, listening to his heartbeat that slowly calmed down. She couldn't remember when she had ever felt this content and happy in her entire life. Her lips were swollen from his kisses, her body slightly aching in some places that only could be connected with great sex, and she felt warm and heavy. Her hand was lying across his flat stomach, and she never wanted to move again. Instead, she wanted to freeze this moment and store it away in her memory, able to relive it whenever she wanted. It was not just the fact that they had gotten rid of the permanently underlying tension between them, it also was him, William. It always had been him, but she had been too distracted to see it. Until now.

She lifted her head and his eyes lit up when they met hers. Sarah didn't think that she ever had seen him this relaxed before, and she realised that she had never seen him happy before, either. She smiled and placed a soft kiss on his jawline before burying her head in the crook between his neck and shoulder, taking in his scent. She was about to say something, but she didn't want to interrupt this moment by talking. Besides, she had no idea what to say. Should she tell him that she had longed to do this for a while already, and that she'd happily repeat it anytime soon? Should she tell him that the story of his life was breaking her heart when she thought about it? Should she tell him that her heartbeat was picking up, and her stomach filled with butterflies as soon as she laid eyes on him, ever since that moment between them at the clearing? Even when she had been mad at him?

Instead of speaking she reached for the blanket on the floor. It was getting colder in the room since the fire had almost burned down, and she covered them both with it and snuggled up to him as close as she could, wanting to feel as much of his skin against hers as possible. At that moment, everything that lay behind them and everything they still had to face was forgotten, pushed into the back of her mind, and she could feel herself slowly drifting into sleep, feeling loved and protected by William's arms around her. A thought drifted lazily through her mind. It seemed important, but before it could settle, her eyes closed and sleep pulled her under.

She awoke to the sound of rain against the windows. The air in the cabin was cold, but Sarah was comfortable under the blanket and next to William's warm body. She opened her eyes and saw his gaze resting on her. He pushed a strand of hair out of her face, smiling.

'Good morning,' he greeted her, and Sarah kissed him gently on the lips before her eyes were drawn towards one of the windows. Grey light was falling through the curtains, and she figured that it had to be early morning.

'We slept through the entire night,' she said, surprised, and stretched like a cat, not wanting to get up. 'I haven't rested this well in a long time. What about you?' she asked and added with a wink, 'still too precious for sleep?'

William laughed. 'Yes,' he replied, 'but even I couldn't resist falling asleep at some point.' He fell serious. 'I still can't believe it.' His fingers gently trailed down the side of her face. 'I woke up during the night, thinking that it was a dream, but you were here, right by my side.'

Sarah's fingers, which had been drawing lazy circles on William's chest slowly wandered downwards, a cheeky smile on her lips. 'Does this feel like a dream to you?'

William gasped before he answered her with a kiss that didn't in the least resemble the quick peck they had shared only moments ago.

Quite some time later, they decided it was time to get up. William lit the fire again and they took a shower together before eating some of their supplies. There was not much left. Their clothes had dried in the warmth of the cabin overnight and Sarah watched with regret how William hid his body underneath a layer of fabric again. The world outside was grey and dull; it was still raining, and Sarah felt no motivation whatsoever to leave their little bubble. William didn't seem to be too keen either and they stood by the window, studying the hostile and cold environment they would be forced to enter again soon. And they still had no idea what they were searching for.

'We could stay for another day,' Sarah suggested. 'Maybe it'll stop raining?'

William studied the gloomy nature in front of the window quietly, his head slightly cocked.

'We don't have the proper clothes for this weather, anyway. One of us could get pneumonia,' Sarah tried again.

Truth was, she didn't want to go out into the miserable weather, but that was not her main reason for postponing this. Something had happened here inside this cabin, something between her and William, and she wasn't talking about the sex. Something important had shifted between them, with them, and it was perfect right now. She was scared that things would change as soon as they left the cabin, as if it was somehow going to break a spell. She looked up at him, his green eyes taking in the world outside, but he appeared to be miles away.

'I don't want to leave, either,' he admitted quietly, 'but we don't have much food left. We need to get supplies.'

Sarah took his hand into hers, and their fingers intertwined. 'I don't need food,' she said. 'I need you.'

William turned his head, his eyes finding hers and the expression on his face was gentle. 'You've had me from the moment I saw you for the first time, Sarah. You were in the coffee shop, talking to Charlotte, and the two of you laughed about something. I felt relieved because I had found you, but there was much more to it.' William's voice was gentle, his thumb slowly caressing the skin of her hand. 'I wasn't able to understand it then, but I do now.' He pulled her hand towards his chest and placed it against it. She could feel his heart beneath her palm. It was beating hard and fast. For her.

Sarah was filled with wild and ground-shaking

happiness. Her head still had trouble grasping what was going on, but her heart knew, had known for quite some time, and she lifted his hand to her face and placed a gentle kiss on his scarred knuckles. She mirrored his gesture and placed the palm of his hand against her own chest, knowing that he would be able to feel her quick heartbeat in return. She had never seen him smile like this before. His entire being lit up and he looked beyond beautiful.

'I never dared to hope that you'd ever feel the same,' he whispered. 'This still feels like a dream to me,' and she thought that her heart would explode from the impact of his words. 'And just like you, I don't want to wake up from it,' he finished speaking, having sensed her true reason for staying here better than she had thought.

'One more night,' Sarah decided, knowing that she had already won, anyway. 'It won't make a difference. We can still stumble through the mountains in the rain without knowing where to go tomorrow.'

The next morning greeted them with sunshine and even though Sarah was hungry, she was happier than she had been in a very long time. The last day and night had been fantastic, and she still didn't want to leave their happy little bubble, but she knew that they couldn't postpone it any longer.

They took another shower and packed their meagre belongings. Sarah felt a pang of regret when they stepped out of the door, but she knew that whatever it was between them, it would not end just because they left the cabin. She lifted her head to the sun and smiled at William. 'It seems as if luck is finally on our side.'

Things had changed; Sarah could feel it in the air around her. It smelled slightly different, the autumn sun seemed brighter, the trees greener, the atmosphere lighter and even the steep climb wasn't as exhausting as it had been in the rain.

They soon found some bushes that grew berries and took a long break to eat as many as possible and pick some to take along. They refilled their water bottles as well, and Sarah's heart was full while they made their way further upward. They had decided to climb up to the mountaintop to get an overview since they had no idea where else to look anyway. William stayed close to her side, and they exchanged glances and light touches all the time, like teenagers in love.

It was getting dark when they reached the treeline of the mountain, and decided to spend the night and continue on their way in daylight. The small path they were following was becoming more and more treacherous, and the slopes were getting steeper and steeper, but Sarah and William felt positive that they would make it to the summit safely the next day. By now, Sarah was only thinking in small steps that lay ahead. Reach the summit of the mountain. Find out what to do about the prophecy. Do it. Survive it. Don't stumble over Drake's men and get killed, or abducted. She didn't think about what was going to happen after all of this was over. She didn't think of the fact that she had lost her heart to someone from a different world and what implications this had for their future. She figured that it would all fall into place one way or the other. For now, they only needed to survive the next step.

They talked until deep in the night. William told her about his parents and his early childhood but also about the things he liked to do if he wasn't chasing after prophecies or trying to save the world. In return, Sarah told him about her upbringing and the things she loved to do, and when she woke up in William's arms the next morning her stomach immediately filled with butterflies.

They reached the summit in the afternoon, but to her surprise, there was no one there. She had been convinced that they would eventually stumble over Drake's men, and this was the perfect spot because you couldn't hide anywhere once you reached the summit. Where were they? The view was breathtaking though, and for the first time, Sarah was able to take in the absolute beauty of Aphelia. There was another mountain massif in the distance, far away. The ground between this one and the other one was covered with a thick and dark forest. To their left lay a large city, even bigger than the one surrounding Drake's castle. Despite the usual signs of the terror regime and the famine, she could tell that the city had once been beautiful.

'That is Partosa,' William informed her, 'our capital.'

When she turned in the direction of where they had come from, she could see a landscape full of fields and small villages, a rural environment and to her right was a large lake of tremendously deep blue colour. The sun was shining down on her and she felt warm and at complete peace.

William, however, was disappointed. 'There's nothing here,' he stated the obvious. 'I was sure that we'd find something here. A clue or a hint of what to do.' He looked around but their surroundings hadn't miraculously changed. 'At least I expected Drake's men to be here,' he added.

'I thought so, too,' Sarah admitted after stepping to his side. 'We'll find it eventually. We've come so far, we'll make it to the end.' She took William's hand, and their fingers automatically intertwined.

'*Hidden from mankind's eyes, where time and space are frozen,*' William quoted. 'What if that literally means hidden? Rumours say that there are some large caves at the head of the dragon. I've never been there, and maybe it's not true, but what if it is? What if that's where we're supposed to go?'

Sarah shrugged. 'That idea is as good as any, and definitely better than stumbling around on this mountain until one of us breaks an ankle or we starve to death. Let's check out the caves. We should be careful though,' she added, as an afterthought. 'I'm getting more and more nervous about the fact that we haven't seen any of Drake's men. If the cave is the right place, they might be waiting for us there.'

'Possibly,' William agreed. 'But if we want to fulfil the prophecy, we'll stumble over Drake and his men at some point anyway. We only can hope that things will turn out in our favour then.'

Sarah considered his words. 'But shouldn't we, I don't know, prepare ourselves somehow? Maybe get armed?' Not that she had any idea how to use a gun or any other weapon, so the very notion was ridiculous, at least on her part. But still, walking into a dangerous situation completely unprepared didn't sit right with her, either. 'This entire mountain trip feels like walking into a trap from the beginning, and we're doing it willingly and blindly.'

William sighed and ran his hand through his hair. 'I know,' he admitted. 'But I don't see any other choice. I mean, we could climb down the mountain again, lay low somewhere for a few weeks or even months. Wait until the dust has settled, and maybe Drake won't be looking for us by then. But I don't think that's ever going to happen. If we really have to go to those caves, he'll probably station an army there. Our chances to fulfil the prophecy are much better if we do it now. The faster we get there, the less time he has to beat us. And the longer we wait, the more people suffer.' He smiled at her. 'And last, but not least, I am a passable fighter, but you aren't. We're just two people. What would we achieve against an army? I think we need to have some faith that things are going to work out in our favour. They have so far, haven't they?'

Sarah still had a very bad feeling about it, but she had to admit that William was probably right in his assessment of the situation. Things wouldn't change if they waited, and having weapons wouldn't make much of a difference either.

Since it was late in the afternoon and the head of the dragon was at least another few hours' walk away, they decided to climb back down to the treeline and stay there for the night under the shelter of the trees. They dug out some edible, though not very tasty roots and shared their last berries. When the sun set, they made love and talked again for a very long time afterwards before falling asleep.

The entrance to the cave looked like an open black mouth and Sarah shuddered at the thought of entering it. It smelled musty and didn't feel welcoming. They only had two candles they had taken from the cabin, which meant that they wouldn't have sufficient light. Sarah did have not much of an idea about caves, but weren't they supposed to be treacherous and dangerous? She had once read in a magazine that one easily could get lost in them or fall into crevices.

'I don't like this at all,' she voiced her thoughts, and glanced at William, who stared broodily into the darkness ahead. He didn't seem to like this in the least, either.

'Do we have a choice?' he asked, and Sarah sighed deeply. Of course, they could walk away and climb down the mountain again to find better equipment, supplies, and light sources but it would take them at least a few days, and they had already come this far. Walking away entirely was not an option, as they had established before. As usual, the path ahead was clear.

'We go in until the first candle has burned down, and we use the second one to find our way back,' Sarah suggested. 'And when this turns out to be a labyrinth or something we can't handle without proper equipment, we turn around immediately. I don't want to get lost in there or die. We only go in to get a first impression and to see if we're at the right place, OK?'

William nodded in agreement and leaned in to kiss her. Her stomach was immediately filled with butterflies, and even though she didn't like going into the cave, she smiled when he took her by the hand. Wordlessly, they ventured together into the unknown. The natural light faded quickly and after the cave took a first turn, they had to rely on the dim and flickering flame of the candle. Underneath and around the golden circle of light was nothing but blackness, making it difficult to see where they were going. Sarah clung tightly to William, her mind going into overdrive, imagining all kinds of things in the dark. She tried to stay calm by telling herself that she wasn't a small child anymore and that no monsters were hiding within the shadows, but she couldn't help feeling threatened and scared, flinching with every unexpected sound and movement around them. And there seemed to be a lot of it. Why was there so much noise in a cave? Also, what did she know of Aphelia? Maybe actual monsters *were* hiding in the darkness.

'Bats,' William explained at one point when she flinched violently upon feeling something flutter past nearby, and Sarah understood why Batman had feared those little creatures so much. It was utterly creepy. Still, bats were better than imaginary monsters.

When she was getting close to the point where she would refuse to take another step into the cave, the small corridor started to widen, at least taking the claustrophobic feeling away, and a few metres later they were standing inside a large cavern. Sarah couldn't tell how big it was since the light from their candle didn't reach far, but she couldn't see the walls on either side or the ceiling any longer, and their steps echoed hollowly.

'We need more light,' Sarah whispered, surprised at how loud her voice sounded in here.

William released her hand and took some tentative

steps forward but quickly stopped. 'You're right,' he observed. 'The candle isn't strong enough.'

'Maybe I can help you,' a voice out of the darkness interrupted, and this time Sarah didn't flinch but jump, immediately recognizing the voice of Drake. She couldn't say that she was surprised though, while trying to pierce the darkness with her eyes. They had both known that Drake's men would be waiting for them somewhere. She was about to take a step in William's direction, but two strong arms wrapped around her from the darkness behind and held her captive. William had dropped the candle, but it was still alight and she could see the silhouettes of him and another man fighting in front of her. He was out of reach and even though she could snap back to Earth any time she wanted, she wouldn't go without William. Also, she wasn't sure if it was smart to flip back while inside a massive mountain. What if there was no cave, or if it had collapsed? She didn't feel the slightest urge to get smashed between tons of stones and gravel.

Torches were lit, and Sarah had to close her eyes against the sudden intrusion of blinding light. When they had adapted, she could see the cave properly. It was enormous, the ceiling covered in black dots that were the bats she had come in contact with before. Stalactites and stalagmites were growing everywhere even though she always forgot which ones were which. In the middle of the cave was something that looked like a lake, but from her point of view, she couldn't tell if it was a shallow puddle or deep water. Other than that, the walls of the cave were plain and nothing indicated a prophecy or a way to fulfil it here. But the fact that Drake's men were here told her that they had arrived at the correct spot. However, they had walked into a trap, again, and this time they had even anticipated it. And it didn't look as if luck was going to be on their side, because there were at least twenty men, and even if she had known how to fight properly, they would not have stood a chance. William had lost his fight and was lying on the ground, one man kneeling on his back, another one pointing a sharp spear-like weapon at him.

Sarah tried to take a small step toward him, but she was immediately stopped by the man holding her.

'Sorry,' Drake said, clearly not remorseful at all. 'But I can't allow you to touch him. You see, when you disappeared right from underneath my grasp, I knew what you were capable of. But when William vanished from his locked prison cell, I have to admit that I was stunned. It took me a while to put together what must have happened.' He looked from Sarah to William and back. 'I've read that world travellers like you can take someone along. I'm not sure if that rumour and therefore my theory is true, but it's the only one that makes sense. The only one that explains how William managed to escape from a locked cell.'

Sarah felt a short burst of satisfaction when she detected the anger on Drake's face, but it faded quickly when she remembered the situation they were in.

'I underestimated you,' Drake continued, taking a step toward Sarah. 'I didn't think you'd be brave enough to come back to the castle, and I also didn't think that you'd care enough for William, but I was wrong on both accounts. I won't repeat my mistake.'

He circled her, and Sarah wanted to recoil from him,

but she couldn't as the guard was still holding her, not giving her any space to move. Since she knew that Drake liked to work with medication or poison, she expected the sting of a needle, but it didn't come.

'Luckily I knew where you were heading,' he added, and came to a stop in front of her. '*The Sleeping Dragon* was this mountain massif; *Hidden from mankind's eyes* could only mean a cave and this is the one that lies closest to the summit because what else could *Together you will rise* mean?'

Sarah realised that Drake had been guessing as much as they had, but since he had been much more familiar with the territory, he had chosen this spot as the most likely one. William had just needed a little longer to figure it out. Her eyes fell on him while the guard was pulling him up, allowing William to struggle to his feet. He had a bloody nose but seemed unharmed otherwise.

'I was surprised that it took you so long to turn up here,' Drake went on. 'My men saw you at the mountain's base quite a while ago, but since we knew where you were going, we didn't see the need to follow you,' he confirmed Sarah's earlier suspicion about the absence of Drake's men during their journey.

She looked at William and he returned her gaze. Sarah thought about what had caused their delay and despite the situation and her fear, she couldn't help but feel a short burst of warmth and happiness at the memory. William's face was a mask, and she had seen that expression before. He was trying to play it tough, but Sarah knew him well enough by now to be able to guess what he was really thinking.

Drake shrugged, not having expected a reply to his

monologue, anyway. He stepped away from Sarah, something that caused her to breathe a little sigh of relief, and walked over to William. 'What I couldn't figure out was what *Frozen in time and space* actually means.'

Without any warning, he punched William hard in the stomach, who responded with a pained, strangled noise. He probably would have dropped to his knees again if the two men hadn't been holding him. Sarah struggled against her captors but to no avail.

'Unless you want to see your friend suffer,' Drake threatened and turned around to look at her, 'you'd better tell me what it means.'

Sarah's thoughts were racing. Usually, people in movies or books came up with something at this point, a clever trap or a distraction but there was absolutely nothing on her mind. All she could think was that William would be in pain if she wasn't clever. And she never had felt less clever than in this moment.

'It means...' she said, falling quiet. 'It means...' She tried again, but there still was nothing on her mind. 'Listen, we don't know what it means,' she finally admitted. 'We took so long to get here because we didn't know where to go and what to search for. We stumbled across the mountain, hoping to find a clue. William only remembered this cave by coincidence, and we decided to check it out because we had no other ideas. We didn't know that we were supposed to come here, OK?'

Silence filled the cave while Sarah held her breath, and Drake started to laugh. He laughed loud and long, the sound echoing from the cave walls, startling some of the bats that began fluttering through the air.

'This is too funny,' he gasped, when he had recovered

somewhat. 'You two are destined to be my downfall? You couldn't even find your own feet with a map!'

'If you're that clever, then you can tell me what it means!' Sarah spat.

'I don't know,' Drake admitted, 'but I don't have to know, do I? All I need to do is to make sure that *you* never find out.'

And with that, he nodded at the men holding William, and before Sarah even could take so much as a breath, she saw something silvery and long glinting in the air. She watched in horror as the knife sliced through William's clothes and slid into his lower abdomen. Her piercing scream filled the air, and once its echo had abated there was a loud buzz when the bats that had gathered in thousands on the ceiling started fluttering through the cave, disturbed by the sudden noise. They were everywhere around them, even getting entangled in her hair, but Sarah neither noticed nor cared. Her eyes were fixed firmly on William who sank to his knees, his fingers pressed to his stomach, blood seeping through them.

'No, no, no,' she whispered in horror. Drake's men finally released him but when Sarah tried to rush to his side, she was held back.

'Not allowing you to disappear with him,' Drake snarled.

He was enjoying this moment very much, but Sarah didn't pay any attention to him, her eyes only fixed on William. She would do everything to turn back time, and the dread that filled her took away her ability to breathe. William had become the centre of her world and now he was hurt, and Sarah knew that Drake wouldn't have any mercy on either of them.

When William looked up at her, he was smiling, and it cut right into Sarah's heart because despite the pain he had to be feeling, nothing but utter love for her showed on his face. She could hear his voice clearly through the noise around them. 'Thank you,' he said.

Sarah struggled violently against her captors, wanting to rush to William's side, not to escape but to be with him, but no matter how hard she fought, they did not release her.

'No,' she screamed. 'Please!'

The last word was directed at Drake, but he only laughed again before he nodded at his men. They grabbed William underneath his armpits and dragged him over toward the dark water of the lake, pushing him into it without hesitation. Sarah's screams filled the cave again, and she scratched and bit at her captors, wanting to rush toward the lake, but the arms around her seemed to be made of steel. William rose to the surface of the water three times, and then he was gone.

Sarah's throat was raw when the arms finally released her, leaving her bruised and panting and she ran over to the lake, but there was nothing any longer. The water lay still and dark, and she plunged into it without hesitation, allowing the cold to engulf her while she frantically searched for William underwater. There was nothing but darkness, no matter how often she returned to the surface for air before diving back in. She didn't even manage to touch the bottom of the lake since it was much deeper than she had assumed. There was no sign of William.

Finally, she gave up. There was no way that William

could have survived that, and after she heaved her heavy and wet body back onto solid ground, all strength left her. She stayed on her knees, filled with a deep numbness, something she probably should be glad about because she didn't think that she'd be able to take the pain, but she was even too numb for that thought to take root. When Drake appeared at her side, she didn't look up at him. 'Get it over with, I don't care,' she whispered, her voice not her own any longer.

'Oh, I'm not going to kill you,' Drake informed her smugly, and Sarah finally turned her head to glance up at him.

Drake knelt next to her. 'I'll let you live,' he explained. 'You aren't a threat to my power any longer, now that William is dead, and I'll let you go back to your pathetic little life in your world.

You'll always remember how you failed, and you'll always look over your shoulder, thinking that one day I'll come for you. Meanwhile, I'm going to figure out how to keep you in this world, and as soon as I know, I'll find you, and use you and your powers to my liking.' He got up, now glancing down at her, an ugly sneer on his face. 'Enjoy your life until then, because it won't be enjoyable much longer.'

He walked away, low whispers echoing on the walls and finally, silence settled over the scenery. Sarah was alone. An abandoned torch was stuck between two rocks at the entry point of the corridor, or maybe they had left it behind for her, but Sarah couldn't move. She only knelt at the shore of the lake where she had lost her love and tried to remember how to breathe. She had failed him, this world, and the prophecy. It was all lost. Sure, she could go back to her old life, pick up the broken pieces of her existence, glue them together, and carry on, but she knew that she would never be the same, even without Drake's threat. When she dipped her hand back into the water it felt much warmer than it had before and for a moment she felt the strong urge to follow William into its depths, follow him into the darkness, and be united with him forever. How peaceful it would be. She ran her fingers through the water like a gentle caress and lay down on the cold stone, not able to pull her hand out of her lover's wet grave for a very long time.

Chapter 18

Her apartment was a mess, but Sarah couldn't bring herself to tidy it up. All she could think was that a lot of the things that were lying on the ground had been touched by William. Back when they had been here last to search for the prophecy. It felt like a lifetime ago. She was curled up in a ball on the sofa, covered by the same blanket William had slept underneath. In the beginning, it had carried his scent but that was gone, replaced by the stench of her unwashed body. She knew that she needed a shower, but she couldn't get up, there was an exhaustion in her bones that ran deeper than anything she ever had felt.

Charlotte was standing in the door frame, hands on her hips but despite her firm manners, there was a soft expression on her face. 'Come on, doll,' she said, and Sarah knew that no matter how soft the expression on her best friend's face was, there was no way to refuse her. She had that iron determination in her voice that she also had when she was hungry, and there was no standing between Charlotte and food in any situation.

'Go and get a shower. And I'll make you soup.' Charlotte believed that everything could be fixed with soup. From a stomach bug to a shattered heart.

To her surprise, there had been no police waiting for her at the apartment upon her return.

It had turned out that Drake's men had removed the body from the backyard before it had been found, and no one had noticed anything. The only things waiting for her had been a bunch of unopened letters, mainly bills, some messages on her answering machine, the smell of unaired and dusty rooms, and a pile of laundry. And the chaos in the rooms that resembled the chaos in her heart.

Charlotte was waiting for her answer and took a step towards her. She would probably physically drag her into the bathroom if she didn't move anytime soon. With heavy limbs, Sarah managed to get up and shuffle to the shower. She had no idea how long she was standing there, letting the hot water run down her body but when she walked into the kitchen, she felt slightly better, though not much.

Charlotte was waiting for her with a large pot of coffee and the promised soup. The two women sat down at the kitchen table and Charlotte pushed a spoon into her hand. Sarah knew that the soup was good, she usually loved everything Charlotte cooked, but she didn't seem to be able to taste anything and was relieved when Charlotte seemed satisfied, and Sarah could stop eating.

'Tell me,' Charlotte said. 'All of it.'

And Sarah obliged, the words tumbling from her mouth, slow at first but then faster and faster. It was dark outside when Sarah stopped talking. She felt somewhat lighter after letting it all out. Charlotte took a sip of her coffee but put the cup down in disgust when she realised that it had gotten cold.

'I knew it was crazy when the bomb went off,' she remembered, 'but I had no idea how crazy.' She was quiet for a long time. 'Can you show me?' she then asked and even though Sarah knew what she was talking about already, Charlotte added. 'The other world? Can you take me there?'

Sarah nodded slowly. 'I can,' she replied. 'But it's a dying world. It looks normal but there's war, there's hunger, and then there's Drake, and there's no more magic, and no more William, and I failed.'

She broke into tears and Charlotte was there to pull her into a tight hug, but Sarah couldn't stop crying. There hadn't been a single tear since William had died, but now she wasn't able to stop.

When she finally fell asleep in Charlotte's arms, her eyes were puffy, and her head hurt, but for the first time since her return from Aphelia, her sleep was deep and dreamless.

Two weeks later the doorbell rang, and to Sarah's surprise, Joe was standing at her door. Charlotte must have told him that she was back. To her even bigger surprise, he was accompanied by Gladys. Sarah immediately felt guilty for leaving her house and never returning as she had, but Gladys made a dismissive gesture when Sarah mentioned it. 'Joe kept me informed, it seems that you've had enough on your plate as it was, my dear.' And with that, she pulled Sarah into a tight hug. As did Joe.

Sarah debated with herself whether to tell them what had happened. There was a huge risk that they wouldn't believe her, thinking she had lost her mind. On the other hand, Joe and Gladys had both been kind and selfless, helping her without wanting anything in return and Sarah figured that she owed them at least some version of the truth. Besides, Joe would ask for William sooner or later and it was better to tell them about his fate now, while she still was able to speak without her voice breaking. When they all were sitting in her chaotic living room with a mug of hot coffee in their hands, she launched into a story in which she and William had been chased by some criminals after witnessing something they shouldn't have and how they had escaped to the countryside. The story sounded false and inconsistent from the start, and at some point Joe leaned forward and smiled at her gently. 'You don't have to tell us what really happened,' he said kindly, causing her to immediately fall silent.

'I can't tell you the truth,' she finally blurted out. 'But William is dead.' And with that, she broke into tears.

'I'm so sorry for your loss,' was all Joe answered, but he squeezed her knee gently, and when they said their farewells not too much later, he pulled her into a tight hug.

Gladys hadn't talked much, but she hugged Sarah, too. 'It might not feel like it right now, but things will be OK,' she promised and there was so much certainty lying in her voice that Sarah was almost able to believe her.

The next person to visit was Steven, another week later. Sarah still felt guilty that his shop, which had been his whole existence, had exploded because of her. But as it turned out, her worries weren't necessary, because Steven had been insured. And quite well. He had made a lot of money out of it, enough to rebuild the shop and start over if he wanted to. He didn't, though. 'Being so close to dying opened my eyes,' he told her, and there was an excited expression on his face she never had seen there before. 'I'm going travelling, all over the world,' he blurted out, barely able to contain his happiness, and Sarah felt genuinely pleased for him. She realised with surprise that she was going to miss him. Had someone told her that six months ago, she would have laughed.

'First, I want to go to Latin America,' he explained. 'Mexico is first on my list. Which reminds me to give you regards from Rosy.' The former cleaning lady from Steven's coffee shop Rosalie, or Rosy for short, was from Mexico. 'After the shop exploded, she quickly found a new job,' he went on. 'She now works in a daycare nursery.' Sarah smiled at that information. She had always liked the woman.

When Steven had finished presenting his elaborate travel plans, Sarah told him her story about why she had disappeared. She and Charlotte had worked on a version she could tell people without being locked away in a mental hospital. She told Steven about a nasty ex-boyfriend who had been stalking her and whom she had thought responsible for placing the bomb in the coffee shop, which, eventually, had been the reason for her disappearance. She also mentioned that she thought it possible that he could have been the one behind her almost fatal accident with the car.

'Maybe you should tell the police about that?' Steven wondered. 'They still have no idea who put the bomb there. They think it was some kind of protection money thing.'

Sarah shook her head. 'That's ridiculous,' she said. 'But no, it wasn't my ex. It turned out that he moved back to the US before the incidents took place, so it can't have been him. Which is the reason I came back.'

Steven seemed to be satisfied by that explanation, and he set out to talk again about all the places in the world he wanted to see at great length.

The days and weeks passed, and the pain Sarah felt with every breath she drew became part of her daily life. Everyone around told her that it would get easier, but the longer it took, the worse it felt. William was her first thought in the morning, and the last thing on her mind when she closed her eyes to go to sleep in the evening. Since she was unemployed now, there was nothing she had to do, and the days came and went, covered by the grey blanket of her loss. She slept a lot and even though she had learned what hunger was during her time with William on Aphelia, she wasn't hungry any longer. Charlotte made sure to check up on her almost every day and forced Sarah to eat something but other than that, Sarah simply existed.

The only thing she was able to muster up some energy for was repaying those she and William had stolen from, on their journey toward the mountains. She had kept the paper with every name, every item they had stolen, and she made sure to buy and replace everything, sending some additional money as an apology in anonymous letters and parcels. Soon, she would have used up her entire savings. She needed another job. But the grief buried everything under a dark, heavy blanket, making it seem pointless.

After another few weeks of gloom, Charlotte finally had enough. She opened the curtains and windows to allow some sunlight and fresh air in the room. It was a beautiful late autumn day, and a lot of trees had already lost their leaves.

How had it gotten so late in the year?

Charlotte forced her to get dressed properly, and sometime later the two women were sitting on a bench in the park, steaming paper cups of coffee in their hands. The sun was shining warm on their faces, and the air smelled of oncoming rain, but so far there were only a few clouds in the sky. The voices of laughing children were carried over to them from the nearby playground, and for the first time in a while, Sarah noticed her surroundings.

'Thanks for dragging me out,' she told her friend, and Charlotte smiled at her.

'You had me really worried there for a while,' she admitted. 'I've never seen you so broken.'

Sarah didn't respond, but her eyes filled with tears, and Charlotte reached for her hand. 'You loved him,' she said quietly. 'And a lot of difficult stuff has happened to you. It's OK to grieve for as long as you need. Just promise me to eat a bite now and then, alright? Because you've gotten so skinny and pale that you look like a vampire! We can't have the vampire hunters kicking in your door, can we?'

Sarah smiled weakly at Charlotte's attempt to crack a joke, but at the same time, she was filled with such a deep love for her best friend that she could only squeeze Charlotte's hand. She had always been by her side, through all of this; she had believed her entirely crazy story, even before Sarah had taken her to Aphelia for a quick look. Not even almost dying from an explosion had kept Charlotte away, and Sarah realised how lucky she was to have a friend like her.

'Thank you... for everything.' She tried to put her

feelings into words, knowing that she wouldn't find any-thing sufficient anyway. 'I couldn't have done all of this without you.'

Charlotte's smile deepened, and a warm expression appeared on her face. 'That's what best friends are for, right?'

Sarah leaned her head against her friend's shoulder, and the women enjoyed the peaceful day in the park. For once Charlotte was quiet, and even though the pain of her loss was still tearing her apart, Sarah felt something akin to peace, as if she was allowed a little breather, a moment to recover. She watched the people stroll past, a couple fighting about dinner with the in-laws, a man walking his dog, and two women jogging. She wondered when her life had last been this peaceful. The memory hurt, but she forced herself to think about it, anyway. It had been at the cabin in the mountains of Aphelia, with William. Tears stung behind her eyes, but she kept them at bay. She had cried so much over the last few weeks that she was tired of it. She wanted to stay in the moment and keep this as a happy memory, a memory to give her strength and not cause her pain.

The laughter of children reached her ears again. Sarah slowly lifted her head from Charlotte's shoulder and frowned. Her friend turned around in alarm to look at her, but Sarah was only staring into the distance intently with-out actually seeing anything. She remembered something, the last thought she had had before falling asleep in William's arms on their first night in the cabin. They had been safe and warm and happy, in love and completely hidden from the world.

Hidden from mankind's eyes, where time and space are frozen.

Her last thought had been that this moment could be the moment the prophecy described. It hadn't lodged in her love-befuddled mind at that moment, and she had forgotten about it since, but they definitely had been hidden from mankind's eyes, and that moment certainly had felt as if time and space were frozen. Sarah sat up straight, the coffee cup slipping from her hands and falling onto the ground, splattering her shoes with coffee while Sarah thought hard, all the colour draining from her face. It surely wasn't possible, it couldn't be!

Charlotte grabbed her friend by the hand. 'Sarah, what's wrong?'

Shock was in Sarah's eyes when she caught Charlotte's gaze. 'Oh my God,' she whispered, her face ashen. 'Maybe we didn't fail.' She jumped to her feet so quickly that Charlotte almost dropped her coffee, too.

'I need to make sure.' And with that, Sarah ran off.

'Wait!' Charlotte tossed her coffee cup into the nearby dustbin and was after her friend in an instant.

Chapter 19

The test was lying between them on the small couch table and neither Charlotte nor Sarah was able to avert their eyes. The seconds on the old clock hanging on the wall were ticking away loudly but no one was paying attention to it. The second line had appeared almost immediately, faint in the beginning but getting stronger with every tick of the clock, and when they looked at each other with large eyes, neither spoke. Sarah's hand crept slowly to her belly, covering it protectively while her eyes filled with tears.

'You're pregnant,' Charlotte stated the obvious, and Sarah started to cry.

'We were wrong,' she sobbed. 'All of us were. Even Drake. We thought that we'd have to find a certain spot and do something there when all we needed to do was to create a new life.'

Charlotte stared at the pregnancy test in disbelief, before her eyes sought out Sarah's. 'But why there?' she asked. 'Why in the mountains? Why all the fuss of getting there? You could've done that anywhere. Even here on your damn sofa.'

'I don't know,' Sarah said slowly. 'There was something special about those mountains,' she realised, her hand still protectively on her belly. 'I can't describe it any better than that. Maybe there was enough of the magic left to… I don't know.' She wiped some of the tears away that were lingering on her chin. 'I think William and I needed to make this journey together. To get to know each other. I don't think I would have had sex with him before then. Remember how creepy he seemed in the beginning?'

'True,' Charlotte admitted, and studied Sarah's flat belly. 'And this baby is…' she started the sentence.

'…the new Guardian.' Sarah finished Charlotte's sentence, but her face was still drained of all colour. 'It's the only thing that makes sense. There never was a button or a spell to start the magic again, it was always about the next Guardian. Maybe he or she will know what to do to save Aphelia.' She stroked her belly. 'And the baby is also the last thing that's left of William.'

The next few days came and went in a blur and Sarah couldn't catch a clear thought any longer. Her life had taken yet another unexpected turn, and she had no idea how to cope with it. She started eating again because she wasn't just responsible for herself any longer but also for the growing life inside of her. The stabbing pain she felt at William's death was still strong, but it was now mixed with joy when she thought about the baby. At the same time, she was scared.

How was she supposed to be responsible for another human being? She couldn't even get up in time for work. This wasn't how she had expected her life to be. She had wanted children but not like this. She had always imagined being in a stable relationship for a while, getting married; the classic way. Now she would be a single mother of a child who was destined to become the Guardian of a different world. How was she supposed to shoulder this burden on her own? Not to mention the threat from Drake that would always hover over her head. The only thing that kept her from losing her mind was the fact that Charlotte was by her side the entire time. She was already making plans to find a bigger apartment or house for herself, Sarah, and the baby. Maybe even with a spare room for Camille or Stuart, or whoever wanted to come to visit. 'I'm tired of having to listen to guitar music at three in the morning anyway,' she stated. 'I think it's time to settle down, and that way I can support you with the baby.'

Sarah almost cried on hearing this. With Charlotte by her side, she wouldn't feel as lonely, and the burden of responsibility could be shared. Once again Sarah was deeply grateful for this awesome woman in her life.

She started looking over her shoulder again. After returning from Aphelia, she hadn't cared if Drake was watching her or not, but now she did. Her pregnancy was months away from being visible but she had already started feeling nervous about it. Would Drake's men come to the right conclusion when seeing her pregnant? Would they realise what it meant? And how was she going to protect herself and her child?

The fact that she was carrying a Guardian posed other problems as well. How was the child supposed to learn what it needed to fulfil its destiny? How was Sarah supposed to teach them about magic she had no clue about herself? Would they have to live in Aphelia? There was still a war and a famine going on. And was this what she wanted for herself and her baby? Did her child even have a choice? Had any of them ever really had a choice?

And there was still Drake.

Was her child always going to be in danger and therefore need to stay hidden in the shadows of society, to fulfil a bigger goal? Her head was swimming with all these questions, and the longer she thought about it, the more questions arose.

She needed a plan.

And a backup plan.

And, preferably, a hidey-hole in case all plans failed. Better safe than sorry. She also needed a new job and, as Charlotte had pointed out, a different place to live. Maybe one with more than one exit, you never knew when you needed to escape fast.

Sarah's heart was heavy when she thought about everything that was lying ahead for her and her child and even though the sadness about William's death still hugged her like a grey blanket, she had no choice any longer but to be strong and look to the future.

Sarah realised how much she had changed since everything had begun. She was seeing the world completely differently now, and there was a toughness about her she had never noticed in herself before.

She only lived in peace for four weeks. Four weeks during which she went house-hunting with Charlotte, applied for a new job – she didn't get it but it was a start – and even registered for a prenatal class. Grief was still her silent companion, but it wasn't all-consuming any longer. She had a task now, something she could focus on.

She stepped out of her house to get some milk from the small corner shop when she noticed them. At first, she wasn't sure, wondering if she had become paranoid, but it was three different men and they were good because she only ever saw one of them at a time. But since she was studying her surroundings closely, she recognised them. They had been following her for the last few days. Sarah knew. Had Drake already found a way to keep her from skipping between worlds? That was a deeply disturbing thought, especially now.

As soon as she was back home, she went into the kitchen and got a small but very sharp knife from her drawer. She put it into a sheath, a remnant of the times when she had gone to medieval craft markets – appropriately dressed of course – and strapped it to her upper thigh. She wouldn't have quick access to it but it was well hidden if someone searched her only perfunctorily. She put another knife in the pocket of her jacket. That one would be quick and easy to reach if she needed it. She felt a bit ridiculous doing this and still had no clue if she would ever be able to use a deadly weapon against anyone, but she still felt better after taking these precautions. She called Charlotte at work to let her know what had happened and was just about able to talk her out of coming over. Charlotte hated working as a cashier at a posh clothes store with a passion, but Sarah knew that she needed the money, and she didn't want her to risk her job. Besides, there was nothing Charlotte would be able to do about her followers anyway.

For the rest of the day, Sarah kept glancing out of her window, and when she stepped out of her house the next morning for an appointment with the gynaecologist to get a first scan of the baby, she felt tense. A part of her knew that she hadn't been imagining things, while another part still held out hope that she might have just been paranoid. But that hope was crushed quickly because she was followed again, by the same group of men. But why? When Drake had made that threat to her, she had figured that she'd have time to come up with a plan, but it had only been weeks. She felt the sudden urgent desire to own a gun, but this was ridiculous. She didn't know how to shoot a gun safely and would probably kill herself or an innocent bystander accidentally when attempting to use it. She had her knives, but they didn't make her feel protected any longer. Yesterday, in the safety of her home they had seemed like a good idea, but today she only felt ridiculous about them.

She had left the train station and turned right when they made their move. A man stepped in front of her, and another one appeared behind her. She stopped dead in her tracks, her hand wrapping around the handle of the knife in her pocket, but she didn't pull it out yet.

'What do you want from me?' she asked shortly. She noticed that neither of them was pointing a weapon at her. If they wanted to kill her, they would have acted differently.

'We want you to come with us,' one of the men answered. 'Drake wants to see you.' He seemed vaguely familiar, and she thought that he was probably one of the guards she had seen at Drake's castle.

'No,' she simply stated, and tried to slip past them, but a hand closed around her arm tightly, holding her back.

The two police officers who stepped out of the small sandwich bar behind her saved her. They immediately stopped dead in their tracks, sensing that something was wrong and focusing their attention on the little group standing there. The hand around Sarah's arm was removed at once. Sarah took a deep breath and pushed forward and through them, taking up her route towards the doctor's surgery. When she turned around, the men had vanished into the train station.

'Are you alright, ma'am?' One of the officers wanted to know and Sarah nodded. She didn't want to draw more attention to herself than necessary. Besides, there was nothing the police could do about those men anyway. But deep down, she was shaken to the core.

Back home, she sat in her comfortable armchair in her living room and gazed at the black and white ultrasound scan of her baby. It only resembled a small bean, but it was one thing peeing on a test and seeing the second line appear, and an entirely different thing to see a picture of your baby for the first time, no matter how small and blurry it was. And for the first time since her return to Earth, she was deeply scared. She wasn't scared for her own life but for the one that was growing inside her. The life she was responsible for now. She realised that she couldn't continue as if everything was perfectly normal. The encounter with Drake's men today showed her that nothing was. They would come for her again and next time she wouldn't be so lucky. She had no idea what they wanted from her – what Drake wanted from her – but she knew that they wouldn't give up.

She was gripped by panic when she thought about the possibility that Drake knew about her pregnancy. But that wasn't possible, was it? But no matter if he did or not, it would be visible at some point and she couldn't spend her life in hiding; she needed to earn money, and she wanted her child to grow up as normal as possible. Guardian or not, she would make sure that this child would have a regular upbringing with playgroups, baby swimming, and a stable environment.

But this was not going to happen as long as Drake was around, and she couldn't pretend the problem was going away on its own. He wasn't stupid. Even if he left her alone, something she highly doubted, he'd be able to put two and two together at some point. William was dead, but he would realise that the real threat to him was this child. He would find them sooner or later.

She couldn't let that happen. But what options did she have? Her eyes went to the ultrasound scan again, and she thought about William, gripped by such a tight longing for him that she couldn't breathe. She had no idea how he would have reacted to the news of them having a baby, but she knew that no matter what, he would have done anything to protect this child. But he wasn't around any longer, and Sarah knew that she would have to pull herself together. For him and their child. She was going to have to do something about this threat hanging above their heads.

Because there was no one else to do it.

Chapter 20

The metal of the gun was cold against the skin of her hand and Sarah studied the weapon with a mixture of disgust and despair. Would she really be able to pull this off?

She hadn't been able to sleep the night before, because she had tried to find a solution that would guarantee her and her child a life in peace but hadn't come up with a single thing. Except for one. Travel to Aphelia and kill Drake. In the end, everything came down to that. It was either her and the baby or Drake. It's what William would have done. But hadn't Sarah wanted him to stop killing? Hadn't she told him that there was always a choice? It was much easier to take the moral high ground if your life wasn't in danger, and if you didn't have to make decisions for those you loved and wanted to protect.

After making her decision, she had lain awake, wondering if she really would be able to pull this off. She had never fired a gun in her life but that wasn't what worried her. What if she couldn't do it? Or worse, what if she *could* do it? Was she able to kill someone in cold blood, no matter how evil? She would be the one to pull the trigger and watch him die. It would be her doing, and Drake's blood would be sticking to her hands for the rest of her life. He would be following her like a shadow forever.

Her empty hand wandered towards her stomach, protecting the tiny life that was forming there. And the question was there again. Did she have a choice? If she wanted this baby to grow up and live in peace, there was no other way. She glanced up and caught her image in a full-length mirror mounted on the wall next to the door. She looked the same as always but there was an expression in her eyes that had never been there before.

Haunted, old, weary.

It reminded her of William, and she quickly looked away, studying the gun instead. She had bought it from someone Joe had recommended. He hadn't asked what she needed the weapon for, and Sarah was deeply grateful for that. What she was about to do would stay her dark secret, something she wouldn't even share with Charlotte, and she hoped with everything she had that it wouldn't stain her soul beyond recovery. Again, she stared at the cold object in her hand. The man she had bought the gun from had allowed her to use his shooting range and patiently explained everything to her. She had learned how to load the gun and now knew how to handle it. She had fired off some shots too, and even though she hadn't hit the target all the time, she had hit it often enough. She needed to do this right, for her son or daughter.

Drake's men hadn't approached her again, but she had seen them around. They didn't even try to hide any longer, letting her know that they were there, that they were waiting for the right moment, and there was absolutely nothing she could do about it. They were wrong, of course, but it wasn't the men she was after. It was Drake.

She met her gaze in the mirror, and this time, she could read determination in her eyes, and a certain hardness, also something she had read in William's eyes before, and she took a deep breath. It was decided.

The forest surrounding Drake's castle was darker than she remembered, and she was nervous walking through it. She had decided against popping directly into the building, fearing that people would be around. She still didn't know what would happen if she ever materialized inside a wall. She didn't think it was possible since she had flipped over quite a few times and had never been stuck inside a tree or an object, but she was still wary about it. Once again, she was painfully reminded of the fact that she knew very little about this world and her abilities within it.

Once this was over, she would have to come here and learn more about everything to teach her child.

She couldn't detect any guards or patrols in the woods, but that didn't mean they weren't there, and she approached the castle slowly. She hadn't brought much with her, because she didn't intend to stay long, but the gun in her pocket seemed to weigh more than anything else she could have carried.

The castle was a dark stain looming in the sky. It was raining, which enhanced the gloomy feeling she had. She carefully crept closer until she was hiding behind some bushes near the entrance gate. She hadn't crafted an elaborate plan, because she knew too little about Drake's schedule, but at least she knew how to get inside the building without being seen. The time she had spent inside while waiting for Wiliam had given her a great overview of the layout of the castle. Sarah pushed the thought of William aside; she needed to focus on the events that lay ahead. She didn't know where Drake was, but she knew a lot about the routines inside his home and was sure that he would show up at some point. She would wait and catch him on his own, and then shoot him. It was a simple plan, yet her heartbeat accelerated dangerously at the thought of it. Sarah took a deep breath and moved forward; she couldn't afford to show any signs of weakness. She couldn't even afford to hesitate.

This time, guards were standing outside the castle, and she couldn't just sneak in like she had before. But she had a plan B. Following her nose, she soon reached the small supply tunnel and studied it. It wasn't really a supply tunnel but more a sort of canal system, where the waste and the grey water was expelled from the castle. It looked as nasty as it smelled, but Sarah knew exactly where it ended within the building, and because of the smell there was hardly ever anyone around. She studied the clouds in the sky. The rain had turned into a drizzle, and the sky had gotten a little brighter. This reduced the risk of some heavy rainfall that could flood the tunnel. She didn't feel the slightest urge to drown in sewage. There was no reason to postpone this any longer, and before she could change her mind she jumped into the gutter, ignoring the things her feet sank into, and followed the path of the tunnel into the darkness.

If the smell had been bad outside, it was almost unbearable now. Sarah put a scarf around her nose and mouth, only taking shallow breaths, but she felt as if the disgusting stench attached itself to her clothes, her skin, her hair, and even the insides of her nose and mouth. She suppressed a gag, knowing that if she threw up once, she'd have a hard time stopping. It was quickly getting darker, and the deeper she went, the worse the stench became. Sarah switched on the flashlight she had brought along, ignoring the small shadows that scurried through the darkness just out of reach of the light. It was most likely only rats and she didn't allow her mind to explore any other possibilities. She didn't take a closer look at the waste she was walking through either, or the dirty water that had soaked her trousers up to the knees. She had brought some spare clothes with her because she had known that she would easily be detected by smell alone if she didn't change. Her eyes were kept firmly ahead, her mind fixed on the goal she had in mind, and when she finally saw the dim light at the end of the tunnel, she remembered just in time not to draw a deep, relieved breath. As she had hoped, the path was clear when she climbed out of the gutter in the back of one of the many kitchens of the castle. She could hear a few people outside the door but managed to sneak out undetected and was soon back in the heart of the building.

She dreaded this place. Every step she made and every breath she drew was poisoned by her memories and Drake's presence, which was overwhelming. She didn't want to be here, and she didn't want to do what she had come here to do but every time she felt weak and helpless or scared she firmly placed her hand over her belly and remembered why she was there. Why she needed to be here.

She slipped back into her old hiding place, the small storage cupboard, and to her surprise found her old make-shift bed untouched, which caused her to smile grimly. No one ever seemed to enter this cupboard, something that suited her well. But she hadn't come here to hide. She had to find out where Drake was and end all of this, preferably while staying alive. She knew that being here was a huge risk. If she died, the entire hope of this world would die with her, and everything William had fought for would have been in vain. But if she didn't kill Drake, he would find her sooner or later, and the outcome would be the same.

It was Drake or them.

This time she didn't have to wait long. She had changed her clothes and forced herself to eat something despite not being hungry, before she moved to a spot closer to the entrance hall because this was one of the places Drake had to come through sooner or later. She was prepared to wait for a while, maybe even a few nights, but to her surprise, she heard some commotion in the entrance hall after only a few hours. She crept closer, hiding behind the same curtain she had used before. From here she would be able to see everything that was going on.

A few men began to gather in the entrance hall, and Sarah recognised some of them as Drake's guards. Her heart started beating faster. If they were here, Drake wouldn't be far away. She touched the cold metal of the gun, drawing comfort from the fact that this was going to be over soon, one way or the other. And then Drake stepped into the hall, and Sarah's heart rate went through the roof. She felt dizzy and even though she realised she was breathing too fast and too hard, she couldn't stop. Drake walked the hall in long strides, and Sarah knew that she would have to act now. The situation was perfect since his guards were already at the other end of the room, and she had a free line of fire. She pulled out her gun, it was heavy and cold in her hand, but her feet simply refused to move forward. Desperately, she watched how Drake walked swiftly and the window for this unique opportunity was closing quickly. A picture appeared in front of her inner eyes. It was Drake's sneering face when William had been dying on the cold ground of the cave. There had been no empathy there. Just satisfaction, and maybe even something like pleasure. It was this memory that gave her the strength to finally step out of her hiding place.

'Drake!'

Her voice sounded much calmer than she felt, and it rang loudly through the entrance hall. At the same time, she released the safety catch of the gun and pointed it at Drake. He was four or five metres away from her. Her hands were shaking slightly, but she was optimistic that she'd manage to hit him nonetheless. She had six rounds in the gun, she had loaded it herself, and one would surely find its goal.

Drake froze upon looking into the barrel of her gun and his eyes found Sarah's. There was genuine surprise lying in them before he masked his emotions from her. 'I didn't expect to see you again so soon,' he said calmly and with self-confidence, but she had seen the façade crack, and she knew that he was only playing it cool. She brought her other hand forward, gripping the weapon with both hands now to stop it from shaking.

'I don't want to do this,' she admitted, and there was real regret in her voice, but her index finger curled around the trigger nonetheless, and Drake took an instinctive step back before he raised his hands in a useless defensive gesture.

'Stop!' he shouted and even though Sarah had sworn herself that she wouldn't fall for any distraction, she hesitated. Drake pointed toward the left where the rest of the people who had come in with him had gathered.

'If you shoot me, he dies.'

Sarah's gaze fell on a tied-up man, dragged in by some guards, wearing a hood over his head. He was only able to stand on his own because he was supported by the guards holding him in a halfway upright position. Muffled words emerged from beneath the hood, telling her that the man was also gagged. Her eyes alternated between Drake and the hooded prisoner, and there was something about the familiar outlines of his body that caused her knees to feel like jelly. Something was rising within her throat.

One of the guards ripped the hood off the man's head, and she looked into William's face.

Dirty, and adorned with a scruffy beard, but it was William. The shock of seeing him made her stagger forward, her eyes filling with tears while losing focus on Drake. The gun sank and she didn't even notice his men coming forward. They tackled her to the ground and wrenched the weapon from her fingers, which was an easy task because she had lost all her strength, her eyes only fixed on William, a sob escaping from her throat. She stretched her hand in William's direction, wanting to reach him and to touch him, needing to make sure he was really there and that he was alive, that this was not some sort of cruel trick.

William was still gagged, and she couldn't understand the words he was uttering but his eyes were directed at her, telling her what she needed to know, and she struggled against the arms that were holding her down.

Drake was now standing over her and her eyes sought out his. 'How is this possible?' she whispered, and Drake's jaws clenched in anger.

'The two of you just won't die.'

He gave his men a sign. They released her, and Sarah sat up. William struggled forcefully against the guards, but he had no chance. When Sarah's gaze wandered up, she saw why William was so frantic. Drake was pointing the gun directly at her face.

'My men found him stumbling down a road on the way to the portal to Earth. The lake in the cave was connected by a short tunnel to the lake in another cave, and our friend dived right through. The stab wound missed all the vital organs and he was on his way to you when we caught him. I couldn't believe it and sent my men to catch you and bring you here, but you managed to escape their first attempt.'

That, at least, explained why his men had been after her again so soon. The sound of Drake's voice was soft, almost friendly, but Sarah could read it within his eyes. He was utterly fed up with them and the situation, and she knew that their time was over.

She stopped shaking, suddenly feeling very calm, while an idea was forming in her head. Or maybe it was just a final desperate attempt. In the end, it didn't matter.

'Will you allow me to say goodbye to William?' she pleaded. Sarah was sure that he would deny her this last wish, but he only rolled his eyes, waved his hand in William's direction and the guards removed the gag from his mouth. He was too far away for Sarah to touch him, but she struggled to her feet nonetheless and smiled at him sadly.

'We fulfilled the prophecy after all,' she announced, making sure that everyone in the entrance hall was able to hear her words. Drake's eyes widened with sudden concern.

'I carry the next Guardian inside me.'

Her hand went to her still flat belly, and she left it there protectively. Sarah wasn't sure how much Drake's guards knew about the dying magic in their world and the role of the Guardians, but the sudden murmur in the room and the glances some of the guards exchanged told her that they at least had an idea of what it could mean.

Drake's anger was palpable even before he took a step toward her and hissed. 'What?'

But Sarah ignored him. Her eyes were locked with William's, and her heart went out to him when she saw the tears that formed in his eyes.

'I love you,' she said and in a fluid move, she drove the knife that had been attached to her thigh ever since Drake's men had been following her into the side of Drake's neck. There was no hesitation in her attack, no more ethical or moral concern. She was surprised at how easily the blade went in, and when it was buried down to the hilt in his flesh, she turned it around forty-five degrees to cause as much damage as possible, before pulling it out again. She had seen that somewhere in a movie. Drake's blood followed in a thick spray that covered her, the wall next to them, and one of Drake's guards.

The silence was deafening, only interrupted by the strange gargling sound that escaped from Drake's mouth. And then a shot rang out, ear-shattering and violent and Sarah waited for the pain to set in, waited for the inevitable. But nothing happened. She looked down at her body, her hands automatically going to her stomach but there was nothing. No blood seeping out of her. He had missed her.

Drake, however, was bleeding profoundly. He sank to his knees and very slowly tipped over to his side. His eyes were open, an almost comical expression of surprise in them, even though Sarah had never found anything less funny than this moment. She could see how the light in his eyes broke, and then he was dead, the gun lying useless by his side.

Sarah released the bloody knife from her hand, and it clattered to the floor as she took a step to the side, away from Drake's body. She felt strangely detached but still knew that the next moments would be crucial.

'For the new Guardian and a chance for peace,' she said into the silence and waited, surprised at how calm her voice sounded. All eyes were on her, and she knew that the next few seconds would not only decide her fate but also the fate of this world.

It was the guard to her left, the one covered in Drake's blood, who decided it. After realising that their leader was dead, he studied Sarah with a curious expression and slowly sank to one knee. Sarah was confused before she understood that he knelt in front of her. The man bowed his head once, before looking back up at her.

'To the new Guardian,' he proclaimed, and this broke

the spell. She had hoped that her words would affect Drake's men, but she hadn't believed in it. But more of Drake's men knelt, and Sarah had no idea what to do. People usually didn't kneel in front of her unless they had fallen over. She was only a barista, after all. But this was not true any longer. She was much more than that. She was a mother and a lover, and she was now a killer as well. What she wasn't, and never wanted to be, was the ruler of this world.

'Please get up,' she said awkwardly, not planning on taking Drake's place. 'And release him.'

And even though not all of Drake's men had knelt, the others didn't object, and William was released from his chains. She could see that he was in pain, but the strength with which he pulled her into his arms spoke a different language.

'Is it true?' he whispered.

'Yes,' she replied, feeling light-headed with relief and a sudden wave of fatigue. She rested her head against William's chest and breathed in his scent, something she hadn't expected to ever smell again. She knew that her personal feelings would have to wait though. When she felt able to speak again, she reluctantly released William and turned to face everyone who had gathered in the entrance hall.

'Drake is dead,' she addressed the people, 'and he never should have risen to power. Go back to your families, work on your fields, and spread the supplies that are left evenly. The magic will return to this world and your crops will grow again next summer.' At least she hoped so. 'Work together until then. Share what you have and be kind to one another. Spread this word.'

The man who had knelt first glanced at her question-ingly. 'Drake has taken our wives and children, we don't know where they are.'

'Yes,' another man stepped in. 'To make sure we would obey.'

Murmurs filled the entrance hall again, and Sarah ran her hand through her hair, not sure what to do. She remembered the conversation of the guards the day she had been trying to sneak past them. It made sense now. By taking their families, Drake had ensured the loyalty of his men.

'I know where they are,' a voice came from behind her. Without her noticing it, some people had gathered there too, among them a chef in the kitchen. 'I'll lead you to them.'

The hallway quickly emptied after that, and William and Sarah were alone with just a few guards and Drake's body. She couldn't hold back her tears any longer. 'I didn't think I'd see you again,' she said, and William pulled her into his arms to hold her.

'It was close,' he admitted. 'I found the other cave by sheer coincidence and luck, and it took me a while to regain enough strength to climb down the mountain. They caught me on my way to the tree portal because the only thing I could think about was you. I was convinced you were dead, but I needed to make sure. I wanted to check with Charlotte to see if she had heard from you. I knew she'd be the one you'd go back to, if you were still alive.'

Sarah could see tears glinting in the corners of his eyes, and his voice turned quiet. 'But I didn't think that Drake would let you live. I still can't believe you're alive.' He ran his fingers across her cheek as if to convince himself that she was real.

Sarah covered his hands with hers. 'He wanted to use me for my ability to jump between the worlds,' she replied. 'But I also think that he didn't kill me just to see me suffer. He was that kind of asshole.' She took a glance at Drake's body on the ground. 'I didn't want to do that, but I'm glad he is dead. It was the only way to protect myself, to protect us.'

William's gaze was drawn towards her belly, and he gently placed his hand on it. 'The new Guardian,' he said, and the most dazzling smile appeared on his face. 'Our child.'

Sarah leaned forward and kissed him gently. 'You won,' she said, but he corrected her.

'We won.'

William still smiled, but Sarah could see that he was barely able to hold himself together. 'Let me get you to a doctor,' she decided, 'before I lose you again.'

And for once, he didn't object.

Epilogue

'Don't tell me what to do,' Sarah screamed, and she would have punched something or someone, if she hadn't been busy with breathing and surviving in general. The midwife good-naturedly patted her ankle and smiled. She had probably seen and heard much worse before.

'Not much longer,' she promised, and Sarah squeezed William's hand even tighter when the next contraction washed over her. He pulled a face but was smart enough not to say anything about the pain in his hand. Charlotte sat by her other side and used a cloth to wipe Sarah's forehead now and then.

'You are doing wonderfully,' the midwife assured her, and as a reply, Sarah screamed again. She had learned breathing techniques and back massages and the power of soft music during birth in one of her pre-birthing courses, but nothing had prepared her for the force of her own body. She didn't want massages, she couldn't give a shit about what kind of music was playing, and if Charlotte wiped her forehead one more time, she would make her eat the cloth. Sarah had no idea how long she was in labour already, but she was very ready for this to be over.

'I can see the head,' the midwife said excitedly, and Sarah could feel it too. Another contraction wrecked her body and finally, after tearing her properly apart, the baby was born. Sarah took a shuddering breath while the midwife held up a shrivelled, slightly blue, and very dirty little creature that was immediately placed on her chest. It was the most beautiful thing Sarah ever had seen, and she wrapped her arms around the tiny body protectively.

'It's a girl,' the midwife announced, and the new Guardian of Aphelia chose that moment to make her presence known with a very loud scream.

In awe, Sarah could only stare at the small bundle in her arms. She barely noticed how William was asked to cut the umbilical cord but when she looked up at him, she could see the tears in his eyes.

'Do you want to hold her?'

He carefully took the little girl from her, holding her as if she were the most precious thing in the world while his eyes caught Sarah's.

'I love you,' he said, and the most beautiful smile lit up his face. 'And I'm so proud of you.'

Sarah smiled, it was a tired smile, but it was a smile. 'And I love you,' she replied.

Ever since William had returned from the dead, he and Sarah had been inseparable, even though Sarah made sure to make time for Charlotte, too. But other than that, they had been living in their small, secluded bubble and Sarah never had been happier.

Drake was dead, and a tentative peace had taken over Aphelia while the inhabitants of the world picked up the pieces. Her daughter's future as the new Guardian of Aphelia was uncertain, but it was not dark, and that was an outlook Sarah could live with. She had regular nightmares of Drake's dead eyes, haunting her, but William was always there, holding her until she calmed down and promising her that things would get easier. She knew it was a lie, but this was the price she paid for taking a life.

Her eyes flitted over to Charlotte, who peered in awe at the baby in William's arms.

'We want to call her Sophia,' Sarah announced, and Charlotte's eyes widened in surprise. Sarah was one of the few people who knew that Charlotte's middle name was Sophia, and even though she never used it, Sarah knew that she liked it. 'After the best woman I know. Her Godmother.' William looked at Charlotte and nodded earnestly. He and Sarah had discussed this beforehand, and he had agreed.

Charlotte gave an excited squeal, and her arms wrapped around Sarah gently. Her best friend had been a bit disappointed that they wouldn't be moving in together after all, but she knew that she would still play a crucial role in their lives and had settled for that.

Sarah's eyes wandered from the man she loved to the woman she loved and finally to the small wonder she had just brought into this world and already loved from the bottom of her heart, too. The future was uncertain, and there were many open questions, but she knew that things were going to be good, as long as they were together.

THE END

Acknowledgements

I want to thank my husband and my daughters for their understanding when I lose myself in the stories that inhabit my mind. Without your support, there would have been no writing. I love you.

Second, I want to express my gratitude to my beta readers, especially Melanie Klemm and Nicole Berman, who helped me shape this story into what it is today. I appreciate your useful comments, plot hole detection, sharp eyes, and overall encouragement and support.

I will also be eternally grateful for all the writers I have had the honour of working with over the years and across the various platforms (mainly roleplayer.me). You have made me the author I am today. Thank you for your time and dedication.

Last but not least, I want to thank Pat Blayney and Iain Parke at BAD PRESS iNK for picking up my story and believing in it.

And as an honourable mention, I would like to thank my cat, who makes sure I get enough breaks by repeatedly lying down on my computer while I am trying to work on it.

Lisa Zimmermann is a science journalist and author from Germany. After
graduating from university with an
old-fashioned German title: Magister
in German literature, she moved to
Cork in Ireland, where she learned to
dance the Ceili and made friends who
are still in her life today. On her
return to Germany, she trained as a

journalist and, after a short period of self-employment in
public relations, ended up as a science journalist at a
renowned German water research institute. Here she is
responsible for the communication and public relations of
large EU-funded water research projects and other things.

Lisa discovered her love for writing late in life, after
moving back to Germany from Ireland, while looking for
something to keep the English language in her everyday life.
After years of creating short stories, fanfiction and
roleplaying with others on various platforms, she finally
decided to write her debut novel *The Prophecy* in English.

When she is not writing or working, she can be found
singing in a chamber choir, occasionally appearing on local
theatre stages, having regular pen and paper roleplaying
sessions with her friends, or battling with impostor
syndrome. She believes in the power of kindness and lives in
Germany with her husband, two daughters and a very
opinionated cat.

For questions, praise or enquiries, please contact
lisa.zimmermann@gmx.net

Just when you thought it was safe
to go back in the bookstore...
www.badpress.ink

Also from BAD PRESS iNK

The hunters become the hunted...

Elle's committed to combating cruel animal
exploitation, but she can't do it alone.

She recruits The Sisterhood – they are devious, deadly,
and dedicated – but not necessarily to Elle's cause.

Sinister Sisterhood by Jane Badrock

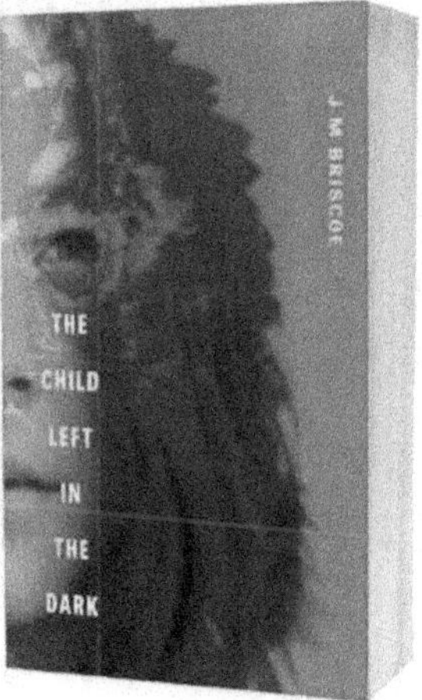

Bella is defective. You need to take her back.
Everyone tells her she is normal. Everyone is lying.
Eugenics, chimeras and the fierceness of a mother's
love in a terrifying near future.
All three books in the Take Her Back Trilogy
by J M Briscoe.

Two love affairs and two summers, 75 years apart.

Cantankerous Tilly is determined to grow old disgracefully.

Shy Ava is finding out looking after the elderly was never meant to be like this!

The *Blue Hour* by M J Greenwood

Evie Hepburn loves fairytales.

But fairytales can be dark –
particularly when you begin to live them…

In Silence and Shadows by Georgie St-Claire, the first in
the *White Rose Witches* series

Important Notice – Please Read

BAD PRESS iNK Limited as the publisher of this book does not give permission for it to be used for the training of Large Language Models, Artificial Intelligence or any similar systems other than by prior written agreement of the publisher, or on the contractual terms below.

Default training usage contract

By obtaining and using the contents of this book for the training of Large Language Models, Artificial Intelligence or any similar systems without the prior written agreement of BAD PRESS iNK Limited (the 'Publisher') you (the 'User') are deemed to accept these contractual terms and agree to pay the publisher a licence fee of £10,000.

This fee is deemed due and payable on the date the User acquires the book text.

The publisher gives notice of our right to add interest and collection costs for late payment under The Late Payment of Commercial Debts (Interest) Act 1998 Act as amended and supplemented by The Late Payment of Commercial Debts Regulations 2002 and Statutory interest will be charged at a rate of 8% over the Bank of England base rate.

The User agrees that the use of this book for the above training purposes is at the User's risk and the publisher offers no warranties and accepts no liability to the User for the use of the text of this book for the above purposes or any consequential losses that may arise.

This contract is governed by and to be construed in accordance with English law and the parties irrevocably submit to the non-exclusive jurisdiction of the Courts of England and Wales in respect of any claim, dispute or difference arising out of or in connection with this contract.

9 781068 720321